FINDER

IN

HELL

WORLD

A LOVE STORY

CHARLES R. STERN

Grey Wolfe Publishing, LLC
145 East Fourteen Mile Road
Clawson, Michigan 48017
www.GreyWolfePublishing.com

© 2018 Charles R. Stern
Published by Grey Wolfe Publishing, LLC
www.GreyWolfePublishing.com
All Rights Reserved

Print ISBN: 978-1628282078
E-Book ISBN: 978-1628282108

Library of Congress Control Number: Pending

FINDER IN HELL WORLD:

A Love Story

A Novel by

Charles R. Stern

Dedication:

For my mother, Mary Margaret Stern.

You are dearly missed.

Acknowledgements:

For Lia Bishop.

CHAPTER ONE
THE STRANGER

The thick, frozen, fickle, and indecisive weather couldn't make up its mind whether it belonged at the end of winter or on the cusp of spring that year. The cowboy boots filled with a drifter were dropped off in a thick fog of anticipation at precisely four o'clock in the morning. An itinerant trucker had picked him up exactly one hundred and fifty miles out. The white logo painted on the dirty green truck said, "Donkey Express." The owner's name, *J. Garland* was painted on the cab door, and the California license plate cover read *Palm Beach* floating over the silhouette of a golden palm frond. The trucker had spewed long monologues about the state of the world, politics, religion, and his family life while his hitchhiking passenger was relegated to the obligation of the listener. The stranger was forced into the position of saying, "Yup" and "hum," accompanied by the occasional nod as if to say, "listening" and head shaking as if to say, "too bad" or "that's terrible," punctuating the appropriate moments in the litany. It was compensatory fare for the ride. The radio was playing *The Weight,* by *The Band, I pulled into Nazareth feeling 'bout half past dead...* The anonymous fence posts and road signs flashing by, *blip, blip, blip* in the headlight beams witnessed that insignificant bit of reality passing by while keeping time to the rhythm of its driver's monotonous palaver. The road was deserted, and the flat land drifted by under the dark starlit sky unaffected by the truck that trundled past. The stranger had been a good listener since he was a fetus and he had only gotten better with practice. In fact, there was a part of him who was always listening, attending to what people were really communicating, underlying their words and deeds, no matter how many times he heard the same story. Human nature was fascinating, and he took every opportunity to strike up conversations with strangers whenever it presented itself. He had mastered the art of hearing the underlying messages buried deep beneath the burgeoning content of whatever topic spewed forth. In fact, everything, animate and inanimate, seemed to offer up a plethora of information as if the universe was engaged in a stream of messages vying for his attention.

He watched the headlights' limited sight distance on the desolate road ahead while he pretended to listen to the chatter of the same story for the third time drifting his way across the cab. The passenger, no longer listening to the teamster's words, heard the loneliness and detachment of an isolated man who had little understanding or interest in his effect on others. The hitchhiker became aware of his own memories flowing by along with the road under the truck.

Without warning, hundreds of toads that had settled on the ruts in the road scattered before the truck in a bizarre, chaotic fury causing the driver to swerve. The truck catapulted through what must have been a huge pothole to avoid hitting them, momentarily rendering the passenger weightless before landing back on his seat in the cab with a silent spine jarring bang, rudely awakening him with a physical bounce that brought him back from his mental detour. He became aware that the driver had not missed a beat in his hyperverbal monologue and was repeating the same story about his homelife for the fifth time. Janice Joplin was belting out *Freedom is just another word for nothing left to lose* from the radio and, miraculously, not a single creature was squashed as if the vehicle had passed through a thin veil of time and space to avoid them. The passenger looked up and saw a dark sky that no longer reflected the myriad of stars he had seen even moments before. Suddenly, the atmosphere seemed strangely cold as if they had passed through a weather front. Now, there were snow flurries marking the windows as the crystalline flakes melted into dots in a race streaking across the glass. He sat up, and looking out the window, read the city limits sign of a town passing by. Something, call it a premonition or an omen, rose up from deep in his guts, traveled through his body and blasted out his mouth. "I need to stop in this town!" he blurted before realizing he had shouted a command, interrupting the flow of innocuous drivel spewing forth, startling the driver. He said, "Sorry to interrupt like that. Please forgive me, but I just realized that I have to stop here if you don't mind."

The disappointed trucker reluctantly acquiesced to the stranger's request and dropped him off.

He had been enjoying the company of someone who actually seemed to be listening to him, something he was not used to at home, and his passenger noticed his CB radio contacts with his trucker buddies were simple warnings of the road, and traffic conditions and detours to take while avoiding speed traps and weigh stations. Otherwise, the discussions were boring because he ended up listening to others when, as men tend to do, they kept cutting him off to talk about themselves or offer useless advice.

He realized that even his wife and kids never really listened to him either.

****

The stranger, who always listened to the subliminal messages, was able to reconstruct the trucker's turmoil. *He is a lonely satellite in his own home,* the listener concluded. *It probably isn't intentional, not consciously anyway, but apparently, his wife is used to being in charge of everything while he's gone on his regular "over-the-road" long hauls that leave him only small amounts of time at home at irregular intervals.* The stranger pieced together the trucker's stories about his life along with what he read in the driver's psyche. *Due in part to his long absences, this man doesn't have any understanding of what is happening in his family and, whenever he is home, he claims, everything he tries to do to discipline the kids is wrong, at least according to his wife. In the past, whenever he disciplined the kids, she reprimanded him in front of them, feeling he was undermining her rather loose system of childrearing of which he was clueless.* The stranger could tell that, if she had explained her approach, he didn't remember it. Maybe it was because she expressed it at the end of a very long monologue, miles after surpassing his capacity to stay with the train of thought that had already derailed. He probably thought she was too soft on them, and she was, but he was probably too harsh as well. The passenger intuited that, eventually the driver retired from parenthood, disappeared into his nasty easy chair and climbed into his beer bottles in total surrender to her. Pouring alcohol spirits on the problem was all he could think to do. He realized that there was an unstated truce between the driver and the mother of his children, and a tiny pocket universe was established around his chair that encompassed the TV. Although he was a talker, he clearly was not good at actual give and take conversation, especially the intimate variety that required him to listen to more than two or three minutes of what anyone else had to say without mentally checking out or getting drunk in front of his TV refuge. The listener pictured him sitting in his old, beaten up, overstuffed chair impossibly stained with beer, coffee, and the ancient unrecognizable remnants of food, his wife refusing to replace the ratty old thing so he couldn't ruin another one. It was beyond the possibility of cleaning without destroying it, but he probably never noticed that the worn, threadbare upholstery had been rubbed to a smooth sheen in spots. She probably kept it covered when he was gone and pretended it didn't exist, in case company came.

His wife, the rider determined through his constant vocal barrage, frequently accused him of having secret agendas behind everything he did or said, but this always mystified him because, like most men, he had none, unlike her and her female friends whose steady stream of gossip he was constantly required to bear witness to, which of course, he generally ignored. It was not that he wasn't interested in her and her life, but he had no clue why she and her friends were always so upset about things he was certain were trivial. A practical man, he was primarily focused on performing tasks and couldn't understand why his wife was always dissatisfied with him. After all, he said, 'I support my family financially and do the major mechanical repairs... when they become absolutely necessary. Besides, I'm gone most of the time making the money she and the kids live on,' he said, obviously believing that performing tasks and supplying the money was enough to express his love. Emotions, in his world, were expressed through the crucible of anger and occasionally disgust, unless the situation called for laughter. Fear and sadness were always hidden beneath his primary machismo vocabulary of anger. "Sometimes," the driver said, "My wife makes me feel dumb as a donkey! She doesn't even want to have sex anymore."

The passenger realized that ordinary people, like the driver, had many regrets and they were often intimidated or emotionally manipulated by others. He, in contrast, was not easily swayed and he did not give up. He sensed that the trucker's wife had long ago abandoned sex and detected the need for the trucker's lost love to be returned to him, but the hitchhiker knew that it was tragically too late. *Sometimes, my ability to read these things in others,* the stranger thought to himself, *is a sad burden.* He looked down between the seats and was surprised to see an abandoned tube of lipstick, but he didn't feel any need or desire for it to be returned to its owner.

Being the man he was, the trucker had so little social grace that he had never introduced himself to his passenger but reluctantly agreed to drop this young man where he requested. He stopped in front of the town's only coffee shop that, according to the sign, didn't open until two hours later, at six.

The stranger emerged from the itinerant truck with a mutual "goodbye, good luck," and "thanks for the ride." His tan was exactly six feet tall, and he brushed back his head of thick dark hair, a well-ordered mop, with his full fingered right hand as if it were a comb. There was a light, well-groomed two-day beard bristling on his face. He had on well worn, but clean jeans along with a denim jacket floating over a blue flannel shirt that was covered by a hoody, and his neck sported a red bandana. He wore an old tattered, faded, and worried royal purple baseball cap with an improbable sports team's logo, the name of which started with a once white letter 'G,' a souvenir of a fond distant past. His boots had the scuffed, stained and well-worn marks of memorable ancient escapades. He carried a large tattered overfull backpack that was about to burst, a worn and barely visible brand name logo, *Mountain Top,* on its side. Around his neck, tucked under his shirt, was a fifth-generation worn-out leather strand upon which he kept a ring, a talisman dipped in good fortune, and blessed by his great or great-great-grandfather, he wasn't sure which, passed on to him from his grandmother through his mother and It kept him safe.

Precisely one minute after his boots touched down in his flight from nowhere, heading no place in particular, a small bird, asphyxiated by the interminable frozen fog that hung in the air like a cold soup, fell with dead weight at his feet. He reached down and gently laid the tiny bit of misfortune in the warm palm of his right hand, touched his talisman with his left, and lending his own hot exhales, breathed the thaw of life back into it. Soon, the bird stirred lazily, looked up at its savior in fearful gratitude, seemingly resigned to its fate in the hands of the stranger. The tiny creature squawked its surprise when, tossed back into the air, it was forced to find its wings. Circling this strange human three times, grateful for its resurrection, as if memorizing his face, it sailed off to find a warm rafter. "Live long and prosper," the drifter quoted, a smile on his face, in part for the rescued bird and partly because of his corny cliché, while sporting the Mr. Spock V-shaped finger gesture.

The stranger's stride was firm and steadily paced with the kind of peacefulness one associates with an individual who is not dragging behind him the ancient worries, guilt, and regrets that encumber most people. His eyes were clear and sharp, acutely focused on his surroundings, and aware of even the minutest details. Observers always had the impression that he was constantly interacting with the universe; seen and unseen.

Finder In Hell World   Charles R. Stern

CHAPTER TWO
EXPLORING PERFECTION

The drifter wandered around the empty town in the ghost-like unseasonable predawn frozen fog, feeling the cold crystals falling on his face, searching for phantoms and clues until the much-needed coffee shop opened at six. Until then he peered into dark, vacant windows of shops at wondrous items he could barely make out in the din, many of which were ten years in arrears from the current fashion. Past, present, and future had melded together for at least fifty years. It was as if the span of time had little meaning within the obsessive drive to meet immediate deadlines. Everything was pin neat, and it appeared that, despite the outdated clothes and accouterments, none were on sale regardless of the season. There were warm winter jackets and cold snowmobiles next to the hot swimsuits and shiny lawnmowers. Merchants didn't seem to discount the out-of-style or out-of-season items, but merely added them to the existing but fatigued stock on display. *After all, the last season will be the next one again soon!* He smiled. Out of the corner of his eye, he detected a mannequin peering at him suspiciously with a judgmental stare. He shook his head. *I must be more tired than I realized. Or is this an omen?* It seemed as though the merchandise resisted being discounted or discarded just as much as the merchants were reluctant to part with them until they were sold. The drifter and the displayed items starred at each other with curiosity in a standoff between suspiciousness and mutual analysis. The shops only displayed, for lack of space, one item of any particular type of merchandise at a time. The customers would see something they liked and ask if there was one in their size or a different color. The computer would happily search the inventory of stocked items to determine the facts of the matter. This pattern of obsessive organization and efficiency had developed, he later discovered, over a fifty-year period that, he realized, coincided with the rise of the use of affordable computers and modern accounting methods.

He and the walls of the buildings closely scrutinized each other, while he searched the layout of the town, noticing all the details he could, but finding no flaws. The filled cracks in the worn sidewalks, the spots where missing bricks had been replaced, and other healed wounds of injured structures, suspicious of the stranger, returned his stare. He explored row after row of awakening shops and warehouses, suspiciously watching him as he passed in the lonely desolate streets, by the houses, apartment buildings, government offices, and a restaurant. The town was inhumanly neat, not one piece of litter or debris anywhere, and it was laid out in an exact ninety-degree grid of streets. Even the public trash cans were empty. Not even a street light was out. There was just the windswept traffic light, swinging in the middle of the main intersection, rhythmically changing colors, directing no traffic at all, save for an occasional dry leaf speeding through the intersection propelled by the misdemeanor gusts of wind, without stopping on red, a flagrant breach of the law. The town was eerily silent with only a lone intermittent breeze. Only the spirits and lonely ghosts who populated the empty streets at night hung around on the corners, no one but a part of the drifter could sense them. His boot steps were returned in mocking echoes from the surrounding structures letting him know he was being watched.

The air had the faint ancient ghostly odor of a lakeshore. An odd thing, given the fact that this town was about as far from any significant body of water as you could get. He stopped and listened to the total stillness that surrounded him. No sound, nothing, and no one in sight. There was a damp odor that seemed to shift between the competing fragrance of flowers and an unidentifiable foul stench with every change in the direction of the wind, reminiscent of musty rotting dead animals, *maybe of birds*, floating in on the westerly wind. *Very strange in such a clean and organized town.* It seemed as if it was an indecipherable warning of some kind for such a flaw in this pervasive atmosphere of perfection, but the meaning would have to be deciphered later. *You could probably eat off any surface in this sterile town*, he thought.

He remembered the city limits sign that said the population was five thousand and six people, and he had no doubt that it was updated the second there was a death or a newborn addition. *Maybe there's no need for updates. Perhaps one birth replacing every death might be the norm in such an orderly place.* He shook his head, *what a ghoulish thought! A town so controlled that even births and deaths were part of a balance sheet. Did the town council regulate when a birth could take place in anticipation of a death?* He tried to clear his head from the runaway speculation that mortal humans tend to engage in when they try to fill in the gaps of information with heuristic shortcuts of near-psychotic confabulation. *No! That can't be true! I'm just making that up! I can't get swept up in my own imagination. I have no facts, merely hypotheses to be investigated.* The even more intriguing thing was the lettering he remembered printed on the city limits sign floating below the moniker "Perfection" that read, "Everything in its place." *Geez! What arrogance!* The stranger paused, shook his head, *what a strange land!* The whole place was asleep but ready to stir awake from the complete and exquisite slumber of the dead. Suddenly, he felt cold, the blood draining from his flesh, and finding himself standing in front of the local newspaper office, hands buried deep in his barely warming pockets, he read each page of yesterday's broadsheets that were taped to the window. There was a report that the Sheriff had apprehended three ten and eleven-year-old boys who had been perpetrating some minor pranks. They broke some windows in two abandoned buildings late at night, and they were turned over to their parents who immediately paid for the damage, but that seemed to be the end of the story. There were no other stories of crimes, just the local town meeting minutes, business and agriculture reports. There was an obituary of one elderly resident and the announcement of the birth of Robert Jason Minus. *One for one*! He shook his head in amazement. Oddly, there was no national or international news, and the paper had only six pages, two of which were devoted to advertisements, and three were reserved for financial matters and reports of local sports teams. The mysterious stranger walked back through town to the desperately needed coffee shop where the beverage was not the only thing drawing him there. A part of him, some might say it was mystical, always serving as an inner detector, felt an ephemeral tug connecting the middle of his gut to something undefinable. It was as if there was an invisible umbilical lifeline like the astronauts used on spacewalks to tether themselves to their spacecraft, but its origin seemed to be the coffee shop.

****

Walking through town, he was reminded that he had always felt like he was outside looking in on life through an invisible barrier separating him from others. He was simultaneously blessed and cursed with a talent for detecting things of which others were unaware. It made him separate and constantly in search for someone or someplace where he would be accepted for who he was and not just for the person he had to pretend to be in public. Early in life, he realized that there seemed to be two of him in one body. The outer self, the self that could read other people, like the truck driver, who was able to manage his environment and social connections. The other was inside, the intuitive self called Finder, who often advised him and occasionally seemed to act without his permission before he could think of what action to take. The actions did, however, always turn out to be the right thing to do. It was like the average person who automatically catches a ball launched at them before they realize it has been thrown. Sometimes, after falling asleep writing in his journal late into the night, he awoke to the realization that he had no memory of writing several of the pages. It was as if his inner-self had located the right words waiting to be written and pulled them out of the pages like Michelangelo who said something like, "You just chip away at the stone to reveal the David within." It seemed that Finder read the need for the words to be liberated from the pages. Miraculously, those pages were always well written. So, Finder was an advisor and a detector of things needing to be found.

****

Suddenly, there she was. Molly Everhart, who stepped up to the door and, shivering in the cold, unlocked the *Wake Up! Coffee Shop,* turned and faced the stranger with her white-sweatered arms crossing over her ample chest, hands buried in the armpits of the white uniform trying to warm them in the open door. She was beaming a welcoming smile that would have blinded him, save for the wire-rimmed sunshades he had put on against the dawning cold rays of the sun peeking at him over the flat horizon. It made him squint, even so. She said, "C'mon in I'm just opening up. What can I get for you on this chilly morning, Sir?" She was unaware of the lilt in her voice and the slight flip of her hair that accompanied the barely detectable dip in her right hip. The stranger noticed it as did the impatient coffee machines jealously waiting, eagerly anticipating her gentle, caring, but exuberant touch to awaken them from their drowsy inactivity, and set them to work.

Molly was a pretty, perky, petite blonde, a twenty-five-year-old vision in white, exactly five feet three inches tall, her beautifully shaped sheer stockinged legs dropping down into her affordable white restaurant worker's tennis shoes. She glided along as if skating on Marty McFly's *Back to the Future* hoverboard, hurrying to load and arouse the ancient fussy coffee machines that ground, groaned, gurgled, and spat to life basking in her loving touch. Molly Everhart glanced over her shoulder and said, "It'll be a few minutes before the coffee's ready Sir, but I can take your order as soon as I finish here." There was an embarrassing gurgle in her voice, coinciding with that of the belching coffee machines, and the glitch in her heartbeat that she was sure this handsome stranger could hear over the cacophony of the noisily extruding apparatus.

"No hurry," he said with a broad eye-flashing, engaging grin as he took off his sunglasses and placed them on the table that supported them with an air of indifference.

She returned her attention to the machines. Although he couldn't make it out clearly over the noise, it sounded to him as if she was talking to them and singing under her breath like a wake-up song you'd sing to gently stir children from their slumber.

Molly Everhart was interested in any stranger in town, especially new men, always longing for something different. Anything interesting in her humdrum, routine, small-town world was more than welcome.

Ebenezer Thornbird, nicknamed The Finder, who had been called Eb since birth, and Finder since he was five, sat motionless, save for his eyes tracking the very attractive and oblivious young woman as she floated through her routine rounds. He had arrived here exactly thirty years from the day that he made his rude emergence from his mother into this shocking and complicated life. That was the day that began a life-long quest which would change everything for him and everyone around him.

The wind picked up and the last snow of the season, desperately trying to hang on to winter, began to flurry in a snowy fog along the unseasonably cold and deserted street. There was a forlorn pickup truck across the street, parked at an odd angle outside the hardware as if frozen in place after a hangover from a late-night bender. It looked out of place in the pin-neat town. A stray mutt trotted by and a multicolored VW Beatle chugged, popped, sputtered, and backfired down the street in the opposite direction. Finder detected a void in the vehicle's driver and alerted him. Ebenezer Thornbird's eyes followed the old wreck down the street until it completely disappeared in a curtain of snow flurries. "That thing is ancient," he commented, not realizing he said it aloud.

Molly Everhart turned toward him slowly and gracefully as if floating on an invisible turntable from behind the counter with a slightly reddened face and said, "Well, these machines are getting older, but they still make the best coffee in town," she defended. The machines seemed to quiet down in support.

He recognized the defensive misunderstanding tone leaking out behind the brightest smile he had ever seen. "No. I meant the VW Bug that just went by. It must be at least twenty years old."

"Thirty!" she blurted before she realized how it sounded. "That old girl has kept running for Junior Ketchum all these years," she recovered. "I think she loves him or something because she never gave up on him." She giggled a little. "He says she's better than a wife because she always lets him know what she needs before she breaks down, he can always fix what's wrong, she never talks back, and she's always there when he needs her. In fact, she is thirty years old today. Junior was in here yesterday and told me all about it. I think he said she has her third engine and the body of a patched and painted beauty made over and rejuvenated with junkyard parts. He said she lets him know just what she needs without crying and manipulating. They have a great connection, a partnership, a pretty good relationship he reckoned. She takes him where he wants to go, and he keeps her happy. A match made in heaven. Isn't that great?"

"I'd have to agree," he said smiling at her wonderful take on life. "The perfect relationship I guess," *I wonder if he has sex with it too.* He shuddered and tried to shake the image of a tailpipe out of his head. She hesitated for a count of five ticks of the atomic clock on the wall and eight beats of her heart while she zoomed back into the present from whatever planet she was on.

She said, "My name is Molly, by the way," remembering her manners before turning her attention back to her mechanical suitors. "You're new in town, aren't you?" she asked over her shoulder.

"Yes, and people call me Eb," he said, "Glad to make your acquaintance. You are the first person I've met here."

"Happy to meet you Eb. Glad I was your first," she said with another blast of her extremely bright grin of perfectly straight white teeth that reminded him of a naked one-hundred-watt bulb. She was multitasking, trying to set up the coffee and boot the computer while wiping the counter. She turned on the music at a low volume. Roy Orbison's incredible voice was singing *Pretty Woman*. "What brings you to our little town?"

"A truck," he said with a fading smile as the joke, his feeble attempt at charm, fell on the floor and died a miserable, embarrassing, and humiliating death before he continued. "Actually, I'm not sure." He was more sober now, "But I thought I might be needed." Pat Metheny's *Off Ramp* was playing now.

"Needed? How would you know you 'might' be needed?" She made air quotes with her raised eyebrows. "Did someone ask you to come here?" she challenged.

"No. The truck driver who dropped me off was going to drive nonstop all the way to Kansas, but I slammed into the sudden recognition that I should stop here; that I was needed. I never understand why these feelings hit me, but I've learned, no matter how strange or scary, not to contradict my instincts. So, I asked the driver to drop me here."

Molly Everhart was fascinated by a man who could follow his instincts and make seemingly correct decisions that had little or no actual data to support them. She wanted to be more like that but felt too anxious to try.

"So here I am," he continued with a flourish of arms, "I did notice something odd when we entered the outskirts of town, though." He was looking off through the front window of reminiscence at nothing in particular. "There's a sign that says, *Perfection*," he continued. "That's a very interesting name for a town."

"Yeah. That is embarrassing."

"If it's so embarrassing, why don't they change it?"

"Oh, I'm the only one who feels that way. Everyone else thinks it's great," she said, "and they did change it, but they changed it from Zanesville to Perfection."

"Well, that fits."

"Fits?"

"Yeah, everything here seems so neat and tidy. I have the image that any litter is retrieved immediately, or it blows out of town to clutter some other place."

"There is rarely any litter or trash on the streets," she said. "I think I saw Jimmy Engelhardt, he's the town sanitation engineer, you know the garbage man, the other day practically break his neck frantically chasing two unruly loose papers that were blowing around the street and practically diving for one before it hit the ground. No one here wants to defile the dirt," she said with a mixture of tongue-in-cheek humor and sarcasm.

"Jimmy looked over the offending papers he accosted intently trying to determine who to report for breaking the littering ordinance, but I suspect they were simply strangers passing through from some other town."

****

Molly Everhart was carried on the wings of memory back to her early childhood when the wind snatched her school paper and deposited it on the street. Her mother said with red-faced indignant embarrassment, "Molly! Pick that up right now! We don't litter!" She was looking around in search of critical onlookers while Molly chased it down. "What will people think of us?" Her mother continued, her voice escalating toward the stratosphere, "What will happen if we all just discard our junk on the streets? Our world will just fill up with it, we'll be crowded out, and have to move to another town to escape the mess for lack of space!" she exaggerated. Molly felt hurt because her school paper was accidental and temporary litter, but it certainly was not trash! She had received a very proud 'A' on it, and she would never have left it in the street. She had presented it to her mother expecting praise only to be rebuffed with, "Well, we wouldn't expect anything less from you." *Nothing short of perfection.* Now, ironically, she was calling her perfect paper junk! It was about that time in her life when Molly began to intuit that there was something wrong with her parents and the town, but she eventually came to believe it was she who was strange.

****

After a three-minute dead space in the conversation, Molly Everhart tried to close the gap and said, "Nothing less than perfection is accepted in this town unless there is some flaw such as a defect in the brain of an intellectually challenged child. Those kids are to be pitied, and their parents are encouraged to send them away, or the family is shamed and pressured to move out of this ostensibly flawless society. It's harder to get rid of adults like that, though." She blinked three times in rapid succession and, as if a taut rubber band in her skull snapped back from her reverie like Dorothy's clicking heels, she returned to the here and now on the plains.

Ebenezer Thornbird's brow wrinkled leaving deep lines on his forehead as he cocked his head to the left slightly as though he was listening for a reply from the Earth's left hemisphere. "Wow! That's extreme," he said. *A kind of social eugenics?! Harsh.*

She thought back again for exactly five seconds through her memories of ancient history to retrieve the vague apparitions of the past. "Actually," she said, "I've never had the nerve to question it aloud. It seems cruel don't you agree?" She stared off for three more seconds in a trance, salvaging dark memories of long ago before she said, "I asked my father about it once, only once you understand, and he mysteriously refused to say anything except, 'That's the way it is.'"

"Amazing!" Eb blurted out before he could censor himself. And then he thought, *anyone would be safer to hide their true feelings in this town if they want to survive here.*

His response shook her out of her reminiscence, her brain shot back from the past to the coffee shop and, remembering her duties, she asked, "So, what can I get you, Sir?" She felt a little uneasy opening up to a stranger as easily as turning the key in the door to open the shop this morning since she normally had to keep her opinions to herself. *What is it about this drifter that makes me feel so comfortable? The only thing I know about him is his name! Yet, it feels as if I've known him all my life. This is weird!* Do you mind if I call you Eb?"

"Call me anything you like Molly. I'm always flattered by a beautiful woman who wants to call me anything but Sir."

Molly's blush matched the red stop sign on the corner visible from the window. "Oh, you <u>are</u> bad!" she said with an unintended gush of happy embarrassment. *He's handsome and charming, <u>and</u> he's flirting with me!* She wasn't used to such straightforward compliments, and she certainly was not used to feeling this tingling all the way down to her toes. She definitely was not used to anyone, let alone an attractive man, focusing his total undivided attention on her as if she really was important. Her nervous system was buzzing! Although he sounded sincere, and he did seem to mean it, somehow this didn't match her take on reality. In fact, no one ever told her she was smart or beautiful or even that they loved her, now that she thought of it. *Sadly, not even my parents.*

Ebenezer Thornbird placed his order. "I'd like a cup of your heftiest house coffee, straight up, as hot and dangerous as you can manage it please." Their eyes met in a kind of unexpected Vulcan mind-meld, a connection neither of them had ever experienced. Even the coffee machines seemed to relax and settle into a soothing thrum.

"Double shot *Wake Up!* Special, black, super-hot, and extra strong coming right up Eb!" Snapping out of her trance-like state, she thought, *Damnit!* silently reprimanding herself for saying it a little too loudly. She had the bad habit of blurting things out at the coffee shop, the only place in the universe she felt even close or comfortable enough to acknowledge her emotions. Feeling his charm, she thought, *still, this guy is fascinating, and we seem to have a mysterious connection.* Then, shaking herself back to her usual reality, *it's probably wishful thinking I'm probably fooling myself. Am I so desperate that I'll glom onto the first mysterious stranger who blows in from who knows where?* But, she couldn't help feeling attracted to him, smiling more broadly now and, although her face had settled a little, there remained a noticeably brighter shade of pink than her makeup had intended. She sailed across the room with his coffee, unaware that her head was cocked slightly to her left exposing her cute left ear and the tasteful dangling earring, or that her hips were subtly swinging making her skirt swish back and forth in a way that was not lost on his anatomy. "Here you are, Sir, uh, sorry, Eb," feigning forgetfulness in an attempt to hide the now open secret of her attraction, unsuccessful though it was, with her unconscious signals radiating through her flimsy facade.

He noticed McCoy Tyner's *The Real McCoy* playing in the background. *Apparently, this station plays all types of music.* He beamed his smile back to her side of the court while he pretended to ignore her unconscious flirtations, at least for now, while trying to put away the hardening force of his vascular anatomy for future reference. "Thanks, Molly." There was that internal signal, the voice of Finder, yelling, *down boy! Later! There's more to discover here.*

"What do you do for a living Eb?" Before she knew it, she was sitting before him with her longing hands palms down on the table extended in an unconscious gesture inching toward him wishing they could experience the intimacy of his touch. The Beatles' *I want to hold your hand* played faintly in the background.

"Well, I do a lot of things," Finder whispered, *back off man! This is too fast.* Oddly, the Beatles, *Let It Be,* was playing now. Ebenezer Thornbird sat back, trying to calm the smoldering coals of desire and, to avoid so much closeness too soon, despite the difficulty of resisting his wood-hardened urges. He knew from experience that women often find a man fascinating at first blush, but find themselves competing with his path in life, rarely receiving the attention they crave, eventually resenting the very things they were attracted to in the first place. *It's rare*, he pondered, *that a woman would be on the same or even a parallel path with mine.* He wanted to avoid repeating that trap. "But mostly," he continued, "I've worked in construction, trucking, salvage, and restaurants around the country. I guess the most profound work was when I hired on for a year in the coal mines of West Virginia. I took those jobs to obtain enough money to move on and pursue my writing and other activities."

"Writing? You're a writer?"

"Yes. I'm traveling around the country writing journal and magazine articles that I intend to combine into a book someday, but people call me by my nickname, 'Finder.' That's what I've always been good at anyway. I think of myself as a locator more than a finder, though.

She stopped and stared blankly. "Finder? You mean you find things people have lost? Or are you one of those people who find financial opportunities for investors?" Her hands began to perspire with the anxiety of deep longing for a physical connection she had been deprived of for so very long. Her desire caused her to squirm a little in her seat. Eb seemed like someone who stepped right out of one of her novels.

"Yeah. Something like that. Not the financial stuff, though. It's more like locating something or someone who needs to be found."

"What kinds of things?"

"Well," he looked her in the eye causing her a mixture of discomfort, excitement, and an increase in the cold perspiration leaking from her hands, hoping she was one of those things. "Just about anything that needs me to find it. In fact …."

"Things needing *you* to find *them*?" Molly Everhart interrupted. "You mean you look for them because of their need to be found and not for the sake of the person who lost them?"

"Yeah, I think I was supposed to stop here because someone or something needed me to locate them and it brought me here to your shop."

"How do you know something or someone needs to be found? How does this Spidey sense work? You seem to be saying that no one told you there was something to be found here."

He sat forward in his chair, crossed his arms, elbows planted on the table, and lowered his head to a forty-five-degree angle as if he were reading memories etched in her inspiring chest. "Well, it's difficult to explain," he said. "It isn't that I hear a voice exactly. The only language I can use that comes close to describing it is that my inner-self, the Finder in me so to speak, hears something signaling or 'calling' and translates it to me in words. I don't hear a voice exactly. To me, it's more of a feeling or a sense until Finder translates it into words. I guess the closest I can come to defining it is that it feels like a longing." There was a silent, but intimate connection between them for precisely thirty seconds of Molly's building anticipation while a noisy panel van spewing gray pollution drove past, and a man with inadequate clothing for the weather hurried by unnoticed before he continued. Looking back at her, Finder whispered, *talk about longing!* "Is there anyone or anything *else* here that needs finding? I feel a pull, an extremely strong one, here."

She frowned, hoping her wrinkled forehead would jump-start her brain and, staring out the window blankly examining the truck parked across the street, she attempted to scan her gray matter, but despite feeling a growing need to be of assistance, searching her memory for anything that might help, she had nothing. Maybe it was because she was a naturally helpful individual, perhaps the stronger motive was to keep his interest in her. *Wait, did he say, "Something else?" Did he already find something?* And after one very long minute of silence, "No," she heard herself say aloud, "I can't think of anything off the top, but I'll keep thinking about it, and I'll let you know if I do." *There's something about this man. I don't know what it is, but he is intriguing and mysterious.* All the men she had met in life so far had been uninteresting. *He is fascinating.* She continued to be deaf to the part of herself screaming to be liberated. It was Finder's fate to discover that part of her long before she would realize it herself.

Ebenezer Thornbird drank his coffee slowly like a man who had little to worry about and yet he seemed to be drifting off into a sea of deep thought.

****

There was the time in the mines when Eb worked miles down in the mysterious primitive underground of the Earth's unconscious realm. *Where the Green Ants Dream* so to speak, referencing Werner Herzog's film where the Australian Aborigines say the Green Ants are dreaming the world. If they awaken, their dreams, and consequentially the world, will disappear. He had encountered all kinds of characters in the mines. Many of them were under extreme stress, largely undereducated, rude and crude. Although open to conviviality and assisting others at times, they tended toward drunkenness, violence, abusiveness, and debauchery. Being adamant Christians, though, they went to church on Sundays unless they were working overtime. He learned to be cautious of the intentions and actions of the great unwashed, the cost of living in the very primitive, uninhibited unconsciousness of mind, and life in the Earth's pre-Cambrian crust.

One Sunday morning, dragging behind the others, he arrived at the elevator after his gang had ascended to the surface and the next shift had already disappeared down the shaft. A light had gone out near the lift and, waiting alone, he heard something moving behind him. He spun around in time to see a figure draped in the vague darkness of the shadows. It was difficult to see him clearly, but Ebenezer Thornbird thought it appeared distorted as if there was some drastic deformity in his physiognomy. Finder said, *his voice has that breath-labored guttural quality of someone in great pain.* It was Finder that heard the figure, but Eb felt the waves of understanding rushing at him, penetrating his consciousness through Finder's interpretation of what it seemed to be saying, "You are my only hope to finally put these weary bones to rest in peace. You will be put to trial by an apparition that must be defeated, encounter more terror and danger than you have ever imagined, but you must face it without fear." The lift arrived and, distracted by the sound, he glanced momentarily at it, but when he turned back to the figure, it was gone. He was puzzled, and Finder said, t*here are real things that no one understands, and people become attached to their beliefs, fantasies, illusions, and metaphors that embellish their experience of reality.* Eb thought before he responded. *But, is this reality or metaphor? Is metaphor just another form of reality?* Tension produced a parade of goosebumps marching down his spine, but shaking it off, he decided that he had been experiencing one of those hallucinations, waking dreams, that occasionally happens deep in the mines... But it seemed so real.

****

After two and a half minutes of unbearable silence, Ebenezer Thornbird was shaken back from the cave of ancient reminiscence when Molly spoke up. "What kinds of things do you usually find? I mean look for or call to you? Maybe that will jog my memory."

"I have found lost animals and people as well as lost items, and I once found water where it was needed."

"Huh." Her shoulders unintentionally revealed a disappointed shrug. As hard as she tried, she couldn't think of any missing person or object that might help him in his quest or keep him interested in her. "The only thing I can think of," she said with a sense of ironic humor, "is that this whole town is missing something." She suddenly realized she had said it aloud and glanced around in terror that anyone else might have heard her. There were no other customers, but the machines seemed uncharacteristically quiet as if they were holding their collective breath, and the fly in the corner stopped its hyperactive face washing. There was a definite feeling that there had been a breach in the order rippling through the place.

"There was a time," he said, "When a child was lost in the woods, and I traced his need to be found in a forest where he had hidden from a wolf in an abandoned oil drum. He was terrified and afraid to come out to me, so I had to go back and find his mother to coax him out. Another child was abducted, but I traced her crying terror to the perp's home and the police retrieved her upon my report, but I disappeared after I made the anonymous call. Do you know how difficult it has become to find a public pay phone? I had to go all the way to the frickin' airport to find one! There was another time when a woman had been robbed of her grandmother's nostalgic locket. It was not worth much, but it was loaded with great sentimental value. I located it, following its need to be returned to its owner, from a pawnshop where it was retrieved, and the thief was caught thanks to the shop owner's report. The Pawnbroker had nothing to lose since he paid five dollars for it and the woman gave him fifty as a reward."

"Are there ever times when you are asked to find things that don't want to be found?"

"Yeah, I'm sometimes asked to do that."

"What do you do in that case?"

"I evaluate whether it's in danger, but if it doesn't wish to be located, it won't usually signal that it needs to be found. There have been times when a person consciously said they didn't want to be found, but unconsciously they did, or they were mentally unstable and unable to make good decisions on their own. Sometimes they were afraid to call out for help aloud because they were under duress. Then, I found them. However, there have been times when a thing, animal, or person would have been abused if they were returned. I don't look for them."

"Wow! The police could sure use you!"

"No. I tried that, and they ended up treating me as though I had something to do with perpetrating the crime or they treated me like I was a wacko. One cop said I was one sandwich short of a picnic when I told him where to locate an extremely expensive set of jewelry that had been crying out to be returned from the thief who had stolen it. He tried to put me in a psychiatric hospital, but, when he discovered my prediction was correct, he thought I must have been involved in the crime somehow until he found out that there were witnesses who confirmed that I was two hundred miles away at the time of the burglary. Fortunately, the District Attorney said there was no concrete evidence to hold me."

"Oh-my-God! That's frustrating... and scary!" She couldn't explain it, but, somehow, they were experiencing the same emotions simultaneously. *Why do I feel so open to him? I have never trusted anyone so easily before.*

He realized their hearts were beating together in a dance of rhythmic synchronization that he had not experienced since he was in his mother's womb. *She's an empath, but,* Finder whispered in his ear, *her skills seem blocked and underutilized for some reason."*

"I don't know of any lost pets or lost people," she finally said. "I suppose people lose small items all the time, but I can't think of any right now." Her awareness returned to the coffee shop while Peter Gabriel sang, *I don't Remember. I don't recall. I got no memory of anything-anything at all...*

"Well, maybe my work is already done," he said with a tone of irony."

"You mean you already found something?"

"I found *you,* didn't I?! Can't you feel it?"

Beaming red so brightly and so intensely that her makeup seemed pale in comparison, Molly Everhart was experiencing the impact of something she was feeling but couldn't articulate. "You sure are a charmer! Do you use that line on all the girls you meet?" She realized how intensely she had been feeling their connection but was resisting it to avoid the disappointment of being wrong. She also became aware that she had implied a closer relationship than she intended.

"No. Just you," he looked her directly in the eye to make certain that there was no question about it, "and I'm always straightforward with people."

Her face beamed an impossibly one hundred watts brighter. "But I'm not lost!" she bubbled. He was silent for a dramatic cliffhanger moment that lasted twelve fluttering beats of her runaway heart while a million miles of uncontrolled thoughts and wonderment flashed by. *Am I?* She was suddenly uncertain. "Am I lost?" she finally said aloud.

"Not any longer, but maybe there's still…" He looked down and away. "You are the first person I found here," he abruptly changed the subject, trying to distract her, "and I was pulled here to the enthusiastic atmosphere in this establishment and that turned out to be you." He had no other idea why he was compelled to stop in this little off-the-track prairie town, but he knew now that it really was, at least in large part, for her. "Well," he said in a matter-of-fact voice, "do you know the etymology of the Greek for word beauty?"

"I have no idea. What does it mean?" *This guy is getting more interesting by the second.*

"It means calling. I felt you calling me."

"You made that up!"

"No. Look it up! Like I said, I'm always straight with people."

They were silent for an interminable twenty seconds. *Did he just call me beautiful?*

Sensing her awkward tension, he tried to divert the conversation, set it on a tangent, and shift the subject slightly away from her for the time being. "I think there is a secondary reason I'm here, but I don't know what it is yet. I'll have to hang around and experience the whole town before it tells me its secrets, but I know part of it is for you."

Relieved to be distracted, she suddenly became aware that she was sitting with a customer, stood up ready to return to her duties and took three steps. "So, you're what? A town whisperer?" She joked, over her shoulder.

"Well, a town can tell you a lot if you observe carefully."

She stopped in midflight and turned toward him transfixed and wondered if this guy was crazy. *A talking town? What th...* She felt a sarcastic twinge. "Okay, mister town whisperer, what has our little town told you so far?" She offered a challenging, skeptical smile standing there with her hands on her hips, arms akimbo. She bent slightly toward him at the waist, looking down into his eyes in a mild confrontational stance, reminding him of the poster with the little girl in the same stance with the caption, "Snap out of it!"

Staring deeply into those deep brown eyes, the ghost of sincerity passing between them, making a connection with an impact that she had never before encountered, he did not flinch. "It told me that there are people here who raised at least one bright, honest and attractive person who has untapped talent and beauty inside as well."

Disconcerting, unexpected, but flattering flames ignited her face in a fiery red blaze; one more opportunity for her to enjoy his admiration. Her eyelids demurred to half-mast, and she felt a drop of hot salty sweat trickling like dripping wax from a candle down her forehead that stung her left eye, *oh God! Now he's going to think I'm winking at him!* She felt so off guard, unable to predict his responses in her usually predictable world, that it was as if he had a kind of hypnotic command over her physiological responses. A mosquito, attracted to the incandescent light bulb above them, burned up in the heat of its desire.

Molly Everhart, unaware of her gaping mouth, unconsciously returned to the still warm chair, where time crawled by, her movements became slow and waxy, and she stared catatonically at this astonishing man, waiting for him to fill her with more wonders. *Is this a living novel?*

"To begin with," he continued, "there's the obvious." He sat back, rolled his eyes forty-five degrees to his left toward the sky and peered into his recollections of the past couple of hours. His head bobbed slightly for two very long seconds while he reviewed the images and conclusions wrought from the impressions he had collected so far.

A stillness blanketed the room as she crossed the diminishing personal boundary between them, used his napkin to rid her eye of the stinging pain, mopped up the pool of anxiety she had shed on the table as the coffee machines silently listened in, and the dust settled quietly in the corner. There was nothing left in the soundless air, save Molly Everhart's rapt attention. *The Rolling Stones' I can't get no satisfaction* was playing in the background, but nobody was listening.

"The town of Perfection told me," he began, "that there are very hard working and frugal people here who take care of things and keep them going no matter the cost of time and effort. It also told me that there is a kind of overly serious concern for rules and neatness. It told me that my finder services are needed and that I should stop here after something called out to me. It told me that it is struggling to be a good town with good people, except for the occasional minor preadolescent acting out, which, apparently, no one bothers to deal with, probably because they don't think it's important. I learned that it is the most pin neat urban environment I've ever seen and that the city does not tolerate anything out of place. There is no mess anywhere, and little is wasted. Every crack in brick or pavement is patched or compulsively replaced as soon as there is a perceived breach. I noticed that there is little interest in the world outside the confines of this city. I also learned that there's the odor of demarcation, an invisible line that divides it into something that conflicts with itself and, in its drive for perfection, it has lost something in the process. The good citizens of Perfection seem to have mixed up the difference between rule-bound perfection and goodness."

"You figured all that out," she said, "in the what? Less than the two hours you've been here and I'm the only person you've met?"

"Well, that's the easy part."

"Only part of it! Easy? Mister, you are something." She had never encountered anyone as observant and intuitive, let alone a man who was so insightful, not to mention so attractive!

"Well, like I said, so are you." He pondered his next words carefully. "In fact, I believe you are a rare and unique individual. Most people don't realize their potential. The only question is, are they doing what their lives intended? You, whether you know it or not, have something very special in you."

After the wave of sinful pride that accompanied the temporary feeling that she was special diminished, she felt a twinge of sadness somewhere deep within, looked away to wipe a single tear from her still stinging left eye, thinking there was more to her life, but she had been too afraid to embrace it. *I haven't been living up to my capabilities, but I don't feel special. How could he possibly be interested if he finds out how ordinary I really am?*

Momentarily, his brain was flooded with thought. "You know," he said, when at last he emerged from his meditation, "if you look deeply enough you can see beneath the surface of things and people. You can look into faces, the cracks in the sidewalk, the clouds in the sky, and see the things behind them; things they are trying to convey to you if you are mindful. I have the feeling you may have ignored what you know, and I'd love to pick your brain some more. I can see that there is a lot more in you, and I'd love to get inside you and discover it on a deeper level, but there are some things I have to do first."

She was dumbstruck. Never had anyone seen so far into the depths of her soul nor had anyone ever seemed interested in doing so. Not even, she realized, had she looked so deeply into herself, *and he wants to know more about me. Probably more than I know about myself!* He was right though, but it scared her and intrigued her simultaneously. She had ignored what she had seen around her as well as the crucible of understanding that had been boiling just below the surface of her consciousness.

After a pause long enough for Molly to digest her thoughts, Ebenezer Thornbird said, "If you look deeply enough, you'll see that there are links between everyone and everything. You just have to work it out. Of course, you must look for it whether it's tangible or metaphoric. There's always a connection. I think that's really what I tune into. This has been known for millennia. I read that Buddha discovered it six hundred years B.C.E. It's been at least that long, but there is evidence that it may go farther back than that. So, everything that is done or said is somehow linked throughout all existence and throughout time. I just happen, for whatever reason, to be able to reach into my small part of it and trace things that need to be tracked. It's my destiny. It's as if I'm standing in the ocean like everyone else, feeling the waves, but I sense the undercurrent, the riptide if you will, that others don't." Molly Everhart, looking through the steam rising from his cup, mixing with the clouds on the horizon, saw the next customer entering the shop through the haze. He had a suspicious eye on the stranger.

Molly noticed the paranoia peeking out from under the camouflage hunting cap and said, "Hi Bill! This is Eb. He's new in town." She knew that any stranger in town had to be scrutinized to prevent any disability they might bring down upon it.

Ebenezer Thornbird stood and shook Bill's flaccid dishrag hand while Molly Everhart got up and headed for her coffee machines. "Nice to meet you, Bill," he said with a smile.

After a faltering hesitation, Bill muttered "Likewise," with the flattest affect Ebenezer Thornbird had ever encountered, clearly avoiding eye contact as if it would be too painful to fully connect with another human being.

"The usual, Bill?" Molly interrupted. Bill offered a slight dip of his head, neck, and shoulders, bending at the waist as a single unit of affirmation, more like a bow than an affirmative head nod.

While he was still shaking Bill's limp, lifeless hand, Eb felt a cold blankness traveling between them, and he politely released his grip before he was sucked into the morass of nothingness. Eb asked, "Bill, do you know where I can find a place to stay for a few days?"

Bill stood ensconced in a paralytic stare into dead air for ten agonizing seconds before he shook his head and said, "No." Bill's empty hand remained suspended for ten beats of his meager pulse after Eb let go before he dropped it. He walked away, arms falling straight down at his sides dangling from his slumped and defeated shoulders like two dead worms, and fled, making his way, dragging his anxiety to a solitary back table.

The walking dead, Eb shivered.

"There's a motel about a mile south Eb." Molly said, pointing in that direction as she shook her head imperceptibly, hunched her shoulders, raised her eyebrows, rolled her eyes and pointed them in Bill's direction as if to say, "Don't pay attention to him that's just the way he is."

"Okay, thanks. See you later Molly." There was a sudden moment of connection between them as if they were of a single mind that startled them both.

"Okay, see you Eb! Come on back!"

Her hopes followed him out the door and down the street until he disappeared from her sight, but not from her soul. Her gut longed desperately for his return while she fell back into her duties, to her jealous and neglected apparatus, and set about the business of serving Bill his usual. She didn't notice *All You Need is Love* playing on the radio, but she did notice a feeling in her stomach like the sensation she felt during the downward slam in the sudden descent following the suspended stillness at the top on a roller coaster.

This was how Ebenezer Thornbird entered Molly Everhart's life and the myths and legends of Perfection and how they both became entangled in his quest.

CHAPTER THREE
EBENEZER

Moirae Clotho, the midwife attending Maya Thornbird during parturition, watched over the thread of life that began to spin when baby Ebenezer slid out of his mother followed by a fifteen-foot umbilical cord that, still clutching the placenta, flabbergasted the supervising obstetrician. Ebenezer Thornbird was a little early, not so much because he was ready but, because he felt his mother's desperate need calling for him to emerge. It wasn't that she actually said anything; he just felt her silent pleas through the fluctuation of their synchronized hearts.

He was the product of the kind of love that only exists in the haze of mind-altering drugs. His mother was just eighteen when, at a rock concert for an amnesic band she no longer remembered, she met a lanky thirty-three-year-old Mexican Native American mix with the Spanish-sounding name of Jesus (Heh-soos). He had long hair and a beard. He and Maya ingested some kind of hallucinogen along with ecstasy and, under the influence, he said he knew for a fact that he was a god. He claimed that he rode a piece of Jupiter that broke off from the fifth planet all the way to Earth and landed near the West coast of Florida which, to her chemically induced state of mind, seemed reasonable. He probably slipped her a Rohypnol, the date rape drug, because she had no memory of anything after they flopped in his van, but she was sure they must have had sex after the concert from the disheveled state of her clothes and the fact that her panties were on backward. Someone else had obviously dressed her in a psychotic rush. She awoke the next morning laying on her parents' front lawn feeling sick and presently vomited before she retrieved her now empty purse and wallet, staggered into the house and collapsed into a two-day stupor. She never saw Jesus again, and Ebenezer never knew his father.

Maya Thornbird awoke two hours after extruding the exhausted afterbirth and scanned the room surprised to find flowers of every variety, mostly white ones sprinkled with lavender and red roses, miraculously blanketing the entire room, but they were covering her too. Their fragrances intermingled and created a blanket of awe and wonder. The mysterious flowers were strewn about the hospital room, a blanket a foot deep, as if they had fallen at random from the sky, filling the bassinette next to her bed burying Ebenezer to the point that only his newborn head was extant. She had no idea where the flowers came from, but she smiled at little Ebenezer swaddled in orchids and then vomited into the emesis basin on the bed table. Reaching for her necklace with her grandmother's protective ring on it, she was alarmed to discover that the nurse had removed it. There was a family legend that it had been blessed by her great-grandfather, a Native American Medicine Man who, she was told, said that it would keep the wearer safe.

No one ever discovered where the flowers came from.

Maya never recovered from the delivery, became increasingly weak and lost twenty pounds in seven days before her death baffled the doctors. She had developed phantom complications from the birth, cried and pleaded for her son when Ebenezer had to be isolated from her when she became septic, and despite the doctors' heroic efforts, she died of a broken heart one week later.

Maya's eldest sister, Pati, took Ebenezer home and adopted him. She was the only mother he knew beyond the eight and a half months and seven days of gestation in the womb. Pati never had any biological children of her own despite the herculean efforts of her husband who, eighteen years her senior, had died of exhaustion when his heart failed in bed in the middle of sexual intercourse. It had been exactly five years and precisely two thousand attempts to fertilize Pati's eggs. Performing the odd ritual after intercourse, of dangling upside down with her husband holding her ankles high in the air, trying to form a partnership with gravity in their attempt to aid his little soldiers to breach the walls of her oval fortress and claim their prize. She continued to feel unfulfilled without a child to dote over until she adopted Ebenezer.

Undifferentiated at birth, Ebenezer Thornbird could have grown in any direction, but his newborn cells began to travel along the tightrope thread of destiny, continued to differentiate into the man he became, and he never questioned his fate, nor did he struggle to change it. He had seen too many people who, trying to fight theirs, had only increased their pace toward the very fate they were trying to avoid and shortened the distance between themselves and the fateful scissors of Atropos. Instead, he let life lead him slowly toward the very distant end of the path. His ability to connect with others at the level of their needs often made people feel uneasy around him, but they didn't know why. That ability to read others and the knack for locating lost things isolated him from everyone else. However, he was never lost, and he never forgot where things were.

Ebenezer Thornbird gained the nickname of "Finder" at the age of five when his adoptive mother lost her car keys. In the nonchalant, confident and matter-of-fact voice of a child much too mature for his age, he said he knew where they were and led her to where she found the keys, in the bushes on the driver's side of the driveway. When asked how he knew where they were, he could only say in his limited five-year-old vocabulary, "I heard them calling me." Of course, no one believed him. They laughed and said he was cute. Pati smiled, patted his head, tousled his hair and said, "He must have seen me drop them." But a week later Pati couldn't find her wallet. He interrupted his play for a moment, and without looking at her, he said, "You left it at that store you went to." When she called the said establishment and discovered he was correct, she was shocked. He had been at home with his Greek sitter, Parcae Lochesis, who said with a matter-of-fact tone, "He's a finder" and the moniker of "Finder" was glued to his totemic spirit and the thread of fate that determined the course of his life. He had begun to feel as if he were two people; Ebenezer and Finder. He knew that he really didn't actually find things, but they found him somehow. They let him know where they were and that they wanted or needed to be repatriated. It was as if they were distressed, felt abandoned, longed to return to their rightful place in the stream of their intended lives, and he seemed to be the only one listening.

Parcae once told little Ebenezer when he was twelve years old, "Make no mistake, someday you will find yourself facing the very danger you will have been preparing for all your life just when you are ready. You'll be faced with temptation, threatened, and lost with little more than the skills you'll acquire in the meantime to protect you. It may be symbolic or mythic, but mark my words, you will be in danger for your life and your psyche and, if you survive it, there will be a difference in you. What that difference turns out to be will only be partly up to you. You'll be distracted by love and anger and wrenched by guilt. It is your destiny to be torn between your good and pure intentions and the unintended consequences of carrying them out. The treatment for this cancer, like all cancer cures, is so toxic that it nearly kills the patient while trying to kill the disease." His nanny hesitated for one minute before saying, "Destiny is like the sun. It's always there. No matter where you run, you can't deceive it, you'll never escape it even when you cannot see it through the clouds of unknowing. There's no sense trying to change it because it can't be defeated. So, acceptance is the only choice if you don't want to go mad denying the unstoppable."

CHAPTER FOUR
MOLLY

Molly Everhart was conceived through sheer mechanical precision drills that, thankfully, only went on for a month before pregnancy caught and peace and solitude reigned once more, at least until the specters of vomiting and eventual backbreaking pain, frequent urination, physical fatigue, and discomfort set in.

Molly was born through an unnecessary cesarean section merely because her mother wanted to get the whole messy thing over with and the obstetrician wanted to avoid being called to deliver the baby in the middle of the night when most children are born. The whole thing was more efficient, and besides, her mother reckoned that she could, with the help of lots of drugs, handle the recovery from abdominal surgery more easily than pushing Molly out through hours of the exhausting and frightening tight squeeze of natural childbirth. Her fears had been exacerbated by the horror stories she read in her conservative women's magazines. *How much more painful can it be than recovering from my appendectomy?*

Molly was born in the nearby town of Orson Wells three miles away, in the only hospital close enough to reach in an emergency or an urgent situation like childbirth. Her parents had always lived and worked in Perfection; respected citizens who intended to bring Molly up by the book. Molly was never sure which book they were talking about or whether they ever actually read it, but they hired a prophetic Native American nanny Artemis.

Artemis had been named by J.T., her Native American medicine-man father, after he read about the Geek god, a protector of the vulnerable. When he told his wife, she rolled her eyes. "I know it is her unique fate to serve the same protective purpose as Artemis," he defended. As Molly's protector, Artemis sheltered Molly from unrealistic expectations, taught her to question the rules and the opinions of others, and served as her nurturing mentor. Although Molly, during her childhood, followed Artemis' advice, she eventually had to stifle herself.

Molly's mother was, through the distant mists and fog of the past and a one half genetic connection, a distant relative of Apollyon Zane, the founder of Zanesville, who had owned most of the town, and was descended from a long line of St. Louis Zanes. Following his death, his St. Louis relatives arrived in Zanesville, took over Apollyon's property, sold the ranch to the granary and liquidated most of his businesses. Only one Zane offshoot remained in town. The Everharts.

Molly was a delightful child full of vigor as most kids were, but she seemed more so than the others. She had friends and spent time with them in play, overnighters, and parties. She was floating through the innocent fog of childhood unimpeded by misfortune but somehow that all disappeared when she turned thirteen. It seemed to her that, without warning, she had been transformed from the girl with many friends into the odd girl out. She was suddenly invisible socially, and her personality began a process of self-imposed implosion designed to regain her lost relationships to no avail. She tried mightily to fit in, but her interests were so different from theirs that she felt exiled within a prison of her own making in reaction to her social isolation. She spent increasing amounts of time alone and occupied her mind in solitary pursuits, in her room or out in the fields looking at the dreaming cloud formations and reading her novels. As an older child, she was able, through persuasive argument, to convince her parents to purchase a magical tablet that she could use to download books, but they didn't realize this gave her access to the internet and exposure to ideas that were foreign to them, and frankly, against their values.

It seemed odd that her parents were so stiff and dry compared to her opposite moist, fluid and flexible approach to life, especially after hearing them talk about their childhood of mischief, the fact that they had been inseparable in those years, and despite the pranks they played on each other. They had formed a bond early in life and carried it through to its inevitable conclusion of marriage and child-rearing. They had wanted to have the average two children, a girl, and a boy, but they were destined to have only one girl and saddled, they secretly believed, with one who was so odd and different from them, and everyone else in town for that matter, that they wondered what had happened. Once she attained adolescence, they did their best to discourage her from expressing her real self in order to avoid social ostracism.

Molly's mother's personality had apparently retreated from the juicy plum of childhood into the rigid, humorless, dried-up prune of her present condition. Compassion and flexibility were not her strong suits since she held the unshakable belief that children should find their own way in life with as little help from others as possible, especially once they reached puberty and presumably had acquired reason. Once, when Molly was small, she fell down on the sidewalk, skinned her knees and cried. Her mother, instead of going to her, picking her up in her arms, and consoling her, said, "Come here, and I'll pick you up," with an emotionless expression. However, instead of eliciting the desired response of shutting Molly up, it engendered the flames of rage, that cold-hearted blackness of bitter despair that widened the gulf between them. Her nanny filled the gap until Molly was thirteen when there was no longer the need for Artemis. Molly loved her mother, but could never feel close to her. Unable to penetrate that cold hard bubble, she sought out her playmates and Artemis for solace, but this only lasted until the other kids fell, she assumed, under the spell of their parent's drive to excel in emotionless financial and social status, and began to compete in cutthroat board games. She had hoped that, as her mother's heart, encased in that rock of solid ice, might melt as she grew older, at least a little, but the stone seemed more stiff and impenetrable than ever.

Her friends were no longer compassionate or supportive, and Molly felt herself sinking into the quicksand of inevitable anonymity. Artemis was grievously missing now too. Molly retreated from the warm, damp, earthly world of childhood, into herself in the losing battle for her soul. She gave in to the foreboding, lofty, arid, and desolate emptiness that she seemed never to be able to fill with her books and the solitude of her field of dreams. She graduated from adolescent novels and sterilized biographies to adult books that became increasingly bent toward the classics and the ones that were more intimate in the details of sensuality and descriptive of sexual relationships. She knew that these were books of fiction, as her mother pointed out, and that reality was very different, but she longed to dive in and swim in the liberated reality she imagined in the unreal world of novels.

CHAPTER FIVE
FINDER

Ebenezer Thornbird intuited his mother's need for him to emerge from her womb and continued to read people by how they acted and what they said. He was a deep listener who could read between the lines. He intuitively understood, so to speak, Chomsky's deep structure of language that he later learned about in college. He understood what people meant through their broken sentences, body language, words, voice inflection and, to a great extent, he could predict what they were going to say and do, often before they knew it themselves. He was good at reading the spirits peeking up from their unconscious minds.

At the edge of five years of age, little Ebenezer Thornbird encountered the first shock of his life since his birth into the cold, rude world when he faced the terrors of separation from his adoptive mother, Pati, during the first day of kindergarten. It wasn't the actual trauma of separation from Pati that disturbed him. It was the even scarier chaos that erupted around him caused by the other children who clung to their mothers crying, screaming, and putting up their strongest resistance against being left alone to fend for themselves against the outrageous misfortune facing them. Eb was so shocked that when he wished with all his might he could escape from the tumult of the intense, overwhelming, and desperate trauma of longing that surrounded him, he felt a part of his consciousness separating deep within. A part that felt the toys across the room wanting, no needing, to be played with; longing for their purpose to be fulfilled. That part of Ebenezer Thornbird, who was later to be labeled "Finder" said, *Hey! Those toys are crying for us to play with them!* Eb turned his head to locate the toys, and said, over his shoulder, "Goodbye mom," and headed across that barren expanse of open floor to rescue the toys from their deprivation, and he had them all to himself. This left Pati wondering if he loved her or if he was simply more mature than his peers. It wasn't long before Finder began to advise Eb when he detected something or someone that needed to be found. It was soon after that fateful kindergarten experience that he began to trail after Pati locating the lost things she misplaced, and his nanny dubbed him "Finder." He had an uncanny sense of where something belonged and when it needed to be returned to its natural place in the scheme of things. It was as if the universe was a jigsaw puzzle that needed its missing pieces put back where they belonged. Finder settled in just behind Eb's left ear, or so it seemed, when he was serving in an advisory capacity. Sometimes, though, Finder would briefly take over Eb's body whenever action was required before Eb realized the need to move quickly, and there wasn't time for advice.

In childhood, Ebenezer Thornbird's adoptive mother used to reprimand him for talking to strangers for fear he'd be abducted or hurt in some way, but he learned from early on how to manipulate any situation, no matter, it seemed, the potential danger it posed.

Once, as a young boy, he encountered a group of three threatening older boys in the late dusky evening on his way home from baseball practice and the boring team meeting that followed. Except for his proud and comforting baseball mitt attached to his belt, he was alone armed only with his wit and mental agility when Finder heard the sinister crunching sound of three sets of foreboding feet following him on the gravel walkway, announcing their presence. Those steps quickened after he heard the echo of whispering unintelligible, but excited conspiratorial voices while the three boys caught up to him. The leader of the group, the alpha male of this wannabe wolf pack, a large boy, two years his senior, stopped him and, with his henchmen surrounding their victim, pushed him hard in the chest nearly knocking him to the ground.

"Where do you think *you're* going?" They all laughed while he struggled to regain his balance. *That's original*, he thought and stood at a ninety-degree angle with one shoulder toward Alpha. He had learned that this was the best defensive stance because it presented the smallest target if an attack was threatened. He was Ben, the main character in *the Night of the Living Dead,* surrounded by mindless Zombies preparing to vanquish him. *Brains! I need brains!* Finder whispered with a mock lugubrious voice in Eb's ear. Remaining pokerfaced, appearing outwardly calm, his heart was *shocked into a gallop, and his lungs came along for the ride. This isn't going well, Finder said. The alpha was already displaying his lack of intelligence. Thought, emotion, and social skill are lacking, and the biggest missing piece is the creativity that he would need to sustain his leadership for long.* Eb intuited this and thought, *that's our advantage.* Alpha was holding his leadership together with bravado, his sheer size, the fact that his cronies were dumber than he, and they were probably a year younger. The long shadows of dusk were lengthening, and there was a cool breeze kicking up. The evening was quieting down, there were few cars to be heard out on the road anymore, and the stench of danger was overpowering.

The voice of Finder said, *Stay calm.* The victim felt scared and tried to maintain a cool façade while putting his calculating brain into high gear and attempted to create a diversion.

With the most calm and matter-of-fact voice he could muster, he said, "You may be bigger, stronger and quicker than me..." trying to align with their vanity, "but you're missing out on something much better than wasting your time messing with me."

The Alpha cocked his torpedo shaped head at a forty-five-degree angle and, pride puffing up his swelling chest like a blowfish, smirking the smirk of a true skeptic, he fired off his expected question on cue. "What are we missing?"

"To get some money the easy way," Ebenezer Thornbird exclaimed.

"What money?" Alpha sneered with a glimmer of interest peeking through the clouds of his unintelligent and pretend machismo.

"I know a store that leaves a back window unlocked at night. You can slip in and grab the cash," he said, "Easy peezy. Neat. No sweat!"

"What if they didn't leave it open tonight?" Alpha had to keep up his snide attitude for show in front of his posse.

"Well then, I guess you'd be too scared to break a window." He channeled Tom Sawyer, trying to get them to do the dirty work for him.

"We ain't scared of nothin'," sneered Alpha.

"Yeah!" The other boys chimed in, trying to cover their fear with clenched fists and wide eyes. They were made of only ten percent bravado. Ninety percent was Fear and tension masked by their facade of fearless confidence.

"Okay then, follow me!" He stepped away from Alpha and walked between his two cronies symbolically splitting them. They closed ranks behind him, forcing Alpha to follow his lead and bring up the rear. Intrigued, they trailed him down the street to the rear of a store, thereby taking the first step toward gaining the upper hand. Now that they were following *him*, he had established himself, at least temporarily, as a part of their group and the authority on this caper. He said, "I'm always the lookout while my friends go in for the cash. They're bigger and much better athletes than I am and can climb and run faster." Playing on their grandiose machismo façade as "better athletes" than he, and the fact that they were beating someone else to it, he said, "but you prevented me from getting to them so here we are." Taking the bait, they were enveloped by the intoxicating fumes of his monetary persuasion, and he was instantly transformed from a victim to a co-conspirator. When they encountered the stubborn, locked window, they insisted that he do the honors of breaking it as an act of trust and implicit initiation. That way he'd be implicated as one of them if they were caught. After looking around and, satisfied that they were alone and there were no cameras, he threw a rock through the window, making it as loud as possible. The boys quickly entered the shop after clearing away the excess glass leaving him as lookout in the alley while the phantom silent alarm he knew was there had been triggered. As soon as they were swallowed up by the building he ran so fast, driven by sheer panic, that he beat memory home with no recall of how he magically arrived there out of breath and sweating profusely, but it was the cold sweat of terror by the time he entered the house.

His adoptive mother said, "You're late."

While his breath was frantically trying to catch up to him, like a trapped animal in a cage, his heart tried to exit his chest as his pulse banged in his ears so loudly that he didn't hear the sirens until he reached his house. "It was a long meeting after practice," he lied.

Later, he told the boys he ran when he heard the cops coming, knowing they must have heard it too, "but," he said, "I yelled to you as I ran away." They said they didn't hear him, but believed him when he said, "Maybe you didn't hear me because I had panicked and started to run when I yelled. My voice probably didn't carry through the window." Miraculously, they bought his explanation.

From then on, they considered him one of their group of budding sociopaths. After all, he did break the window, and there really was cash in the till, even if they didn't get away with it, so he hadn't steered them wrong. It was just bad luck that the silent alarm had nabbed them. They never turned him in, they hadn't asked his name anyway, and they were merely placed on probation for six months on the charge of breaking and entering. They were minors, and this was their first actual arrest, probably in a long eventual rap sheet just waiting to chronicle their ill-conceived deeds. They seemed proud that they had a criminal record. To them it was "street cred," and by some odd quirk of illogic, it made them seem like dangerous legends in their tiny little minds. He kept a distance and a low profile so no one would think he really took any part in their stupidity.

As he matured, he became more competent at persuasion with the help of his inner advisor, and talked himself into and out of situations as needed, partly because he was a good listener and, more importantly, he knew what people needed. The other part of him had the knack of determining what others lacked or wanted, and he could determine what they had lost. He wasn't a con man though because he never used his abilities to harm anyone or steal anything; but instead, he merely used his talents to obtain work or to extricate himself from a bad situation and rescue lost things and people that needed finding. The universe was made of waves of circumstance flowing in an ocean, leading everyone to their destiny like a whirlpool sucking everyone and everything toward a fateful end. He knew, as he grew older, never to question his fate, but this left him a stranger in a strange land.

Everyone else seems to be struggling against their destiny. The whole universe is in flux, but no one else seems to see or sense it. I'm alone in the world. No one feels or sees things the way I do.

****

There was an incident two years ago, he remembered, that was a summary example of his interpersonal abilities.

He was winning at the poker table with a group of individuals with rather elastic morals who were unhappy losers, upset about losing so spectacularly to a stranger that they suspected him of cheating. One man, who said his name was John, leaped up, pushing his chair back, pulled a gun, and yelled, "You cheated me!" Everyone jumped up, flying out of their chairs that tipped over, and backed off elbows bent with hands out in front of them as one of them said, "Woah!"

There was nothing to do but drop his cards and raise his hands high while the others searched him for hidden cards and secreted cheating devices. When they came up empty, they made him strip naked while his irritated clothes longed to return to their rightful place on his body. They turned them inside out and made certain there was nothing taped to him, but again, they found nothing.

"I haven't cheated you! You have been cheating yourselves!" he was redressing them while he re-dressed himself.

"What do you mean we cheated ourselves?" John said with a sarcastic eye-squinting tone, his head cocked to one side, pointing his weapon directly at the chest of the accused.

"Well," he said, "for one thing, you all have tells."

"Not on your life!" said John.

The others asked, "What tells?"

He spent the next twenty-three and a half minutes, after he put his clothes back on, pointing out each character's Tell. "You," pointing at John, "look right and then left when you have a poor hand. You," pointing at the next victim, "hunch in your shoulders slightly when you have a winning hand. And you," shifting his pointing finger to the next man, "tap the toes of your right foot when you have a good hand."

The others laughed, "Thumper!" they teased, embarrassing the man, but this served to break the tension, causing John to slowly lower his flabbergasted weapon, accompanied by his jaw, in an aghast open-mouthed expression. They ended up asking him to teach them to improve their play.

He spent the next three hours doing so before he feigned exhaustion and said, "I'm beat, see you tomorrow," collected his winnings and left town on the first conspiratorial bus, purposely forgetting to mention the fact that he had been counting the cards all along. Realizing that Finder had detected the money longing for liberation from those thugs, he smiled himself to sleep.

****

Ebenezer Thornbird had been a top student all through school, got along with most of the other students and professors, and achieved his college degree. He had several brief sexual relationships with coeds. There was one waitress at an off-campus restaurant who seemed to present herself with hips pushed against his infatuated and lustful table every time she waited on him. The table, it seemed, nearly orgasmed in response because it always rocked slightly and his water glass sweat more profusely with each encounter. She waited on him no matter where he sat, so he eventually gave in and took her to bed. Despite the good time he had with all of the women, none of which were particularly close, he always felt so different from them that those relationships were short-lived. He longed for a girlfriend with whom he was compatible, a relationship of mutual understanding.

This feeling of being left out on the fringes extended to his academic goals when his major concentrations in journalism and in psychology did him little good since there were few jobs in journalism at the time and none in psychology without advanced degrees. Following an urge to head out on the road of freelance travel writing, satisfying the need to roam and explore his interest in people, interacting with them in their natural settings, he decided to write travel articles and books. He took his old laptop, a pen and notebook, began his prophetic journey across the country, picking up odd jobs as he went along to supplement the meager income from his articles about the places he visited and the experiences he had. He was neither interested in accumulating a lot of money nor in amassing material goods.

****

Ebenezer Thornbird and Finder worked together seamlessly. Eb reading people and circumstances on the spot, and Finder detecting the needs of the lost and the misplaced. Finder heard Molly calling, and Ebenezer Thornbird was able to develop their relationship with his genuine intuitive charm. But, in her case, he knew that it wasn't just Molly's need to be found, but her need to be understood, loved and liberated. These were the very things he had longed for all his life as well, and Finder knew it as much as he did. There was a part of Molly Everhart calling, begging to be liberated from a kind of internal exile she had learned to perpetrate on herself.

Finder In Hell World

CHAPTER SIX
RESTAURANT SECRETS

Ebenezer Thornbird returned to the *Wake-Up! Coffee Shop* at precisely two o'clock by the atomic clock on the wall, and walked straight to the confident counter behind which Molly stood with anticipating breath. Dolly Parton's *Little Bird* was playing in the background.

"Hi, Eb!" Molly cried out before she realized she had expelled a few too many decibels, and thinking she sounded more exuberant than she should have, she looked around self-consciously at the three customers, but there was no significant reaction.

"Hi Molly, can we talk later?" he said in a soft and husky voice that sent her emotions spinning.

"Sure Eb. What do you have in mind?" There was that smile again!

"What time do you get off work?"

"I get off at three-thirty today." Her eyes had dilated into deep staring pools of desire inviting him to dive in. He looked into those very alluring orbs but held back at the edge of those waters until he was farther down the stream where he felt destiny was compelling him to go. Besides, his inner voice, Finder, said, *there's danger here.* He knew it wasn't in her, but he feared involving her, or anyone for that matter, into his quest, at least until he understood it clearly. He was drawn to her, and that made him feel protective. "Is there someplace where we can talk in private?" he asked. "I'll buy you dinner."

An unfettered smile blasted from her face, so loud and broad that it would have burst his eardrums if it was audible, and it would have hurt her face, but she was too distracted by her excitement to notice it. She was stretching facial muscles she had probably never used before. "We can meet at the diner down the street," she said, pointing in the direction of the anticipated sanctuary for a potentially intimate discussion. "It's called the *Dine Inn.* We can sit in the back where no one will bother us, and I don't think anyone can hear us there. How about five o'clock, so I can go home and change?"

"Okay, but don't change too much. I like you just the way you are." His joke was such a stale adolescent cliché that, making him blush a little, it caused an awkward hour-long two-second pause while she stood there not comprehending, giving him time to reboot. "Okay," he finally said, "I think I passed it earlier in my walkabout. See you there," he said, offering an engaging, compassionate smile and, waving over his shoulder, Ebenezer Thornbird left the coffee shop carrying his self-assured and very experienced backpack slung over his shoulder.

Little Peggy March was singing *I Will Follow Him* in the background.

"See you Eb," she said while her smile and racing heart followed him out the door until he was out of sight. Although he disappeared from view, her thoughts and feelings followed him all the way to the end of the street before she was distracted by a customer, her unconscious mind taking over the task of mentally stalking him while her heart flopped around in her chest, and she turned her conscious awareness to the customer. "Yes Ms. McDonald, what can I get you?"

****

When Ebenezer Thornbird arrived at five o'clock, Molly Everhart was sitting at a very happy back table of the *Dine Inn* with two smiling glasses of water and expectant menus. Classical music softly played in the background. "Hi, Eb!" Molly heard herself say with a spirited impact of way too much gusto.

"Hi Molly!" he said with a matching grin that was a little too enthusiastically wide for their brief acquaintance, but his expression put her at ease. Eager to accommodate him, the booth opened up, pulled him into its embrace and, with a single smooth stroke of confidence, he slid into the welcoming seat with a steady and congenial attitude. It was just the refreshing breeze she needed to cool the climbing temperature of her anticipation and the longing in her belly.

****

Molly Everhart was born in the neighboring town's hospital and had only left Perfection to commute to the college ten miles away where most of the students were Perfection High grads. Even though she had lived there all her life, some part of her knew instinctively that there was something wrong with just about everyone who lived in this stale and stuffy town. However, she had suppressed this knowledge as if it was a terrible sin for which she never confessed. She ended up turning it against herself as though she was the one who was so badly flawed. If she was so different than everyone else, she concluded, she had to be the odd piece that didn't fit an incomplete puzzle. *Perhaps it's a piece of a different puzzle.* She had always been a highly active child, like most preschoolers until they hit the wall of school rules and socialization with other budding peers; and again, in middle school when the merciless dangers of adolescence struck. However, she didn't realize that her peers suddenly started developing differently than kids in the rest of the world. She did realize that she was traveling a divergent path that increasingly set her apart from the others. Everyone in school seemed to resemble their parents more and more every year after sixth grade. Although the others did not make fun of her, it was as if they didn't notice her either, which made her recognize her increasing distance from them and everyone else in town. She often felt ghost-like in the midst of a crowd. She noticed that everyone else was encapsulated in an organized and steady bubble compared to her openness to life and its emotions. She wondered if she had been adopted or snatched at birth from another mother's loving embrace. Maybe there was some sort of disastrous genetic misfire or birth defect. Whatever the reason, her tears burned her bed at night amid the outbreak of her teenage passions that created intense angst and belied the war between her repulsion for the attitudes of others and her desire for acceptance. She knew that there was something wrong with her so she tried to fall into step with all the other runners by subduing her emotions during the day, but she always felt as if she was losing the race. She felt like the victims of Tourette's syndrome who have learned to suppress their barks and epithets all day only to relieve themselves of the tension by spewing them out in the privacy of the solitary, lonely night. She drained the gasoline of her tears silently into her consoling pillows that were in tatters from excessive hugs, kisses, floods of misery, and ignited by flames of passion.

Molly Everhart had always endured her isolation with especially intense anguish in her increasingly insomniac bed at two in the morning. She knew she had been condemned by some malevolent force in the universe to a solitary life, drowning with angst in the depths of loneliness and despair. She kept her emotional ballast below deck away from the fresh air of life and love, trying to keep herself afloat on an even keel in the attempt, at least on the surface, to appear as if she belonged to the rest of the fleet, but her mental seas were rarely calm.

No one seemed interested in Molly Everhart and, despite her physical attractiveness, she was rarely asked out on a date; and then only by boys and men who were so emotionless and distant that she couldn't tolerate their company for long. She did have one date that almost set her on a different trajectory with a young man from out of town, a transfer student attending the same college for a semester, her only sexual encounter. It was brief and wholly unsatisfying because, in addition to his emotional availability to her, his availability extended to too many other girls and to an irresistible wanderlust. He soon disappeared into the sunset of her memory, turning it from brilliant purples, pinks, and yellows to black and white; an old noir film playing in her mind of him riding off in his pickup truck and cowboy hat over the horizon with another girl. She thought of Rick's last line in *Casablanca* "*We'll always have Paris.*"

Starting in her early preteen years, Molly Everhart began reading exciting novels, some of which smoldered with the agitation of dangerous passions. The kind her mother called "trashy" even though many of them were classic prize-winning novels. At age sixteen her mother caught her masturbating in bed after reading the particularly sensual section of a novel. She was told that those books were simply myths and fictions and "no one is really like that," so she shouldn't believe anything she read.

"Besides," her mother added as a parting shot when she slipped out the door, "touching yourself down there will make you a hunchback."

From then on, despite her mother's attitude and her own increasingly secretive compulsive reading and related activities, Molly tried to straighten her posture whenever she slumped, fearing everyone would realize what she was doing in the sanctity of her own private room.

She tried to save her soul by attending the local churches, to no avail. There was the Catholic Church, St. Josephat, whose rituals and Latin she couldn't understand probably because she was not raised Catholic and had never attended catechism. This was the same for the Greek Orthodox Church, St. John the Devine, with their services partly in Aramaic or Greek. The Missouri Synod Lutherans were way too conservative, and they practically squeaked in their constrained and stifling strictness. The Episcopal Church, St. Jerome, was a hybrid of the others. There was Emerson Unitarian Church in Orson, but it was too intellectual, more philosophical than theological, except for the sermons that included all religious traditions and philosophies that sometimes confused her, but in any case, they didn't seem to focus on her needs. She found them all dull and boring. The only thing the sermons inspired was somnolence and loud snoring of at least half the congregation. No other denominations ever took hold there probably because they were too emotional and charismatic. *There is no room for stomping, yelling, falling out and Bible-thumping in Perfection,* she thought with a sarcastic tone.

Nothing exciting or even interesting ever happened in this little buttoned-down hamlet of Perfection. There was little crime, except for the minor mischief of the occasional juvenile stunts of a few later elementary and early middle school boys who, largely ignored, were remanded to their parents for exactly no punishment at all, and confined to their fantasy and toy-filled bedrooms where they spent most of their time, anyway. Everything was by the book, data-driven or "evidence-based." Little was left to speculation, intuition was looked down upon, and inspiration was practically nonexistent. Couples got married not for love, but for practical reasons such as procreation or for tax deduction status. The meaning of the word 'love' seemed to be a rote cultural acknowledgment of statistically determined compatibility to be confirmed publicly by legal contract. An arrangement in which, during an argument, only a skewed sampling of their gender-matched friends agreed that each of their opposing views was correct.

****

Ebenezer Thornbird seemed to be a misfit, just as much as Molly Everhart knew she was, with the profound exception that he seemed at ease with himself, compared to her overwhelming self-doubts, suffering the lack of self-confidence since the onslaught of adolescence.

Now he was sitting across from her in the booth at the unimaginative *Dine Inn* and he, to her delighted surprise, had asked her there. She felt her needs awaken from their secret caves of banishment but tried to keep her hopes in check in order to skirt any inevitable disappointment and heartache. As always, she feared opening up too much, despite the lack of awareness that she was unconsciously telegraphing many of her feelings anyway. As had always been her custom, in her attempt to place the attention on other people, she spoke first. That way, she could connect with them while, at the same time, avoid the spotlight and thereby hide from any scrutiny of her true nature. Distracting people in this town by getting them to discuss anything but personal matters was a snap for her since they were obsessed with topics that were, for the most part, floating somewhere in the social and emotional ozone external to actual human experience. "So why did you ask me on this dinner date?" she asked with a certain tongue-in-cheek humor to put him off guard.

"Date?" he choked, "well, I a...." He looked down to shade his eyes until they had adjusted to the brightness of her smile, paused for exactly fifteen seconds, and slowly raised his head in time to see his own reflection in her eyes.

"Just kidding. About the date, I mean," she said.

"Well," he reluctantly revealed, "for one thing, calling it a date is just fine with me, and I felt called to you before I even saw you. Wait, that's two things. Anyway, you were the strongest pull I've felt in a long time, stronger than any human or any woman, ever."

Her breath caught, her heart skipped precisely three beats, and she felt a little light-headed from the diminished blood flow to her brain. She had wished hard nearly every night since she was a lonely teenager for someone who, leaping out of her novels, would come to her rescue; someone to whom she could relate, and who understood her. Her novels had stoked the flames of longing for the characters that seemed more human, or at least, more like her than those around her. *How did he know?* She was wrapped in her shock mixed with excited surprise. *Things like this don't happen to me. Am I dreaming and will I soon awaken in my empty and disappointed bed?*

"As a secondary matter," he said, "I thought, once I met you, that you could help me understand more about why this town is also calling me here. In addition to meeting you and your needs, I mean."

For the first time in her life, she didn't know what to say. She always had something she could say even though she held most of it back. This time, though, she found herself suspended in the silent vastness of the expanding space of her psychic universe trying to make room for his alien spacecraft. She stared at him blankly long enough for her mind to descend back to its original launching pad in her skull.

The spider in the corner of the ceiling detected the hapless fly caught in its web, but no one noticed, nor was Molly aware of the waitress standing next to her ready to take her order.

Eb told the waitress they needed more time and politely sent her away.

"Well," Molly said, shaking herself back from the rigor mortis of suspended time and a dead pocket in space, "I'd love to help you, but I don't know how to begin. How can I help you get what you need?" Her smile had become nearly a grimace. Despite his positive view of her, Molly's anxiety belied her troubled mind; her difficulty letting go of her life-long self-image. She clasped her hands together on the table to hide their spasms of excitement. Her pulse was pounding in her ears now, and her palms were leaking so profusely that they were beginning to form a puddle on the table. She quickly drew them away and picked up a napkin to absorb her anxiety, but the flood was unstoppable.

He said, "I've been wandering around town, meeting as many people as I could, and I've had several strange encounters with residents and business owners."

The waitress floated blankly back into the picture, and they placed their orders.

CHAPTER SEVEN
NOSEY EBENEZER

Eb said, "Molly, there's something odd here, I've been poking around town talking to people, and it made me realize another reason why I needed to meet you. You are so different from the people I've met so far."

The shudder swept through her that confirmed and reinforced her rather lonely self-view. She looked down shyly and studied the now embarrassed and profusely sweating water glass, telling herself, *I knew I shouldn't get my hopes up. I should have known such an insightful man would see my worst flaw right away.* Taking all her strength to recover from the back pressure building up inside, she managed to respond, "yes, I've regretted the difference all my life, but I'm flattered that you think I can help you," her discouraged balloon deflating more rapidly with every passing second. "Since I'm so different, I don't know how I can be of service to you." She hesitated to reveal more, but after two uncomfortable seconds slogged by, she felt compelled to fill the gap. "All my life I have had to hide my true feelings to be accepted here." She explained how her parents, her mother, in particular, disapproved of her emotionality and her general approach to life. "As a child, she continued, "I had to hide under the covers at night with a flashlight to read award-winning novels because of my mother's attitude that they were frivolous and even, in some cases, dirty or disgusting." She looked away for an excruciating sixteen seconds with what seemed to Eb a tear in her left eye behind her faltering voice, "I've never been accepted by anyone, even my parents." Her trembling hands were still extended on the table with her napkin still absorbing the remainder of her anxiety, and they turned upward in a gesture of pleading to the gods for understanding, but she was used to there being no one to console her. "Please understand," she said after a poignant suspension of time, "I love my parents, but I've always felt unreal, an observer from a distance, and there's an ever-widening chasm between us the older I get."

Eb would have sworn in court on the Bible of public opinion that he heard the crack of a stubborn heart explode in her chest. Her façade of self-esteem crumbled right in front of him, and he reached for her hand to catch the falling star of dignity as it fell through the storm clouds of sadness before the deluge.

She put up absolutely no resistance to his surprisingly tender touch and began to leak tears. After an eternity of ten seconds, she pulled her hand away for no other reason than to wipe the tears that started flooding down her arms, onto the table. They mingled with the ever-increasing tide of her sweaty hands that had already overwhelmed the exhausted napkin. He got up and hastily retrieved twelve napkins from six tables leaving a cacophony of perturbed silverware strewn across the tables in an attempt to stem the tide that, when he returned, made him slip in the lake that had already begun to form on the floor.

The snow began to fall more heavily outside, and a car accidently skidded on the last bit of ice of the disappearing winter season while a young boy took his last chance to purposely slide on the sidewalk as if trying to flee the burgeoning spring weather waiting in the wings.

Molly's tears subsided, and Eb's hands resumed their position after she blew her nose three times on the now useless sopping napkins, and she began to speak again, miraculously picking up where she left off. "My mother's attitude was not constructed of direct knowledge from reading those novels, but from reviews in conservative and religious magazines that condemned fiction as filth and the root cause of the degeneration of society and its institutions." She looked up expectantly with still damp orbs and felt herself disappear into his dark eyes.

"You've been through a lot all your life," he said, "and you've had to hold it in all these years." Eb's heart went out to her, and Finder gained a clear understanding of what was calling for help from within. "I can't imagine what a burden that has been, and that's why I need your help. You are a participant observer here, and I need your input to assist me in my task. I need your support." Pausing in mid-thought, calculating the correct thing to say for fifteen beats of her heart, he finally continued, "Thank you."

She stopped mid-breath and stared at him, her mouth falling open in shocked surprise. *This was unexpected!* "You're thanking me?" she sniffled. "Why would you be thanking me? What do you mean? Are you making fun of me?" Her confusion caused her to stiffen a little when she noticed she had started to slump in her seat. She was used to people misunderstanding her, and she had just poured out her most secret self to this stranger. The fear of buyer's remorse gripped her, and her mind wanted to run, but her body wasn't even close to letting her leave. Mired in her quandary, she felt glued to her seat.

"Don't misunderstand," he said, addressing the fears he noticed in her question. "I thank you for opening up to me. It is painful I know, but I'm honored that you picked me to bear your soul; your true self. It's refreshing to bask in the presence of such honesty. It isn't often that anyone gets to experience such intimacy." He saw her body collapse into a melting pool of relief and gratitude. Her tense shoulders let go and dropped down a foot as the gravity of the situation tugged at her heart. When she was back to as close to normal as she was going to get that day, she wiped her brow, and her still damp brown eyes stood out, rimmed in bright crimson sclera.

Eb, realizing that she took his comments the wrong way, knew better than to tell her she wasn't different, so he said, "I think your difference is refreshing, and I don't see you as damaged, like you seem to see yourself. It is because you are so different that you can help."

"Thank you," she said in barely a whisper, unconvinced, looking down at the water glass where the ice had already melted from her warm tears and the radiating heat of intimacy stoking up between them. "Eb," she finally said in a normal, but quiet voice, "I still don't know how I can help you. What can I do?" Her voice revealed her desire to help mixed with uncertainty along with her attraction to him. Uncomfortable having the focus on her, she reverted to what she always did, threw the switch from the train of thought they were on, and focused on the sidetrack of Ebenezer Thornbird and his needs.

He reached for her still damp hand. "I'd like to pick your brain, but are you sure you're up to this right now?" he countered.

"Yes," she said, not believing that he still wanted to focus on her needs until they were fulfilled. "I want to help you more than ever." *He has been so kind, insightful, and understanding like no one has ever been for me.* Following a thoughtful, but self-conscious silence, she said, "You know I've never opened up to anyone like this." *I hope this wasn't a mistake.*

"Thank you, Molly. It's always easy to be with such a caring, mindful, and special woman."

Letting the moment mature for what stretched out to fifteen seconds, he returned to the previous discussion. "For starters," he said, "you know everybody in town and the surrounding area in a way that I can't, so I need your take on my impressions and whether they fit the pieces of the puzzle."

"Okay," she said, thankful to finally let herself become distracted from her own self-doubts, "anything I can do to help, Eb." Her voice was more confident now. She peered at him through the grateful pools of her still wet and expectant eyes purified by her tears like the sweet breeze flowing through the windows after a spring rain.

Ebenezer Thornbird explained his experiences on his walkabout through the town, but unlike the Australian aboriginals who see the spiritual significance in every landmark, he saw none. There was no hint of the friendly connections he encountered in other towns. "I examined the physical structures as well as that of the interpersonal interactions of the people in the central district. Even the buildings and the items stocked in the stores were suspicious of me. I smiled and extended my hand in a friendly gesture to everyone I encountered on the street and in the stores, but I was met with blank faces staring back at me and, feeling like a ghost, I was uncertain whether the ones who didn't shake my hand actually saw me."

Sounding skeptical with a questioning face, Molly asked, "Did you have any success at all?"

"Only about sixty percent success of positive automatic responses from others. That is, sixty percent responded with a reciprocal handshake. Some, however, were wary upon seeing a stranger approaching on the street, they resisted the urge."

"I'm surprised anyone talked to you."

"I didn't say sixty percent of them actually talked to me. I knew from experience that people, especially men and most women, will automatically extend their hand in response to someone extending theirs in a friendly gesture often without realizing it, or vaguely so, before they find their hand has been grasped."

"What happened when they did shake your hand?"

"Most wanted to know what I wanted, jerked their hand away, or just sailed on by like two ships unseen, disappearing into the fog of denial, momentarily distracted by something unseen before they instantly banished it from their minds, as if I was invisible."

"Yeah. That's more like I would have expected. Did anyone actually talk to you?"

"Yes, I think about fifteen percent of them did. Maybe the others thought I was an insurance salesman or peddler of some kind trying to sell them something, or worse, to rob them."

"Wow! I'm amazed you had that much success. You must have something going for you."

"I thought this was odd, though, in a small town so far from any large city. In my experience, small-town folks were usually more welcoming to strangers, at least on the surface."

Molly was stunned and finally said, "Really? Other towns are that different? This town is tighter than a constipated drum, especially if they think you want their money, or worse, some sort of control over their lives. They are truly rigid, paranoid and skeptical. You can practically hear their sphincters slamming shut."

"Regardless of the response people gave me, I would say, 'I'm Eb, and I'm new in town. How are you today?' If they stopped, I continued with, 'I'd like to get to know your amazing town a little better. Would you mind if I asked you some questions for my travel journal?'"

With eyes springing wide in dilated enchantment, she asked, "Who actually talked to you?" *This guy has something. I don't know what it is, but there's a kind of aura about him. It's not a visual aberration or anything, but there's a vibe or something. It's more than mere charm.*

Finder said, "She looks like a deer in the headlights." Eb just smiled.

"The fifteen percent who spoke to me were mostly the unsuspecting proprietors of various establishments I cornered in their shops, but when I shook the hands of the willing, I felt the same emptiness of disconnection pass between us that I felt in the coffee shop with Bill. It wasn't reluctance as much as a kind of extreme bizarre disinterest in their fellow human beings."

"Boy, are you spot on!" Molly Everhart confirmed.

"This town, it seems to me, is filled with loosely connected individuals who reluctantly interact with each other out of necessity," Ebenezer Thornbird continued.

"Who did you meet?"

"There was one man in his seventies, part Mexican mixed with Native American genes I think, who seemed to be roaming around inside his oversized shirt and pants that were three sizes too big for his very skinny and diminutive body. His clothes desperately hung on, and it was all they could do to keep from sliding off. Apparently, he had been a much larger man before age, osteoporosis, and muscle debility diminished him to a shadow of his former self. He had long gray hair, and he appeared demented because he often seemed lost in the labyrinth of his own mind. His recent memory was difficult for him, but I thought his remote memory might be more intact. Stories of the past were just what I wanted anyway, a history of the town from the viewpoint of its residents, especially the older ones. But his responses to my questions were disappointingly superficial and concrete. When asked if he lived in town, the man, who called himself J.C., pointed down the street and said, 'In a house down there'." Ebenezer Thornbird was frustrated in his attempt to engage this man on a more informative level.

****

"Where did you come from originally?"

"Jupiter."

"The planet Jupiter?"

"Yes. I hung on to the piece of it that broke off until it landed in Florida. That's why they call the town Jupiter Florida."

"How did you make a living?"

"I worked."

"What kind of work did you do?"

J.C. stood and stared at Ebenezer Thornbird for exactly thirty-seven seconds trying to remember. "I did lots of things."

"What do you do now?" Eb tried again.

J.C. said, "Just waitin'."

"Oh? What, if you don't mind me asking, are you waiting for?"

"Waitin' on judgment day I guess."

"Do you have a family in town?"

"Just me and granddaughter Elise. She helps me. She's eighteen, I think."

"What will happen after judgment day?"

"I'll be gone... Heaven, I guess."

"What about Elise? What will happen to her?"

"Well..." He seemed confused, frozen in time, looked at his hands waiting for them to answer and, when there was no response, he half said, half asked, "Well, son.... maybe you'll stay with her and keep her company for a while?"

"I'm sorry J.C. I can't, but maybe you or she have friends or relatives elsewhere who can take her in or maybe she can take care of herself. After all, she takes care of you." Eb became aware that he had given J.C. too many things to think about at once for the old gent to process, and it probably overwhelmed him.

J.C. stood there shifting from foot-to-foot, right to left, and left to right, spat, lifted his hat, scratched his gray head balding in the middle, pondered all aspects of the inquiry, and tried to string his thoughts together without finding a solution. He finally said, "Well, I guess that'll be all right." He seemed to forget what he was talking about or that he was talking to anyone and wandered off following his empty stare down the street of vacuous senility.

****

Molly said, "I've been told that J.C. was a drifter, a kind of hippy-type, a little crazy, burned out on drugs when he came to town years ago and worked at the granary outside of town where the Zane ranch used to be. In fact, it's still called The Zanesville Granary. Once he was laid off, he started picking up odd jobs as a handyman until about five years ago, when he was diagnosed with Dementia. Now his granddaughter watches over him, but sometimes he embarrasses her by wandering around town acting strangely and saying strange things. He is grudgingly tolerated because, although he was a little weird at times, he was a rather anonymous but hard-working citizen and, as a handyman, he had helped everyone in town at one time or another. They just want him kept away from strangers to maintain the Perfection image."

Eb said, "Molly, It was odd speaking with him. He seemed familiar somehow. I can't put my finger on it, though. I'm certain I never met the man before, and I thought at first blush, J.C. was an exception because of his senescence, but most others I encountered had the same bland and blank expressions. Even though they had no memory problems, were fully oriented, and most were not religiously preoccupied, there was a concrete and superficially vague countenance about them. It made them all seem drab and uninteresting." He thought for two seconds, "Actually," he said, "they seemed disinterested in most of the accouterments of human relationships with the exception of guarding their money, their control, or of specific verifiable facts. They seemed largely expressionless and mildly inappropriate."

"Inappropriate?" Molly asked, with raised eyebrows. She couldn't believe that there was anyone who would let him think they were imperfect.

"The extreme example was a man who called himself Eddie who asked me, 'Will you take Jake, my dog?' He didn't ask me if I liked dogs, or was I interested in having a dog, rather, he cut directly to the chase, to get rid of Jake."

****

The dog growled, snarled, and pulled at the leash, determined to get at Eb until the bite of Jake's stench penetrated Ebenezer Thornbird's entire existence, beginning with his nose and shuddering through his body, raising the ugly head of disgust. It was a mix of burning rubber, nasty dog smell and a hint of" … *what is that?* "Sulfur I think." His heartbeat doubled, and his feet wanted to run, but he knew better.

All we need is to be chased by one of the dogs from hell, Finder whispered in Eb's left ear with pressured urgency.

Ebenezer Thornbird's voice quavered when he said, "As much as I'd like to have a dog Eddie, and I would love to have one, I really would, but I can't take him. I'm a traveling man."

Eddie said, "That's okay, just feed him whenever you can."

Eddie seemed desperate to rid himself of the cur, but he didn't seem to know why. Finder said, *there's something missing that Eddie's looking for. Even he doesn't know what it is. It seems like a cry for help, but something's blocking him from articulating it. He seems trapped inside himself.* He was suspended in wonder for three beats. *That dog isn't real either! It seems like he doesn't belong in this world; a demon.*

Ebenezer Thornbird declined to take the leash when Eddie, assuming he would, reached out to hand the dog to him just as Eb stepped into a nearby store, leaving Eddie standing in the street, mouth open, extending the leash in his hand, suspended in a state of catalepsy holding the bag. "See you, Eddie. Good luck with Jake." *He must know that no one would want that vicious beast unless they were involved in some violent illegal business, like dog fighting.*

****

"Oh, that's Eddie Renfield," Molly said, "He's always trying to unload that mutt on anyone he can, I guess because he can't afford to feed himself let alone Jake. The dog is so dangerous that everyone avoids him. Fortunately, he only comes to town once or twice a week."

Eb looked confused, "I thought this town got people like him out."

"Well," Molly said, "Eddie doesn't actually live here. His family was forced out of town by peer pressure, but they moved out to just beyond the town limits when he was about twelve, and that's when that old stray dog found him. His parents died mysteriously, burned up in their bed in the fire that consumed the house when he was about eighteen. Some say they were murdered, but an autopsy was inconclusive and the sheriff at the time couldn't pin it on anyone. Eddie was found with Jake protectively sleeping on top of him in his bed, the house having burned to ruins everywhere except where Eddie slept. It was very strange.

"Eddie was always odd, but he grew stranger over the years. At the time, though, he was eighteen and stayed there in a lean-to that was still standing until he was able to build a rather primitive rickety house around it. No one knows what really happened, but, most likely they were dead already or rendered unconscious before the fire was set. Maybe someone killed them and set the house on ablaze, but it's a mystery how they didn't wake up, and Eddie and the dog slept through the whole thing too. At least it looked like they did.

"Eddie Renfield doesn't come here very often because people ignore and avoid him and Jake as much as possible. I'm told that Eddie has had that dog since he was about twelve or thirteen years old and he has gotten weirder every year. He always seems desperate to rid himself of the dog, but never took him to the pound in Orson or anything. Jake has lived longer than any dog I've ever seen. He must be at least twenty because I remember Eddie having him when I was five or six and people were saying that Jake was old back then, even before he found Eddie."

"He does seem ancient like a single-headed version of Cerberus the three-headed dog that guards the gates of Hades, fierce and ugly.

"That description fits, no one knows what Eddie does when he's not here. He seems to eat very little and doesn't seem to feed the dog much. Jake always looks sick and emaciated. I wonder, does Jake fend for himself for food and catch small animals and birds for his meals? I've seen him with feathers around his mouth. Maybe he catches food for Eddie too, but he is so dangerous that he has to be on a leash whenever he's in town."

"It's no wonder Jake is so vicious," Eb said, "He'd eat you if he could, I guess." After a fifty-second pause, he asked, "What about J. C.?"

He's been here since around the time the name of the town of Zanesville was changed to Perfection," Molly said, "but he was diagnosed with dementia only five years ago, a rapid downhill slide. His granddaughter tries to keep him out of trouble, but he's harmless, and no one pays attention to him. When he gets away from Elise, his granddaughter, he can't remember the way back home and either she finds him, or the Sheriff takes him home. When he pointed in the direction of his home, he was probably guessing."

****

"One man I spoke with was visiting a relative in town. When I asked if he ever lived here, he tensed up and loudly proclaimed,

'No way!' Then, when realizing he had said it too loudly, he looked around to see if anyone heard him. In a quieter tone, he said, 'I rarely come here.'"

"Why do you say that?"

"This place is weird."

What's weird about it?"

"Well, I'll give you an extreme example of how uptight this place is."

"This town is so tight and sexually repressed." He went on to explain, "that when a prostitute calling herself Candy came to town, she only serviced one man, a widower, one time before she became unemployed for lack of business, went broke and left town with a passing trucker whose fire she lit, for a large fee, all the way to California. She had tried everything she could to stir up business in Perfection. She even went to the extreme of showing a few men the certificate of commendation she had received from the mayor of a small Texas town in appreciation for her 'meritorious service' as a 'consultant' to the all-male town council. However, it was to no avail, it didn't inspire the townsmen of Perfection who couldn't see spending their good money for sex when they had perfectly good women at home.

"It wasn't that Candy's professional skills weren't good enough, so no one actually sought her out. It wasn't that the men in town didn't want sex either. It did seem to be a grudgingly natural need that sprung up from time to time. It was just, they reckoned, 'why should we pay for sex when it would only distract us from our usual business dealings?' Besides, their wives and girlfriends performed well enough on those occasions, at least in the mechanics of carrying out their wifely pretend orgasms once or twice a year when it seemed required. They had read articles citing scientific discoveries that regular orgasms kept you healthy but, to their way of thinking, that was about every six months.

"The good people of Perfection," he continued with a more than subtle sarcastic tone, "had little use for sex for pleasure or for sensuality, except to procreate, occasionally to relieve stress or, once in a while, in the line of duty. Of course, children are tax deductible," he said with a sarcastic smirk.

"When it came to procreation, however, sex was a sour obsession performed several times a day, garnished with boredom and salted with the race to get it over with, clean up, and put the disgusting experience behind them for a few hours before the reluctant schedule called for them to start all over again. This rigid pattern continued unabated until *Thank God!*" He rolled his eyes, "pregnancy took root, and that was always followed by the relief of abstinence sometimes lasting for years.

****

Ebenezer Thornbird told Molly Everhart, "I've noticed a pattern lacking in human emotional connection in most all of the good citizens of Perfection. There was one very large woman in her late fifties with a huge umbrella she used as a cane. She wore too many layers of unfortunate clothes, a demented queen on a float in a Mardi Gras parade, festooned with three layers of huge flowing outer garments printed with very large flowers. She was so large underneath them that life itself was surprised at her unexpected girth, and her walk was that of a giant bloated duck. The kind of walk former ballerinas have developed from years of standing in unnatural positions and walking heel first in toe shoes. She seemed to take two steps before her dresses moved forward and, brandishing her scepter umbrella, she dropped down hard with a loud *thud* gracing the groaning bus stop bench that served as the reluctant temporary throne for her royal derriere. She said her name was Lilith. Her attitude was haughty and surly with her nose pointing up in such a way as to reveal the hairs that stuck out like needles in a pincushion from her nostrils. Her breathing was labored, and she seemed completely uninterested in anyone else but her pathetic self."

When Ebenezer Thornbird approached her, she was cordial, if resistant to talking to anyone, let alone a stranger, and spoke in a fake British accent. He said, "There she sat on a public bench awaiting her limousine, the only bus that ran through Perfection."

"Yes." Molly interrupted. "It takes her to the mall in the next town, Orson Wells, where she rides her chariot, one of those electric scooters, circling around and around each store until the batteries run down, ignoring the fact that, despite her tonnage, she could walk just fine."

"She was some piece of work!" he blurted.

"She was born," Molly continued, "just prior to the town's reincorporation as Perfection."

"But," Eb said, "she wasn't sure why it was renamed. When I asked her if she could tell me anything more, she would only say, with a curt 'I suppose it's because the town is perfect.' When I asked how she knew this and what evidence she could supply, she added, 'I just know it that's all,' with an air of disgust just as her limo pulled up. She arose with great difficulty during all manner of groaning and knee creaking from the bench, leaving it in a more blessed and perfect state than before she graced it with her bottom line, despite the permanent significant dent she left behind in the structure. 'That's the end of that story,' she said as she boarded her coach with royal difficulty, suffering the indignity of needing the assistance of her bus driver chauffeur/charioteer before she vanished behind the door and her thirty-seat limousine disappeared in the distance. *She is the pumpkin in this Cinderella story!*

Molly Everhart said, "That's Lilith Lugosi. Everyone calls her the Countess because of her name along with the fact that she acts as though she's royalty, a queen or something, not to mention her unusually long canines."

"In fact," he added, "most people told me essentially the same story whenever I inquired about the town's name." When he spoke to business owners, they felt he had trapped them in their own self-created situation standing behind the counter or next to their merchandise. They only had the relief of escape from his buttonholing when another customer entered, but most were trapped in their reluctance and felt obliged to take the time to answer his questions. "They were not exactly what I would call warm and friendly. They exuded more of an odd emotionless cordiality as though they were reading a script that someone else had written." There was irritation underlying a polite countenance as they answered his questions, but they really didn't want to make more than a superficial connection. "They were stiff with their Spock-like rationality," he said. "Human relationships, I concluded, were merely instrumental; things to be tolerated, tools to be used. They could better understand the needs of inanimate and mechanical objects. They are true materialists, taking excellent care of their things, probably more for the practicality of good business, financial stability, and order than for aesthetic value or to simply enjoy them."

Molly's eyes were even wider now. "You really put your finger on it! I've lived here all my life always feeling that there was something wrong, you've brought it into crystal clarity for me." She shook her head as though to rid herself of something nasty that just flew into her hair.

"It's as if they need things to be in a certain order," he elaborated, "or they'll be ravaged by anxiety, guilt, and confusion until order is restored. The shopkeepers all said they had no idea why the town's name was changed. There seemed to be no clear explanation, but everyone exhibited anxiety, their hands seemed tremulous, and their voices quivered when the topic was broached."

"I bet that rattled their cages!" she chuckled.

"Yes. It was as if they were reacting to mass hypnosis or something, their reactions were so similar."

"Now that you mention it, I've spent most of my life trying not to notice it. I thought it must have been normal."

"I also observed," he explained, "people having what ostensibly were conversations, but, it was more like the parallel play of two and three-year-olds who are simply playing in the proximity of each other, but haven't yet learned to play in coordination and cooperation with each other.

One shop owner, an example of this, said he heard that the town was renamed because it was trying to be perfect and, in his opinion, it had achieved that lofty status. He quickly tried to interest me in his merchandise and, or so it seemed, to distract from the subject as if he was mechanically reciting a memorized script. His hands were tremulous and sweating despite the cool air. This was typical of the other entrepreneurs as well.

****

Ebenezer Thornbird approached a woman sitting on the park bench at the playground where her grandchildren were playing and sat next to her. She was slim, a polite way of saying anorexic, with graying hair. It was difficult to gauge her age given her gaunt appearance. She wore extremely expensive but very conservative clothes. She appeared rather aloof. After introducing himself with a friendly smile and offering his usual patter about his travel journal, she was willing to talk, probably from the boredom of sitting there for so long on those butt-busting planks. She blankly explained, with no modulation in her voice, that she and her husband owned most of the businesses in town and that their goal was to purchase them all. When Ebenezer Thornbird asked her why she needed so much wealth, she said, "Oh it isn't for the money! That would be crude and useless. We aren't in it for the money alone. The money is nice you understand, but no." She stared off at the jungle gym for three seconds. "You see, it's about winning and money is simply the vehicle we use to measure it. The money is simply the point score." She paused for another contemplative minute, turned, and looking him in the eye she said, "Why do you think multimillionaires and billionaires run for president or congress? It certainly isn't from the goodness of their hearts and certainly not for the money!" She laughed, staring off at nothing in particular, formulating her thoughts for fifteen seconds and, without looking at him, she asked, "Did you ever play Monopoly?"

"Yah. As a matter of fact, I have," he said.

"Well, that's the idea. You play until the winner, the last man standing, has all the money and property, and everyone else goes broke. The money is the score! Not the goal" When Ebenezer Thornbird asked her about the name change, her demeanor began to break into a sweaty confusion etched on her face accompanied by a mild tremor in her hands before she broke off the conversation and turned to her grandchildren saying, "We have to go now. Come along kids" as she stood and walked away without as much as a "By your leave." Her lack of social skills and disinterest in others was astounding.

****

"Yep! You sure tapped into the essence of the town there," Molly Everhart said. "She's Gertrude Johnson. Man is she tight! Everyone looks up to her and her husband, Kurt, because of their control and their success. Kurt and Gert, what a hoot! The whole town would salivate, if they had any saliva, to think they could even approximate their wealth and status." She gazed off for two ticks into her dawning mind and said, "Wow! I'm surprised that she lost her cool. I don't think anyone has ever seen that! You really got under her skin."

Eb said, "The only thing that unnerved her was when I asked about why the name was changed to Perfection. She was so upset that she didn't even excuse herself, arose from the bench like a zombie, and walked off into some distant trance-like place. It was as if she was leaving one world behind and entering another. "But," he said, after another nine-second of recall, "The children seemed oblivious to it all even though they were close enough to hear our conversation. They played like normal kids do. Did their parents play like that as children?"

"Oh yes. Everyone was like that until after about sixth or seventh grade." Molly Everhart's tone was matter-of-fact.

"You mean they magically changed that drastically at the age of what? Twelve or thirteen?"

"Yes, they did, and it was practically overnight, too. I remember that by Thanksgiving of my seventh-grade year, there was such a stark difference between my friends and me that I fell from grace and, bingo, I was suddenly out of the loop, and I plummeted into a wasteland of anonymity."

"What the...?" He looked confused. *Did puberty hit them so hard that it knocked childhood right out of them all at once? Just like that?* He thought for two tics. *There's more to it than a lost childhood. Most normal adults have more civility and emotional flexibility.*

"Now that I think of it," he continued, "they apparently skipped adolescence completely. Besides, what about normal adult emotions? They have none of it."

Thinking more deeply for a two-second tic on the extremely accurate atomic clock, on the wall, he frowned and said, "Wait a minute!" He looked up abruptly and, staring into her eyes, he said, "That didn't happen to you. You obviously survived adolescence unscathed by it."

Wrinkles appeared as she leaned forward and her forehead knitted into an irritated unibrow. "Unscathed?" she said with a little too much intensity "Are you kidding? I have had no close friends ever since seventh grade, and I've had to stifle myself just to get along."

"But you smile, you are bubbly, and you connect with people publicly in your job. People seem to accept you in that role," he pointed out, "and you seem open with me."

"That," she said, "is only because the business manuals all say that you should always smile and act happy when interacting with the public. They go by the book because it's evidence-based even if they can't comprehend why anyone should do such a thing. They simply say, with a shrug and a hint of resignation. 'That's science'."

"Geez!" Eb joked, "Do they give lessons in how to smile too?" There was a loud silence. "Well..." she started to say before he interrupted incredulously.

"No!?" His eyes grew too large for his head, and his jaw drooped while his face jutted forward.

"They have business seminars on how to act," she admitted. "I saw one manual that had diagrams of the facial muscles and information on the physiological effects of different kinds of smiles."

"Wow! Is that why you have a college degree and work in the coffee shop? You can express your need for emotional connection with the customers, and they only accept it because they believe you're faking it by the book, believing your genuine feelings and intentions are fake?"

"That's about it," she nodded. He laughed so hard his stomach hurt, and it was so contagious that she followed suit. After exactly three minutes of belly-busting mirth, she became acutely aware that the other two customers were looking at them. An elderly couple who always ate in the silence of two people who had lived overlapping lives for so long that they had nothing new to say to each other. The couple, and now, the waitress and the proprietor were all staring at Molly Eberhart and Ebenezer Thornbird with eyes of disgust, but Molly couldn't stop until her tightly wound spring had run down and she ended up in a puddle, as flaccid as a ragdoll.

She cleared her throat, he took a deep breath, and they tried not to look at each other while their laughter finally came to a sputtering halt. But, when they raised their water glasses and looked at each other across their simultaneous first gulp, an outrageous guffaw exploded in the rapture of water spewing out their noses, despite the eight disgusted lasers beaming at them. Molly Everhart felt the liberation of the ancient impacted emotions burst forth as if she was giving birth to something that had been gestating in her belly for more than a decade. It hurt her physical body, but the emotional relief was worth the humiliating stares. It was the first time she felt such a close connection with another human being beyond the fictional characters she imagined in her novels. And it was fun! *When was the last time I actually had fun?*

After three minutes of uncontrolled uproar, they had regained a modicum of composure for the second time. They distracted themselves by wiping up the nose water with their napkins. Ebenezer Thornbird gasped to replenish enough of the air that had escaped his lungs nearly causing him to faint, but he had swallowed so much air that he burped instead. This ignited their uncontrollable laughter again, but it only lasted a minute because they ran too low on energy. He had to catch his breath to remain conscious and wait for speech to reemerge. He looked at the silent couple across from them, leaned in across the table and whispered to Molly, "I bet those two have talked about the same topics so many times that they have them numbered to save time."

"Numbered?"

"You know, one means "how was your day?" and two means "terrible" and three means "good," four means "shut up" and so on."

Molly said, "Oh you really *are* bad!"

"Number four!" he blurted.

She tried not to laugh again but ended up with a restrained snort that caused her to blow her nose on now useless, exhausted, shredded, and very wet paper napkins. They sat in the relief of a five-minute silence.

"I talked to quite a few people," Eb managed to finally say, trying to grim up and change the subject, "and they all had the same basic approach with minor variations."

"Well," Molly said with amazement, "I think you captured the essence of the people around here. They're the norm. So, if you want to know about them, why talk to me if I'm the exception to the rule?"

"I have talked to some of them, but, like I said, I can't talk to them all. I need your take on it since you and I are, in our own ways, the outsiders. You can confirm my views or refute them. You see things they can't due to the very fact that you are *not* like them.

They can't see themselves the way someone who's different can."

'Okay," she said while regaining a little more energy now.

"Besides," he said, "I need more information than just about the people here."

"What do you mean? What else?"

"As I told you, I have the nature of a finder in me. It's my blessing and my curse. When I'm called by lost things and people I must seek them out, but I sense danger nearby more than I've ever encountered. I was attracted to this place and, I'm now convinced, it was to find you, but there's something else, too."

****

Ebenezer Thornbird, Finder, met a couple with their kids in the supermarket and immediately felt he had entered two separate worlds simultaneously. Two of the children were seven and ten, the other two, also a girl and a boy, were thirteen and fifteen. There was such a stark difference between them. The older ones were clones of their parents and even dressed similarly. His impression was that they wouldn't dress exactly the same way for social purposes, but they made absolutely certain that they dressed exactly unlike each other in a kind of reverse obsessive-compulsive manner.

They were like one of his roommates in the college dorm.

His roommate had to keep the window blinds at exactly the same level and measured their exact distance from the floor, but when the roommates made fun of him for this, he measured those shades to be absolutely certain that they were exactly *not* the same distance from the floor.

****

Finder In Hell World   Charles R. Stern

"The older girl, Eb explained, "wore a blue top with a gray skirt and her stockings and shoes matched. Her brother had on a gray shirt with blue slacks and socks and shoes to match. The older kids were, like their parents, sober, distant and lacking in empathy. They were all business, but the younger ones were exuberant like the normal healthy kids I've encountered just about everywhere else."

"You are astute! I feel like I'm just waking up from a bad dream!"

Ebenezer Thornbird sat for a minute waiting for her to recuperate from the thunderbolt of enlightenment before he continued.

"The younger boy had on slightly mismatched socks," he finally went on, "and his shoes were dirty. The girl wore an odd colored blouse that was buttoned incorrectly, and her hair was slightly disheveled. So, if the adults and the older kids were like that as children, they had made a drastic change somehow."

Molly said, "Yeah, all the parents try to raise the young ones by the book, so they tolerate their behavior because that's what they read."

"But what about the older ones? Eb puzzled. "Don't they go by the book with the adolescents?"

"No. They don't have to because the kids act exactly like their parents by then." Thoughtful for a minute, she was struck with a glimpse of the spirit of recognition that flew across the room and whispered in her ear before she said, "Sometimes, I think the parents can't tell the difference between their older kids and themselves. There are no discipline problems, but no one seems truly happy after they reach puberty. They don't exactly seem unhappy either. Just sort of emotionless. Maybe it's just ordinary puberty, and I missed it."

Eb said, "I think it's the other way around. *They* missed it. You have developed in a normal, healthy way, but there's more to it. The adults here are more inflexible than normal adults. Actually, I'm thankful that your parents didn't read any further in this so-called 'book'." *Maybe the book doesn't cover adolescence, and they don't bother to buy the one that does.*

"How can you believe such a thing?" Molly fell back into her old self-view. "I'm so different, and there are so many of them that..."

"That's why," he cut in, "like I said, you developed, and the other people in this town didn't, so they are the ones who are different. You were more like the normal, healthy kids everywhere else. As a grown woman, you're much more like the adults elsewhere. You're basing your opinion on what others have communicated to you here and not on the big picture from the perspective of the rest of the world. This place is different, and somehow, you've escaped the ravages of this town's adolescence gap. They seem to have missed puberty completely, and they missed something else as well, but I can't quite put my finger on it. It's as if they were replaced by clones from another planet." He hesitated for precisely one minute and thirteen seconds on the atomic clock above their heads and risked saying, "This town of Perfection is definitely not perfect! Far from it!"

Molly Everhart sat back and slumped in her seat, but, startled by her posture and the ramifications it might signal to him or anyone else who might notice, she straightened up despite the discomfort it engendered. She stared at him, without really seeing him for precisely three minutes, wrenched by the sudden uncontrollable ghostly parade of her entire life passing in flashes for review before her mind's eye. She found her entire worldview revised in a single stroke, no longer seeing herself as the unhealthy one, but the one in which others, living their pitiable lives, hadn't a clue about the reality it presents. They had changed, she realized, around October or November of the year they entered seventh grade when they were about twelve or thirteen years old.

"Now that you mention it," she said, "it's as if they entered another world passing through an invisible force field like the ones I read about in those sci-fi novels."

"Yeah, apparently, they went from childhood directly to adulthood, but the adulthood they acquired was even stranger than the normal adults everywhere else."

Maybe this is some kind of space alien experiment or something, she thought.

He spoke again, "I feel the call of something needing to be found out there. Something that wants me to find it. Something that needs to be rescued from its anguish."

"Where? In town?"

"Nearby somewhere, he said, "it is a very strong feeling, but its direction is still unclear." He felt a yearning swelling deep inside him that was not his, but an external tug at his gut. After an eternal two minute silence, he said, "I never fight my instincts when it comes to finding the things that need to be found. This time, I feel the cries of things that aren't merely lost, but imprisoned, more strongly than anything I've ever encountered." Ebenezer Thornbird didn't mention that Finder knew there was still something in Molly Everhart that was crying out to be liberated as well. "It's my destiny." Finder was firing up inside and felt compelled toward his fateful track.

CHAPTER EIGHT
SHERIFF BUCK

Leaving the restaurant, Eb and Molly noticed a shiny, but older model police cruiser, the kind with the red gumball dispenser flashing on top, sporting the Sheriff's logo in the form of a pentagram on the side, and an antenna that reminded Ebenezer Thornbird of a fishing pole, passing them by. It continued on for one hundred feet before making a sharp U-turn, pulling up by the curb next to them facing the wrong way, the fishing pole whipping back and forth making a *jub, jub, jub* sound, helplessly slicing the wind when the vehicle slammed to an abrupt stop. The driver's door flung wide and, leaving it open, the Sheriff stepped out with the engine still running, the dashboard lights visible, and the radio crackling. *Boy! This town is still in the last century!* The constable was square-framed, five feet nine inches tall, and nearly as wide, with a star on his left breast pocket and one on his Stetson. He was overweight by the one hundred pounds that had been unsuccessfully stuffed into his uniform, a full size too small, spilling out over his typical police utility belt complete with a Glock and a Taser along with a flashlight and handcuffs. *Talk about a muffin top!* There was a radio clipped to the belt with a tethered microphone on his shoulder attached to his right epaulet. Approaching Molly and Eb with a thumb in the belt swagger, Eb couldn't see the officer's eyes behind the wraparound sunglasses, odd for that time of the late afternoon. Molly noticed a small bird that landed on the squad car; a bobble-headed spectator studying the scene.

"Evenin' Molly." The Sheriff touched his hat.

"Sheriff." She smiled. There was a three-second pause while the Sheriff looked suspiciously at Eb, his eyes darting back and forth between him and Molly before she took the hint and said, "Oh! Forgive me, Sheriff. This is my friend Eb. Eb this is Sheriff Buck."

"Sheriff," Ebenezer Thornbird said as he reached out for a handshake. The Sheriff took two suspicious steps back off the curb with a riveted, almost paranoid gaze, aimed firmly at Eb while keeping his left thumb securely stuck in his belt and his right hand at the ready on his Glock. He said, "slowly remove your wallet son, if you have one, and hand me your ID." A nanosecond later, he threw in, "Please" as an after-thought. Eb felt his heart racing as he slowly reached into his back pocket to retrieve his wallet when he saw Sheriff Buck's hand on the pistol. Eb said, "Here you are Sir," as he handed the driver's license to the officer. The Sheriff took his time scrutinizing it.

"Ebenezer Thornbird. Is that a Native American Name?"

"Probably. I don't really know for sure, Sir." Eb said trying to appear calm. "It might be, but my mom died a week after I was born and I never knew who my dad was. My adoptive mother said she thought her father's grandfather or great grandfather was some kind of Native American healer or something."

"Massachusetts huh?" Sheriff Buck regarded his suspect with deep suspicion, "Long way from these parts." Eb felt his heart throbbing in his neck and heard its *thump, thump, thumping* in his ears. Handing the license back, the Sheriff asked, "What's your business here, son?"

Son? He looks like he's around my age! Maybe within a couple of years. Maybe it's his way of projecting his authority. "I was passing through and thought I'd stop here and see what this interesting town has to offer, and Ms. Everhart here graciously agreed to show me around." He looked the officer in the eye: at least where he thought his eyes should be behind the shades baring any deformities, beyond his personality that is, trying to communicate his sincerity. "I'm an itinerate freelance journalist making my way across the country writing a journal that I'll use as a basis for articles that I intend to publish in magazines and later in a traveler's guidebook."

Sheriff Buck smiled, "An unemployed drifter hay?" The constable frowned while Eb played go fish in his backpack. Sheriff Buck's hand tightened his grip on his weapon. Eb moved slowly to eliminate any suspicion.

"Here, I'll show you my articles." He pulled out his journal and some clippings of articles he had published. The Sheriff grabbed them, nearly tearing the pages, thumbing through the journal so quickly that he couldn't possibly have read any of it, in a furious lack of interest, before he handed them back. He didn't bother to look at the articles.

"How long are you planning to stay son?"

"Well, I don't know how long it will take to thoroughly cover this town." Eb felt an icy sweat forming on his neck and a river of anxiety running down his back. The sun was setting behind the clouds on the horizon, the day birds were coming in to roost, and the nocturnal birds prepared for the night shift. "I'd like to talk to a lot of people to get the whole story, you understand, I want the whole picture and not just the sketchy stuff other travel writers put out."

Sheriff Buck's frozen, stoic face barely moved a muscle before he disconnected from Ebenezer Thornbird's gaze, looked down for a fraction at the thumb in his belt. His hand was still on his weapon, and he stepped one foot back on the curb, "Yeah, that's why I'm checking you out," the officer said. "I've had several calls from citizens complaining that you were harassing them."

Eb was shocked, "Oh no, Sir!" he realized his voice was too loud for comfort, too defensive for the situation, and he feared Sheriff Buck would think he doth protest too much. "I would never harass anyone," he said in a lower decibel. "As a journalist, I ask questions, but I never impose myself on anyone. If they say they don't want to talk, I leave them alone."

"Some people feel you were harassing them," the officer repeated.

"Well, they had every opportunity to say no because I asked if they were willing to talk to me; but if they didn't object, I probably continued to ask questions." He felt the false accusation trundle through him, and while tempted to, he realized he shouldn't put his cold hands in his inviting pockets while talking to a lawman with one hand on his weapon. Crossing his arms, he warmed his hands under his now damp armpits, trying to hide his anxious tremors.

"Be sure you do from now on," Sheriff Buck warned, "or I'll have to ask you to move on," he threatened. As he said it, he closed his left eye, smiled, pointed a finger, took aim, and with a click of the tongue, snapped his thumb forward, firing it at Ebenezer Thornbird with laser-like accuracy.

"Yes, Sir. I think I do, and I'll be very careful, as always." *What a dick!*

"You okay, Molly?" the Sheriff asked, watching her very closely for any sign of hesitation or a subtle signal for rescue from this questionable stranger.

"Oh yes, Sir, Sheriff Buck Sir," she said with a faked accent that was a cross between a southern drawl and an East Texas big hair feigned sincerity. "I'm sure I'm just fine. Mr. Thornbird here has been a *perfect* gentleman, bless his little heart, and, if I may say so Sir, I have observed him approaching people and what he said is true. He is very respectful. Yes, Sir."

The Sheriff touched his hat with his right thumb and forefinger without getting the joke, nodded and grunted, "Molly, Mr. Thornbird."

They said, "Sheriff," in unison.

He swaggered back to his car with a bowlegged stride reminiscent of John Wayne with a horrible rash. He looked back over his shoulder briefly as if to say, "I've got my eye on you." The bird took flight, but not until it left its guano calling card; a comment on the sheriff's demeanor. The Sheriff had trouble getting into the car when his overloaded utility belt caught on the edge of the seat back. He turned the car around, gave it its head, spun the screeching tires as loose gravel flew in an impressive signal of power.

"What was that all about?" Eb said under his breath, "and your accent!"

Waiting until the cruiser was out of sight, Molly doubled over in guffaws while holding her stomach.

"What's funny?" Ebenezer Thornbird's face wrinkled.

"The Sheriff. He's so macho! The truth is, he's the only cop in town!"

Eb choked out his surprise. "You mean...!"

"He has no deputies and no dispatcher," she interrupted.

"But he had a radio on his belt, and I heard the one in the patrol car hissing. It was lit up like a Christmas tree, and that big antenna...!"

"I know! Right?" Molly was looking at Eb wide-eyed, eyebrows raised, face jutting forward accompanied by a high-pitched voice as if sending him a signal to recognize the joke. "Get it?"

"Man! This is why my forehead keeps getting flatter!" he said as he struck his forehead with the palm of the right hand of enlightenment. "I thought I had heard everything!"

They both roared uncontrollably again while they walked, weak-kneed with laughter, toward Molly's home holding each other up arm-in-arm. "Seriously?" Eb said after controlling himself, having trouble deciding whether he was being Punk'd. "You mean he has radios that no one calls him on, and there's no one to talk to?"

"Yes!" she said through the veil of her mirthful tears. "He was supposed to get a new deputy, but they haven't hired anyone in five years! The town council didn't think there was enough crime in Perfection to warrant a deputy and a dispatcher.

"And," she continued, "He washes and polishes that stupid patrol car every day. I'm surprised it still has any paint left on it! Wait until he finds the calling card that bird left on it!" They laughed a little more until their psyches were too exhausted to continue; and besides, their faces and bellies hurt. Molly Everhart took advantage of the moment, spontaneously wrapping herself around

Ebenezer Thornbird's left arm while they walked. He offered no resistance. When they reached her house, she said, "Would you like to come in for some coffee or ice cream? My parents don't drink so there's no alcohol."

"I don't drink anyway, it clouds my senses, and it's late." He was looking her in the eye with a sincerity she was not used to, "and I'd like your help tomorrow." He said with an eagerness in his voice that thrilled her.

"Okay, but I have to work until noon tomorrow," she reminded. Then she added, "I've had more fun today with you than I've had in all the years since I was a child combined!"

"I'm glad. I had a great time too." He hugged her and kissed the top of her head. A ripple of passion squirmed down her back, and a glow of warmth grew well below her navel. All right, I'll see you tomorrow

"Okay, I'll pick you up at the Motel," she replied. "Can I give you a lift back tonight?"

"No," he declined, "I'll walk back through town and see if there's anything I missed. It's a nice night, and it's getting warmer."

****

Ebenezer Thornbird walked through Perfection, through the crowds of unseen phantoms, souls only Finder could feel. Finder felt a shiver flash down his spine, took the time to look around. Despite his feelings and crowded sensations, there were only three people out there, but he noticed that they appeared to be pursuing a specific purpose. They were headed to a restaurant or home after working late. No one was just hanging out on the corners chatting, none that he could see, despite Finder's feeling as if there were lost souls somewhere nearby. Eb turned and saw the cause of his trepidation. There were headlights coming in his direction. Sheriff Buck pulled up beside him and said, "Evenin' Mr. Thornbird. Leaving town on foot?"

Ebenezer Thornbird stopped and said, "Evening Sheriff Buck. I'm heading back to my motel room, Sir."

"Hop in and I'll give you a ride," Sheriff Buck said with a malevolent grin.

Aware that he'd be trapped in the back seat if he did so, he declined. "No thanks," and, making the next move in the game, he smiled, "but I appreciate the offer. I'd like to just enjoy the walk through your perfect town. Besides, I'm sure you have important duties as the local constabulary."

The Sheriff hesitated for three seconds and three suspicious beats of Eb's heart, but flattered, he said, "Okay, whatever you like. Have a good evening Mr. Thornbird," he said with an irritated tone of disappointment.

Ebenezer Thornbird responded with a two-fingered Cub Scout salute. A snub that the Sheriff missed. "Same to you Sheriff," he said as they took leave of each other.

The Sheriff mimed his finger pistol again, shot Ebenezer Thornbird through the heart, winked, and repeated, "Mr. Thornbird."

"Sheriff."

This is a clear omen, said Finder; *The sheriff is going to follow us around, he has nothing else to do, and by the way, no one to talk to.* Ebenezer Thornbird was the only potential threat to the ostensible perfection of the perceived but pretend, flawless community, simply because he was an unassimilated stranger.

Finder In Hell World   Charles R. Stern

CHAPTER NINE
A FLASH OF INSIGHT

Molly Everhart pulled up in front of the Motel room at exactly one fifty in the afternoon. No one in Perfection was ever late which explained the ubiquitous precise atomic clocks and watches. When she knocked on the door, it startled a small bird that had been sitting on the windowsill.

"Come in!" He was sitting on the bed. "I'm just putting on my boots. Is there somewhere else we can eat lunch? I don't like the looks we get at the *Dine Inn,* and maybe we can go where the paranoia with a badge can't follow us around."

She thought for a minute, "Well there are restaurants in Orson," She agreed.

"Can we talk there where we aren't overheard, and there isn't too much noise?"

"Yes," she said, "I know just the place, it's private, and the Sheriff has no jurisdiction there, but it's more expensive."

"That's okay," he replied, "I'm game for a quiet, intimate conversation and good cuisine."

The last time Molly Everhart had been in that restaurant, or had a quiet, intimate conversation, for that matter, was on a date with her itinerant cowboy student womanizer. Difficult memories lurked there, but she wanted to appease Eb, there was nowhere else nearby that fit the bill so perfectly, and her attraction to him trumped the previous boyfriend debacle by a mile; maybe ten. The restaurant was in the opposite direction from the one which he arrived on riding the *Donkey Express*. The Sheriff could be seen in the rearview mirror, but neither of them noticed. He stopped at the county line and turned around, but still, no one noticed... or cared, save the bird that landed, hopped to the middle of the road, a border guard, watching Sheriff Buck's Cruiser kick up dust in the opposite direction. The radio was playing music when the news came on just as they passed a very big rock on which someone had painted "Hell World" in big red letters. Eb saw that the land behind it appeared to be barren and Finder wondered, *what's that all about? Maybe some kids painted it as a joke. Maybe a college fraternity prank. Something's out there, and it feels malevolent.*

Following the farm report and the financial results of the various commodity markets, the weather announcer on the radio said, "Spring has finally arrived, and there's going to be a blue moon tomorrow night." The music returned to the *Marcels* singing *Blue Moon* just as Molly pulled into the restaurant car park.

Requesting a private table, they were ushered to the back booth where there were no other customers in sight. They perused the menu, ordered, and Molly said, "This is nice. I've only been here once, and that was a few years ago when I was in college."

"It is nice," he conceded. Then, after exactly thirty seconds of silent reflection, he said, "I noticed that we passed by a large rock on the way here. It had *Hell World* painted on it in big red letters. Is someone planning to build a roadside attraction or theme park like the *Mystery Spot*, *Brea Tar Pits*, or the giant ball of aluminum foil?" he asked in a half-serious tone that she didn't seem to notice.

"No. At least I hope not!" She looked away as if she had something shameful to confess. "That was a part of town back before it was abandoned."

"Before it was abandoned?" Eb's head shot up so fast that it would have flown off if it wasn't attached, but it merely left him with an irritating kink in his neck.

"It was a part of the town before they changed its name to Perfection. You already know the town used to be called Zanesville after the founder in the 1800's, but that part of the official town borders was a small forest. The rock was painted a few years after the name change."

Ebenezer Thornbird's puzzled frown announced his difficulty wrapping his head around the reason for the change and why no one would talk about the town's name. It didn't seem worth the hassle of reincorporation, so it seemed rare to change the name of a town after all those years. Now there was an additional puzzle. "I still can't understand why they changed the name. Was there something wrong with Zanesville? Did they find out years later that Mr. Zane embezzled the town coffers or something? No one, so far, has been able to break through their barrier of anxiety enough to tell me why the town is named Perfection. It's almost as if they don't know why on a conscious level, and unconsciously they're anxiously avoiding something upsetting as if it's dangerous; a kind of mass denial."

Molly said, "I don't think Zane had anything to do with it. It was fifty years ago, he was long dead, and I wasn't born yet."

"Well, I guess it fits," he said. "Everyone here, present company excepted, seems to think they are perfect or close to it." He hesitated for six seconds. "But, I see that these people in this so-called perfect town have something missing. This town is a shell; far from perfect. Like I told you, everyone I've met so far apparently has lost what you have somehow managed to keep. Their search for money and control isn't driven by passion, but by a goal-oriented motivation to carry out and win a kind of game just because it's the only logical and emotionless thing they can think of." He thought for six seconds, "and now there's another question."

"What do you mean?" she asked.

He thought for a moment before he spoke. "You said that *Hell World* used to be a wooded area, but it looked barren to me."

"Well, it used to be, but something happened to it. No one seems to know exactly what." There was a long silence while Molly Everhart could almost make out the gears grinding away in Ebenezer Thornbird's head.

Finder whispered, *that barren place has something to do with the shift to Perfection and it has affected the kids too. These are dramatic changes and that rock has something to do with it.* "Tell me more," he said, "About when you were in the seventh grade when everything changed. There has to be an explanation for such a profound, abrupt, massive personality shift and a reason that you escaped it."

She thought back through a flipchart of memories to the seventh grade when the spin of her world shifted to a different axis. "Well," she said, "the only thing I can think of is full moons and Halloween."

"Halloween? You mean a ghoulish prank or a werewolf thing during a full moon?"

"Well, not exactly, but sort of," she said, "I don't mean to be vague, but there is a tradition in Perfection that kids who are entering adolescence go there around Halloween. The kids spend the night, in what I learned in college is a kind of 'rite of passage' that started about fifty years ago. Supposedly, if you survive the night there, you have become an adult and, presumably more perfect."

"But," Eb interrupted, "they didn't just leap into adulthood. There's more lost than adolescence alone. There's a deeper inflexibility."

After a five second pause, Molly said, "There are all kinds of stories of witches and demons out there to scare the younger kids." Her eyes rolled up forty-five degrees while she reviewed the documentary of her past flashing through her memories for one minute and thirty-five seconds before she continued, "I think what confused me is that occasionally someone would go there at other times. I remember thinking that there had been a blue moon one of those nights, so maybe it's Halloween and blue moon nights when they go there, maybe just on regular full moon nights and I happened to see some kids go out there under a blue moon."

"Is that why the rock has *Hell World* painted on it?"

"No, I think that was painted around the time of the disasters."

"Disasters?" Ebenezer Thornbird's eyes bugged out, round and white as golf balls, eyebrows shooting north into deep wrinkles of confusion, wondering what else she hadn't told him.

"Okay," Molly Everhart was suspended in her thoughts for fifteen seconds before she said, "maybe I'm not explaining it very well. I'll start from the beginning. My grandmother said that over fifty years ago, it was a forest filled with all kinds of wild flora and fauna."

"In that barren land? What the hell happened? You said disaster struck?"

"Well, there were some land speculators and builders who bought up the whole place and built houses, but nothing would grow after that. The trees and plants died and then there was a wave of pestilence."

"Pests?" He said while his eyes grew an impossibly wider look of shock.

"Yes. Termites, and carpenter ants and fires as well as tornados until nothing was left. The builders called the tract Westland because it was the western half of the city, but people started calling it Wasteland and eventually somebody, probably some teenagers, painted *Hell World* on the rock near the entrance. I guess that was to scare the younger kids who hadn't gone through their overnight ritual yet. No one ever discovered the truth."

Ebenezer Thornbird said, "It does sound Biblical, but why didn't the plants grow again? Did someone salt the Earth?" he asked, with a tongue and cheek reference to ancient scriptures.

"No. The soil was thoroughly tested. My father said that the State geologists along with the researchers from the University studied it, and they saw no reason why the plants didn't grow again, especially since they had grown in abundance before. They took soil samples from there and planted seeds both in their lab and in *Hell World*. The seeds in the lab grew, but those that were planted in *Hell World* did not, even though all environmental factors were controlled to match; the plants were watered in the lab exactly like the ones in *Hell World,* and the temperature was coordinated as well. He said that even the researchers seemed changed somehow after they left the place, too.

"Changed? How so?" He cocked his head to the left again as if listening for a response from the Universe.

"They seemed confused or shocked, and when they were asked about their findings, they simply said that the 'soul,'" she made air quotes, "just didn't want to yield any life there."

"They said, 'soul'?"

"Yes, my father thought maybe they mispronounced the word soil, maybe it was someone with a deep Southern accent. Either way, isn't that a strange thing for scientists to say?"

"I'll say! Very strange. Even if they meant soil."

"And you say that all of the kids around twelve or thirteen go there to spend one night?"

"Yeah and..." she stopped in mid-thought, eyes glazed over, staring off through the window of memory into the myriad of past images, and her breathing quickened. Eb saw the glint of her rhythmically accelerating pulse reflected in her necklace chain draped across her carotid artery. He noticed too that her breath was fast and shallow by the rise and fall of her chest.

"What's the matter?" he inquired, trying to pry her back to Earth.

"It's just... I had a revelation!" Her eyes widened, and her eyebrows lifted high while she leaned a little farther forward.

"Molly, what was it?" He was completely focused on her now. *What could be affecting her so intensely?*

"The rite of passage, or whatever you call it, is when everyone changed!" she said with a difficult breath.

"That's what I was starting to wonder," he said. "You told me that the other kids changed around that time."

She sat up even straighter, but not out of self-consciousness this time. She was a balloon of understanding inflating with the shocking air of enlightenment. "No!" she said, a little too loud. Ebenezer Thornbird flinched and blinked at the force of it. "It didn't happen *around* then, it happened *exactly* then!" She swam back upstream toward the headwaters of her history and arrived at the exact space and time where it all happened while he waited for her to clear the waters of recall. At long last, she said, "Now that I think of it, all the kids who went in there, to *Hell World* I mean, were kind of foggy for a few days afterward. I think it must have taken a month or so for the adjustment to fully develop. I thought it was from a lack of sleep and from being scared, or that it just took time to complete the rapid development to adulthood, but now that I'm thinking of it, they have been increasingly very different since then. It was as if they suddenly became clones in lockstep with the adults in town. They definitely weren't any fun anymore." She peered for a fraction further into her expanding awareness. "I think what threw me off was the fact that most of the kids went into *Hell World* at Halloween, but a few went in when the moon was full.

There was a weeklong suspension of activity for the next five minutes. The waiters stopped, the other customers were frozen in place, the cooks were paralyzed causing the food to overcook, and the phantom odors of recognition permeated the place. Eb said, "I have a very strong feeling that something or someone is calling, imprisoned, needing to be found, and the signal has something to do with that rock or *Hell World* itself." Suddenly he perked up. "But," he said, "How did you get through it without ending up like the other kids?"

She glanced away, a look of shame and embarrassment appearing on her face, and she confessed, "I never went in there. I chickened out, I was too scared." The air leaked all the way out of her balloon, she looked down at herself, and she no longer cared that she slumped in her seat.

Eb said, "Well, I am happy you didn't go. You would never have developed into the wonderful person you are today." She was visibly calmer now, a secret burden lifted, her deepening breath slowed, and she sat back up without self-consciousness, her face relaxed. *She seems more beautiful than ever.* Of course, he couldn't tell her that directly because she'd just think he was simply trying to make her feel better, but he meant it. He was thoughtful for two minutes. "There's a full moon soon isn't there? I have to go in there."

Her eyes widened, her flopping heart propelled her terrified body forward, and her mind and emotions leaped across the table to save him. "Oh, my God! You have to stay away from that place!" she pleaded.

"Why?"

"I don't know exactly," the mere thought of it made her tremble slightly, "but I've always stayed away from it. All the other kids went there, but I was too scared. Assuming I went there since everyone did, they never noticed that I avoided it, and though unsuccessful, I tried to act like them. I seemed to be invisible to them,"

"Why were you afraid to go?"

"Well, first of all, everything in there was dead." Her eyes glazed over while she dove back into her reminiscences. "That by itself scared me, and there were the stories the older kids told about the demons. Besides, people say they sometimes see a fire burning in *Hell World* at night. In fact, I overheard one of the boys say that that is the signal for the kids to enter. They say that it's a demon. I don't know who or what it is, or whether it's just another story to scare the kids. I always thought that one of them set the fire just to scare the uninitiated but, now that I think of it, I've never heard of anyone going there after their assigned night, and I've never gone anywhere near it."

She was looking at him, but no longer saw him due to the documentary flashing through her mind while she ventured more deeply into her memory banks and said, "Oh! Now that I'm thinking of it, Mr. Edelson said the wheel cover of his vintage Cadillac came off, and he saw it roll into *Hell World* last year, but he couldn't find it when he got out of his car to retrieve it. Maybe it rolled behind a rock or something, but he said it disappeared and he was afraid to go into *Hell World*, to search for it. That was an adult who had no reason to make up a story. Of course, no one believed him, at least that's what they said. They assumed he was hallucinating or something, but they did seem a little unsettled. Maybe he fell asleep at the wheel and had a dream despite the obvious missing hubcap. Maybe he was just too caught up in the idea of there being something out there. I just thought their reaction was because it didn't fit with their drive for perfection, but maybe there was something more to it."

She stopped again and stared off for a fifteen-second lapse into the middle distance of the past few years while a memory elbowed its way into consciousness. "Looking back on it though," she added, "as far as I know, none of the kids who went there ever returned to *Hell World* Just like Mr. Edelson wouldn't go in again. You know, now that I think of it, the only adult that went out there was J.C. you said you met him."

"Yes," Eb said, "I remember that he was demented. Do you think he's demented because of his incursion into that barren land?"

"His granddaughter was about thirteen when she went into *Hell World.* Well, she isn't really his granddaughter. Her family rented him a room when Elise was little, after he was laid off from the granary, and she adopted him, as sort of a replacement for her real grandfather who died around that time." She thought for three seconds. "Anyway, I remember that Elise went in there and didn't come out right away the next morning." Molly stared off at, but not reading the sign on the wall offering a Thursday eleven to two lunch special. "J.C. supposedly went in after her when she didn't return on time. He loves her probably more deeply than anyone ever in his life." A two-minute silence of struggling thought ensued.

Eb asked, "What does J.C. stand for?"

"My father told me once that it stood for Jesus. You know, the Spanish pronunciation heh-soos. I think his last name was Spanish too; something like Calderon. "J.C. must have been diagnosed with dementia soon after that foray into *Hell World* to retrieve Elise!" Molly Everhart's eyes rolled north in pensive calculation, "she's eighteen now, and it was about five years ago, so Elise was thirteen at the time. Maybe something happened to him like it did to the kids. Maybe his age made it different for him than for the adolescents.... Or maybe, it was because he was already a little bit unbalanced to begin with." Suddenly, she sat up straight as if she had just realized that she was sitting on the tack of revelation and blurted out, "Oh God! What if that happens to you?" Molly's eyes were pleading pools of dampness, and with trembling fingers, she reached for his hand. "Please don't go there."

"I can't help it, Molly. I have to go," he said with compassion in his voice, empathy in his eyes, and a gentle squeeze of her hand.

Molly was terrified. Here, sitting before her, was the man of her dreams and fantasies right out of her novels, who understands her more deeply than she ever dared to hope, seeking out a danger that even he senses, a danger she has always felt out there in *Hell World*. She was trying to hold back the rising tide on the edge of an ocean of tears building just below the surface, a tidal wave of emotion about to erupt and drown her in a sea of despair. Her eyelids were blinking rapidly as she looked away. *How come I get so easily emotional?* It took her two minutes before she could martial her vocal cords into the beginning of gurgling speech. "Eb," she managed to gargle, sounding like a flowing brook, "If you're determined to go out there, I'm coming with you!"

"No Molly, it's my job, my fate, and it's what I do. It's what I'm destined to do. I don't want you to jeopardize yourself. Besides, I will need your help in other ways."

She thought with a silent and extremely wrinkled brow for a minute. *He needs me to help.* Her head nodded slowly, unconsciously. Pondering this, she said, "Okay, as long as I can be with you."

"Those stories about Mr. Edelson and J.C. confirm it." He said, "That's when and where the transformation took place."

"I see what you mean. I guess that is why, because I didn't go there, I always thought I was left behind condemned to the chaos of childhood immaturity while everyone else grew up."

"That must be it!" Eb was energized. "*Hell World.* There's something they left out there on the threshold of their adolescence, just as something happened to the houses, animals, and foliage. It's all yearning to be found and liberated, and I'll have to go there and find it." He thought for a moment and said, "Didn't you say that wasteland was destroyed fifty years ago?"

"Yes. Why?"

"Is that when the rock was painted?"

"Yes."

"And, was it soon after that that the kids started going there?"

"Oh, my God! That's right!"

"And it wasn't long after that the town was renamed?"

"Yeah… Actually, it was about a generation later."

"So, it was after the first generation of kids went through that ritual?"

"That's right!"

Ebenezer Thornbird and Finder thought for twenty seconds. "I have to go there!"

"Oh geez. I'm afraid you'll end up like the others, I'd lose… I mean you'd end up like the rest of this town or worse, like J.C.!" She grabbed her head with both hands trying to minimize the impact, her elbows planted on the table, her blood pressure shooting up twenty points, the ringing in her ears warning of a pending conflagration, and her head felt like it was going to explode in terror. Molly looked out the window and thought she saw a small bird take flight from the windowsill. The little thing had been looking at them and seemed to calm her, but she shook her head slightly while her nerves settled. *I'm just being paranoid,* she rationalized.

"Molly," he said, "it's my path in life. Please don't ask me to abandon my destiny. I can't be in the position of choosing between that and my feelings for you."

Wait! Did he just say he has strong feelings for me? Molly's heart took two somersaults, one backflip, and ended her Olympic routine with a one arm handstand that ended in a standing ovation followed by the ceremony awarding her the gold medal.

They finished their delicious meal savoring its taste at the excited sexually charged table and drove back toward the motel.

Molly said, "Unfortunately, I have to go home. My parents are expecting me and my mother wants me to do some chores and errands for her."

"Okay, but in that case, can you drop me at the library after I change clothes? It'll only take a minute to change," he said.

"Sure. No problem. I'll wait in the van for you." She saw that bird again. It landed on the hood of the van, hopped back and forth, scrutinizing her, until Ebenezer Thornbird emerged from his room. She swore its head nodded its approval before it chirped and took flight.

It was only three minutes before Eb returned and mounted Molly's van. What time are you off work tomorrow?" he asked.

CHAPTER TEN
THE ARCHIVES OF REVELATION

Driving up to the library, Molly Everhart noticed Sheriff Buck's cruiser following. "Buck is following us," she said.

"I know. I saw him through the side mirror." Eb zeroed in and gave her a quick squeeze, a kiss on the forehead, and was out of the van while she was still trying to catch her breath, all within five heartbeats and four blinks. "See you later!" he yelled over his shouldered backpack as he strode away toward the library.

"See you later! I'll come back after I finish helping my mother," she yelled back much too loudly, but there was no one else there to hear her, save the bird that had just landed in the small tree next to the entrance. *That bird seems to be following Eb around, watching over him as if it was indebted to him or something.* She pulled out of the lot and waved to the Sheriff as she passed. He frowned but politely returned a crisp but casual salute.

The sign in front of the building simply said, "Library," but the cornerstone read *Zanesville Library. Estab. 1920.* Ebenezer Thornbird walked into a dark, lonely and dusty place, a step backward in time where, to save money, the librarian burned only the lights that were needed, since the few leftover patrons were spirits of past readers and they required very little light. There were computers in the library of course, but they were outdated by several cyber generations, and most people owned more current versions. Most everyone could download books and information via the internet on their tablets or phones, and the sad, long neglected, and dusty hardcover books were not in demand except when their contents could not be obtained online.

The lonely unfulfilled librarian sat in front of her very ancient slow computer behind a creaky old desk lit with a single, dim, energy efficient desk lamp. When he stepped up to the counter, Ms. Jacqueline Oddmeyer looked up, startled to see, what at first seemed to be a ghostly apparition, but turned out to be an actual visitor step out of the darkness. She stood and walked to the stool behind the counter. She was so short in stature, five feet tall exactly, without her three-inch platform heels that made it difficult for her to mount the stool in a two-rung climb as if it was a ladder. *She's obviously self-conscious about her height* Finder whispered. Without those stilts, no more than the top of her head would have been visible over the very high counter, obviously designed by a tall man without regard for the fact that the majority of librarians were women when the library was built. A throwback to the nineteenth century, she had on an old-fashioned high-collar white blouse that buttoned all the way up to her chin, a black skirt with stockings to match and a gray sweater that all but made her seem to disappear into the dark gray-black background reminding Eb of a Rembrandt portrait. Her hair was the combination of a dull brown with reddish highlights mixed with a vague gray that made it appear ashen. Staring at him through huge lenses that were tethered to a chain around her neck, her eyes leaped out at him and he had to stifle a flinch. *Better to see you with my dear*, Eb silently joked to no one but his own brain before he realized it and, once he became aware of it, he continued his humorous self-delusion, *Thank you. Thank you. Thank you very much* in the very poor internal Elvis imitation to the applause of the invisible mental audience.

Around Ms. Oddmeyer's neck was a matching necklace of little beads of various colors and a lanyard with a key and her nametag fighting for position between her ample breasts. Her long hair was stacked in a bun atop her head revealing dangling feather earrings and a face with little makeup. *She'd be more attractive if she wasn't so bundled up,* he thought. It was as if she was trying too hard to subdue any hint of sexuality, except the feathers seemed out of place. Maybe a sign of her hidden lustful self or maybe a link to a Native American heritage.

A pleasant, but slightly smug voice said, "Hello Mr. Thornbird, welcome to the Zanesville library how can I help?" She smiled a smile that seemed more mischievous or maybe a little diabolical as she flicked a switch to illuminate Ebenezer Thornbird in a kind of spotlight that was unexpectedly bright. It caused a squinting and eye-watering encounter which merely encouraged his feeling of being a performer on a stage with an audience of one. He flinched at not only the sudden brightness but the fact that she knew his name.

Hello," he said, "I'm at a disadvantage mam. Have we met?" *man! Has she got secrets!* Finder exclaimed.

"Oh no," She intoned with the taste of irony on her lips. "You're the only stranger in town, and the town council met and brought up your suspicious travel journal."

"Suspicious?" he asked, "What's suspicious about it?"

"The council only meets when the need arises and mostly for concrete, practical matters such as zoning, property taxes, and repairs to the infrastructure. They're unaccustomed to dealing with human resources or social issues because, well... because there never are any. The sixty-three citizens who attended were suspicious of you and especially what you might report about their town."

"Huh? What the..."

She opened her notebook and paraphrased the minutes, "One man said, 'What if he finds flaws in our Perfection?' Thirty-two of them welcomed your report because, as one woman explained, 'It might be good for business if travelers wished to explore a perfect town and of course, spend their money here. Perhaps it would be held up as a model city. If he does find flaws, all the better so we can address them and remedy the situation.' Thirty-one members of the crowd wished to get rid of you in case you did find flaws, or worse, if your articles attracted strangers to move here. Another man said, 'He should be politely asked to leave, if you catch my meaning.'"

Ebenezer Thornbird protested to the empty library loud enough through his teeth that the librarian heard him. "I'm just trying to write articles and books about the towns and cities across America. I'm a freelance travel writer." His voice, traveling like an echo throughout the ancient structure, unintentionally carried with so much intensity that the ghosts of past readers and researchers, who forgot to join their hosts in the afterlife, abruptly looked up from their phantom books, and the universe seemed to take offense.

"Shhh! she hissed. This is a library!" Despite the fact that they were the only two living beings around, she seemed to be protecting the phantom readers, maybe the entire town, maybe the world, from strong vibrations in the ether. After a seven-second pause, regaining her composure, tugging at her clothes and smoothing her perfectly unrumpled hair, Ms. Oddmeyer continued, "yes, that's what you say, but the Sheriff said that it only means that you are..." searching her notes, "quote, 'a jobless drifter.' That's what he said, anyway. I'm just reporting what was said. I always attend the meetings to stay abreast of town activities as the official librarian, archivist, curator of the historical records, and recorder of the minutes. I don't have a dog in this fight, and I don't have a vote either. Now how can I assist you Mr. Thornbird?"

Unsuccessfully trying to clear his head and calmly re-focus on his intended task, he said, "I searched the online databases for a history of this town, and I only found a very short summary, a kind of propaganda put out by the Chamber of Commerce, seemingly designed to keep people from coming here. I'd like to find out more about this town of Perfection, and frankly, why the Chamber of Commerce, of all things, would discourage, prospective residents tourists or, for that matter, prospective businesses from stopping here. Do you have information that isn't on the Internet?"

"Yes, we do. I'll show you to the archives." She turned to a console mysteriously secreted behind the counter, and the lights flickered on, lighting their way to the stacks, precisely those lights that were necessary and no more. Passing various stacks, Eb noticed that there were open books lying on the tables as if someone was reading them and, he thought just for a nanosecond, out of the corner of his eye, he saw a page turn. *There must be a breeze.*

"Here is a history of Zanesville written by a grad student at the nearby college for his master's thesis," the librarian said, "and here is the biography of Apollyon Zane. There is also a stack of local newspaper articles that have been scanned into the computer's hard drives as well." He cruised through the articles and was about to read the Zanesville thesis while the biography of Zane was waiting in the wings, just as Molly returned from her errands.

"Hi, Eb! How's it going? Did you find what you needed?"

Before he could respond, Ms. Jacqueline Oddmeyer approached, floating in from the mysteriously dim recesses of the building, with official-looking folders. "I thought you might like to see this copy of Apollyon Zane's Will and Trust. I found it here in the library quite a few years ago, long after the Westland tract had removed the flora and fauna. That was never supposed to happen because the Trust stipulated that that area was to remain wild, but by that time it was too late." Ms. Oddmeyer stood silently hesitating, her engines caught in a momentary stall, trying to determine whether to say more. "Oh, what the hell!" She jump-started, "I made copies to keep here along with the original and gave a copy to the town council. I believe they put it in the safe at city hall, probably to hide their mistake lest anyone accuse them of mismanagement and thereby revealing their imperfection. Of course, someone could charge them with malfeasance, but that would reveal an imperfection, and we could never have that! They don't realize that I have the original and this copy," she smirked, obviously pleased with herself for pulling one over on the town council.

One more move in the game, Eb thought before he thanked her, turned back to Molly and resumed his explanation of what he found so far. Ms. Oddmeyer took a few steps nearly disappearing into the dark recesses, stopped, turned slowly for dramatic effect, and interrupted again. "There's a genealogy of the citizens there as well." She offered an enigmatic smile that was almost a conspiratorial smirk. Molly's stomach began to feel the green jealousy monster rising deep within; a growing competition for Ebenezer Thornbird's attention. But, was Jacqueline Oddmeyer's attention sexual or simply a narcissistic need to be the center of the discussion, and in some kind of control?

Ebenezer Thornbird read the page of the Trust that she had left open for him and said, "I see. It does spell it out in no uncertain terms that the wilderness must remain untouched." She reached over and opened the genealogy to a certain page, pointed to a specific spot where a name jumped off the page, caused a double take that flashed through both shocked cerebral hemispheres, traveled through his very surprised body, causing him to flinch; "*Thornbird!*" he said aloud.

The librarian smiled, diabolically proud of herself. "I thought you might be interested in this. As you can see, a local Native American Medicine Man named Jay Thornbird was believed to have mystical powers."

****

Everyone knew from the moment he broke free into this world that Blue Jay Thornbird, later called simply Jay or J.T., was a born Medicine Man. There was something mysterious and other-worldly about him, a kind of glow you could see if you looked at him In just the right way. When his mother's water broke, a terrible raging thunderstorm was boiling, and the heavens opened up In a deluge, but when she went into labor, a great flash of lightning signaled an abrupt end of the storm, and soon after he was born the Sun was smiling in a cloudless sky. Blue Jay Thornbird was born at midnight, stayed with his mother in a darkened room for the rest of three days and three nights until the time was ripe. His uncle came to fetch him just before the Sun's spirit began to break above the flat horizon into the most brilliant dawn anyone could remember. It was as if Father Sun held back until just the right time before bursting into a spectacular display of power that enlightened the world. The infant remained with his mother in the darkness, save for a small fire, barely illuminating the room, swaddled in a special blanket with his face completely covered. He was taken by his Uncle Raymond Shining Star, the tribe's Medicine Man, to a sacred rock in the woods where his entire tribe was waiting.

Uncle Raymond had traveled to study with representatives of nearly every major tribal group and band in the country, learning from their Medicine men and thereby gaining the mystical knowledge of many native peoples.

He climbed the boulder with his tiny bundle, held the baby, face still covered, toward the East. As the orange and yellow sun began to stream its light over the horizon turning pink and blue just as the Face Uncovering Ceremony began. Raymond Shining Star slowly revealed his nephew's face just as the sunrise turned a royal purple. The boy's eyes were closed in a serene countenance, and he did not fuss. Instead, the soothing rays seemed to be infused into his body. The Medicine Man said, "Feel the warmth of Father Sun," holding the child toward the spectacular dawn for a full minute, for one hundred and twenty beats of the baby's heart. The boy's eyes opened. Turning him to the West, his uncle said, "See the Earth. See the animals in the forest." Turning him to the North, "see the mountains. See the shining waters." The boy's eyes seemed to smile brightly. He slowly turned the baby's face to the South toward the assembly, "See your people. You will always be rich for these." The boy's arms reached out. Blue Jay Thornbird did not cry. Instead, he looked around at everyone, burped and gave a simultaneous tiny squeaking fart. Everyone laughed, someone said it was a sign, and everyone spent the remainder of the day exuding gas until a mysterious bluish fog covered the ground. Blue Jay Thornbird was handed over first to his mother and then, one-by-one to each member who welcomed him into the arms of the tribe. He drifted off to the safe, comfortable sleep of contentment as the sweet aromas of the ceremonial food wafted his way. Everyone said his eyes were large, old, and wise. A true gift of the Great Spirit. They remarked that he did not cry and that he seemed to be observing everything and everyone like a wizened elder. The drumming had begun, but the baby slept through it for hours while the blue fog rose to the tops of small trees.

As he grew, Jay Thornbird attended school during the day where he learned English, but as the afternoon shadows stretched across the land after the evening meal, he was taken to a Kiva. In that underground place of ritual, mystery, and spiritual preparation, sacred ceremonies were performed and learned, along with his native language.

"You will carry on these traditions after the old ones and I are gone," Raymond Shining Star told Blue Jay Thornbird.

"I will not fail you, my teacher; my uncle."

At the age of twelve, just as the boy's voice was cracking, Raymond Shining Star said, "It is time for you to become a man." In anticipation of the full moon, he was silently loaded in Uncle Raymond's old rickety pickup truck, driven to a remote place where they camped. They built a sweat lodge, fasted for three days, performed a cleansing ceremony of chants accompanied by ritual smoke, before Blue Jay Thornbird was sent off naked wearing only a loincloth into the mountains to find his spirit animal.

"You must remain awake as the full moon rises. Drink only as much water as you require to sustain your life." After a ritual chant, Raymond Shining Star said, "Take this medicine pouch. In it, there are some dried plants. As the sun sets, place them in your mouth and mix it with a little water before you swallow it. Then you must wait."

"What must I wait for? What will I see, Uncle?"

"That is for you to know; I cannot tell you, but you will know when you see it."

Blue Jay Thornbird built a fire, hunkered down, and waited. His throat burned a little as the sacred concoction went down with the sunset while sister full moon rose in the clear sky. Struggling to remain awake, his mind seemed to stretch on forever, when he heard a sound behind him. Turning his head, he saw a small bird on the branch of a thorny bush surrounded by a glowing light. The bird, his spirit animal, spoke to his mind saying, "You will perform well for your people, teach a stranger the skills you possess, and one of your descendants will spawn a protector who will help to keep her charge safe." Groggy at first, sleep captured him, and he did not awaken until the rising sun peeked over the horizon, and he ran to his uncle who told him to remain silent, savor the experience, meditate on all its ramifications and discover what more it reveals.

Blue Jay Thornbird grew into a towering figure in the tribe as he learned the deep healing powers and wisdom passed on to him, the accumulation of the wisdom and experience of the Native American diaspora. He picked up the skills so rapidly that they seemed to be passed on through the genes in the Thornbird bloodline.

Billy Thornbird, Son of Jay Thornbird, achieved a high school diploma, and despite never pursuing advanced degrees, he was well read. He loved the Greek myths and took a course in Greek Mythology at the local college. "I find mythology fascinating, but the Greek ones seem to call to me." When his wife, Shining Waters was pregnant with their daughter, he said. "The child will be called Artemis after a Greek goddess, the protector of the vulnerable." She rolled her eyes toward the heavens, shook her head, and made *titch, titch, titching* sounds with her tongue. When the baby girl was born, he remained steadfast in naming her Artemis, the Protector. He remembered what his father's spirit animal had told him. "Your descendants will spawn a protector." He knew this child would be that descendant. He had seen the omens and trusted his attraction to the Greek myths, and the Goddess Artemis.

****

Molly was thunderstruck. "Thornbird? Wow, what a coincidence!" She said, "You and that Medicine Man have the same last name!"

"Apparently, Billy Thornbird had two children; a boy, Adam,

and a girl," said Ms. Jacqueline Oddmeyer "Adam Thornbird moved somewhere out east. I lost the trail when I was trying to fill in his line in the genealogy. His sister remained here until she moved away about thirteen years ago,"

Ebenezer Thornbird thought, *has fate been beckoning to me and somehow delivered me here?"*

After a three-minute span of thought, Ms. Oddmeyer said, "You may be interested in another fact. It appears that J.C. was probably the illegitimate grandson of John Crow, a Native American who had been raised on a reservation out west but was taken to a mission school, stripped of his Native name and saddled with his 'Christian name', John, from the Bible."

****

John Crow, a Native American boy of ten, was taken away from his parents and his local band, a Native American group smaller than a tribe, by the US government. His parents were told, "This young man needs an education that you cannot provide. His mother cried and begged them not to remove him, but they paid her no mind. She thought, *these white men must be deaf because they didn't even look at me or even blink.* They made no acknowledgment of her presence and dragged the boy away, forcing him to live at a mission school, taught to speak English, and punished if he tried to speak his native language or practice any of his native customs. He was made to follow the mysterious and confusing Christian ways of his Catholic keepers.

The mission's groundskeeper, Running Fox, a Native American, who was re-named Billy Joseph at the mission, took John Crow under his wing and assisted him in circumventing the Monks' and Priests' harsh punishments and beatings, secretly maintaining at least some of his customs. Although there were some similarities in each other's languages, they communicated mostly in English, carried out some of the rituals late at night, and took forays into the wilderness for days at a time with the excuse of hunting for game. They brought back animals for food and pelts to avoid suspicion, but they trapped most of the game and spent the majority of their time practicing native rituals and in sweat lodges. Billy Joseph told John Crow, "They can beat your body, force you to worship their god, and make you speak English, but they cannot take your spirit."

"What do you mean?"

"Your spirit is not just your own, and it doesn't belong to them or their god. They do not understand that our spirit is everywhere. Their's is owned by their King God in his sky-heaven. Our heaven is everywhere. You can never be lost because your spirit is part of everything around you."

"But we can die. "

"That's the Spirit Walk you take from this life, leaving your body behind to mingle with the Earth and the sky and step through a thin veil into the pure spirit world. The difference is that your spirit joins The Great Spirit."

"But isn't that like the Christian God?"

"No. The Great Spirit is everywhere. You are always part of it, but the difference is that you are no longer restricted by a mortal body; you are everywhere. You are one with the trees, plants, and animals; the Earth and the sky. The Christians die and go to some place in the sky that is separate from this world or to a separate place underground for punishment."

John Crow's original Native American name was Screeching Crow apparently because of his ear-piercing cries as a baby. Billy Joseph said, "You will always be Screeching Crow no matter what the Monks call you. Besides, you must seek your spirit animal guide to become a man."

As John Screeching Crow entered adolescence, their disappearing acts into the wilderness provided him the opportunity to climb to the top of a small mountain after preparing for his quest by fasting for three days. He hid his food and later fed it to the animals to hide his fast from the monks. He was told by Billy Joseph to climb the mountain and sit there singing a sacred chant, taking with him only a small medicine pouch containing a few magical fetishes, and flint to make a fire along with some dried plants. These were designed to keep him safe, but, more importantly, to attract his animal spirit. He was allowed some water to stay hydrated and he swallowed a small amount of dried plants with it, on the second night, at dusk.

That night, he witnessed a wondrous sunset dipping low over the landscape reflecting off the barren desert planes in a mirage, a reverse sunset, looking to John Screeching Crow like two mirrored sunsets disappearing into each other. As soon as the last shard of light disappeared over the horizon leaving only the full moon, the stars, and his small fire, he vomited his anxiety over the cliff. Turning slowly toward a growl he heard behind him, fear arose from deep in his belly when a Puma, starring at him from the darkness, nearly caused him to fall over the precipitous edge of his consciousness into the dark abyss. He saw the creature as clearly as if it were daylight and yelled, "Aaaaeeee!"

The creature licked its chops and spoke in his mind, "You are a Medicine Man, and your dreams will guide you to your teacher." The Puma leaped, disappearing into John Screeching Crow who fell into a deep state of unconsciousness until the next midday. Weakened from malnutrition and dehydration, but feeling the energy of a mountain lion and a mature sense of confidence that he had never known, he was no longer a child. He hurried as fast as his debilitated body would allow to find Billy Joseph. When he tried to tell his mentor what had happened, Billy held up his hand and said,

"That is yours and no one else's. Keep it to yourself until you find your teacher."

****

Molly had picked up the book and, surprised, she read on, "It says here that John Crow escaped the mission school at age thirteen and he sought his kinfolk only to discover that the entire band, including his Medicine Man grandfather, had all died out under mysterious circumstances. Probably from famine and disease."

"John Screeching Crow was the only living member of his band." Ms. Jacqueline Oddmeyer added, "He still spoke their language, but he was left alone in a world where no one else did. Fortunately, he spoke English and, somehow, he made his way to Zanesville, probably hoboing on trains guided by his puma dreams.

****

Since John Screeching Crow's grandfather was a Medicine Man, he was taken in by Jay Thornbird, who taught him the practice of Native rituals just as his Puma spirit had prophesied. Before they even spoke, Jay Thornbird knew there was something special about John Screeching Crow. There was a glow around him, and he carried himself with the confidence that seemed unshakable. Introducing himself, he said, "I'm Jay Thornbird, and I see that your bright spirit brought you here. What spirit protects you?"

John Screeching Crow hesitantly revealed his spirit to be that of the Puma. Jay Thornbird smiled and said, "Yes, yes, you carry yourself like a Mountain Lion."

"My grandfather was a Medicine Man, but he and the rest of my band were wiped out by famine and the White man's diseases. The children, like myself, were taken to the mission school."

"How did you escape?"

"Billy Joseph, his native name was Running Fox, helped me through the passage to adulthood, and with his help, I ran away to seek my family."

"Come live with me, John Screeching Crow, and learn your grandfather's craft."

Without hesitation or questioning his path, he obliged, eager to follow his fate.

Revered in his community for his spirit powers of healing and his wisdom, John Screeching Crow became a highly-accomplished Medicine Man. There was little written record of his intervening years since they were rarely transcribed and they were sacred to the local Native American community.

****

"I read," Ebenezer Thornbird continued, "that John Crow eventually married Little Moon, had a son, James Crow, who also became a Medicine Man.

"Apparently, according to this genealogy, James Crow met a beautiful Mexican woman at the granary," read Ebenezer Thornbird."

"Allegedly, he had an affair with Maria Calderon, a Mexican woman. According to the unsubstantiated story," Ms. Oddmyer said, "when he saw her, even though he loved his wife, he was immediately attracted to her, and in a dream, his spirit animal said, 'You must pursue Maria. The fate of many people depends upon it.' They had a secret affair, and Maria Calderon soon became pregnant, but James reluctantly told Maria, 'I'm married, and you must leave before the baby is born.'"

Maria cried and begged, "I will stay and have the baby! I will tell no one who the father is. I promise."

James said, "I've had a prophetic dream foretelling a larger purpose that we must pursue despite our emotional connection." He prevailed, Maria relented, and she moved away before giving birth to a son.

James said, 'I will send you money every month until the child is eighteen' and, watching her leave a trail of tears behind, causing a downpour of such proportions that the mud rose to his ankles, he added, 'I love you, but there is a sacred purpose to be fulfilled. I cannot jeopardize my standing in the community for the sake of the tribe and that of Zanesville nor can I bring public shame to my wife and children.'"

"Ms. Oddmeyer said, "Maria Calderon apparently moved to Florida, Jupiter Florida if memory serves, to have baby Jesus and he was given her surname, Calderon."

"It says here," Molly chimed in, "that James Crow supported her and their son in secret until J.C. was eighteen."

Jesus Calderon, J.C., apparently had been involved in drugs and alcohol and probably damaged his brain in the process because people said he was a little strange when he came to town; a virtual alien here.

"The records state," Ms. Oddmeyer added, "that J.C. traveled around aimlessly, but eventually was forced to seek rehabilitation by a drug court when he returned to Jupiter, Florida where his mother still lived. He eventually had psychiatric treatment for his delusions, the primary one being that he was a god and that he lived on the planet Jupiter, probably because of his name and his city of origin. It was speculated that his brain had been damaged by the myriad of illegal substances he had consumed over the years."

Molly said, "Here's a note that J.C. was arrested on a charge of disorderly conduct, apparently in a blackout since he had no memory of the entire day. Now straight and sober, he visited his dying mother who revealed that his father was James Crow."

"Yeah," Ms. Oddmeyer cut in, "he subsequently traveled to Zanesville, just before it became Perfection, seeking his father, James Crow, who, as It turned out, had died. No one believed him since he was so strange, probably from brain damage due to his long history of drug use, and because James had apparently hidden J.C.'s existence so well that no one knew of him. His crumpled and barely readable birth certificate had no name for the father, but proved that he was born in Florida."

"According to this book," Said Ebenezer Thornbird, "it looks like, even though James Crow had died, and the remaining Crows denied that J.C. was a relative, he stayed on to work in the granary until he was laid off."

"He had been renting a room from Elise's family," added Ms. Oddmeyer. "She grew up believing he was her grandfather, and he took on the part with gusto. J.C.'s name was added to the genealogical archives, but I had to add an asterisk that meant, according to the footnote, there was a question of whether Jesus Calderon was actually related to James Crow."

"How did you obtain the information about his substance abuse and his legal problems?" Eb asked.

"I obtained some of J.C.'s records several years ago from the court and the clinic where he was rehabilitated, Ms. Oddmeyer continued, puffed up with pride from her sense of accomplishment. He was already getting confused at times and readily signed a release for the records. There was a very detailed history, and among the official documents, a birth certificate, but, as you can see the father's name was left blank."

Is this why I've been drawn to this place? Finder and Eb thought simultaneously, *I may be connected to Jay Thornbird, the Medicine Man. My mom, Pati, said my father called himself Jesus. Is J.C. my father? I'll never know for sure since he's too demented to remember a drug-induced one night stand over thirty years ago.*

CHAPTER ELEVEN
ZANE

"Listen to this! According to his biography," Molly began reading aloud. "Apollyon Zane was born in Philadelphia with the assistance of a hospital midwife by way of mysterious circumstances. The baby was breach, and the labor went on for three grueling days that left Mrs. Zane near death from exhaustion and sheer frustration. The doctor was busy attending to several emergencies at the tiny hospital, and came at the last minute, presumably when that emergency trumped the needs of his other patients. Mrs. Zane had become so exhausted, debilitated, and near death that he had no choice but to attend to the birth. He performed an episiotomy and used forceps with great difficulty to extract the very large head, left the remaining task to the midwife, and returned to the other patients. It was speculated that the forceps left the child with physical distortions of some kind, but this was never confirmed."

"Geez! What an ordeal!" Ebenezer Thornbird's face displaying several shades of yellow and green as Ms. Oddmeyer slid a wastebasket toward him with the toe of her right foot.

"Just as curiously," Molly read on, "No one was ever privy to the reasons for the abrupt move, but Apollyon's family fled to Texas immediately after his birth, literally overnight." She looked up from the book, "One day they were living in the house they had called home for many years and the next, shockingly, they left no evidence that they were ever there!"

Returning to the book, she read on, "Mrs. Zane was faint, wan, and at death's door after three days of being torn apart by the labor and from the perilous episiotomy and partial forceps delivery. Legend has it, this says, she had made a pact with the devil for her firstborn to insure her survival after three days of excruciatingly hard labor."

"Yes," Jacqueline Oddmeyer added in the rather superior tone of a know-it-all, "The midwife tried for two of those harrowing days to turn the breach baby and finally succeeded on the third, but the doctor was worried that all that pushing and tugging might have caused spinal deformities. The day the Zane family left the Philadelphia hospital the midwife was mysteriously found dead in Zane's delivery room from no natural cause the doctors could deduce."

"There was no cause?" Eb was stunned. "Was her life traded for that of the midwife?"

Molly continued reading, "It says here, the look on her face was that of horror, and the coroner's report had no choice but to clearly state that she had died of fright." Silently, she read a little further. "Listen to this!" Molly continued, "There was a never disproved rumor that fraternal twins had been born that day and the first one out, tagged by his mother's pact with the devil, had killed the midwife. The mother was so weak from the murderous trauma of the birth that she couldn't have perpetrated the deed herself."

"What about his father? He could have killed her."

"No," said Ms. Oddmeyer, "he wasn't in the room. He was asleep in the exhausted languid, smoke-filled lounge of expectant fathers at the time, typical of hospitals of that era."

"Yeah," Eb said, "it would have been impossible for anyone to believe that a newborn infant, or even two, had the means, let alone the strength, to kill anyone."

"But there she was," Molly continued, "lying dead on the floor refusing to confess or reveal any other explanation. She even defied the interrogation of an autopsy and kept her haunting secret to herself."

"Although, I was told," Ms. Oddmeyer said, "that a nurse swore she saw a screaming ghost resembling the midwife on the midnight shift, but everyone believed she was probably hallucinating from lack of sleep. Mrs. Zane was exhausted and close to death when they fled the town, but no one suspected foul play."

"It says right here," Molly inserted, "that Apollyon Zane was a vain and secretive child who kept to himself for the most part. He was tutored at home rather than attending the local school and played very little with the other kids. However, all five of his tutors were periodically replaced and mysteriously disappeared one by one without a trace. No one ever saw any of them again."

"Geez, mystery upon mystery!" Eb piped in. "What about the suspected physical distortions from the difficult birth trauma?"

"Yes," said Ms. Oddmeyer, "I talked to some of the people from that area, and they told me the family stories. They said nothing about any physical disabilities, but the Zanes were distant and made little effort to engage with the community. They were mysteriously reclusive, and no one knew what went on beyond the gates of the Zane compound. When the last Zane patriarch died, the Sheriff had to arrange an auction for the back taxes on the property. Apparently, the Zanes had become impoverished after Mr. Zane died, and no longer managed the finances."

"The records I reviewed there read…"

"You went there?" Molly interrupted.

"Yes. I'm a historian and a genealogist by training, so I was curious about the founder of this town and the Zanes' mysterious background.

"When the assets were inventoried, they found an outlying solid brick windowless structure on the property in which, or so it appeared, someone or some thing had lived there for many years. I was able to go inside, and it was very strange; creepy in the extreme."

"What do you mean 'strange' and 'creepy?'" asked Molly, unaware that her mouth was hanging open and that she was sitting on the edge of her seat

"There were odd things there. The caretaker showed me the shackles and chains that were attached to the walls, but they didn't appear to be designed for an animal. He said, 'They seem to be made for a human being. The cuffs are too big for the nasty dog they once had, and there are two leg irons and one for the neck. The attached chains allowed free access to the entire interior, but anyone wearing them would be stopped short of the only exit, such that the captive could just reach the food delivery hatch at the bottom of the door.'"

"Holy….!" Eb was speechless for a full thirty seconds. Then he said, "What the heck! Did they have a slave in there or a wild or dangerous human?"

Ms. Oddmeyer said, "No one knows, but I was able to view the building, the only original structure left of the compound. It was eerie with all of the rusted old chains and shackles still there. No one had ever dared to purchase the thing, apparently out of fear that it might be haunted by the poor creature who once dwelled there.

"The door to the dwelling had to be broken open since it was festooned with a myriad of long dead locks, the keys for which were nowhere to be found as if they had imprisoned someone there and threw away the keys. I saw the slot, a small wooden flap in the bottom of the door just large enough that food and other items such as a chamber pot, could be passed through and locked thereafter. There was an old electric cattle prod leaning against the wall near the door.

"This biography says," Molly continued to read, "when Apollyon Zane was a child, he was rumored to have an imaginary friend way beyond the age that most children outgrow such things. Some people speculated that he was crazy because, when anyone happened to be walking by the tall hedge that surrounded the property, they thought they heard him talking to himself in two different low voices. Apparently, the other kids stayed away from his house because it had a very high fence behind a tall hedge and behind that a very angry dog that would like to tear your leg off or go for the throat."

"Yes," Ms. Oddmeyer added, "and Apollyon Zane practiced drawing and shooting his toy pistols until he graduated to actual firearms, learned to draw fast and shoot with a high degree of accuracy. The gunshots were blasting from behind the hedges until he left home at the age of eighteen. He worked as a range hand until the cowboy's nightmare ménage à trois addiction to his good friend Jack Daniels, who gripped him by the throat, Lady Luck, and the habit of gambling took him over. However, his quick draw and accurate aim of childhood and adolescence served him well."

There was a short silence while Molly read more of the biography, "According to this, there was an unsubstantiated legend circulating that Zane killed seven men in gunfights."

"Yes," said Ms. Oddmeyer," but the well-respected historian of Western gunfighters, William Gaunt, could only account for three such incidents and one wounding. He did find that Zane also fought briefly in the Civil War on the side of the Confederacy with Quantrill out of Texas, and killed many men in the heartless justification of war."

"He left the Raiders when they tried to carry on fighting, killing and raiding after the war was over." Molly read on silently again before she added, "He saw the futility and the lack of profit in it so, in his middle thirties, he found work on the ranch of Phineas Exelon, a wealthy rancher whose wife had died of scarlet fever. He signed on as a cowhand at first, but was quickly promoted and, due to his skills with weapons, he was appointed the old man's bodyguard and confidant. Exelon's two sons and only heirs were ghosts of the war, and he began to treat Apollyon as a third and only living son."

Looking through the biography, Eb said, "Apparently, Mr. Exelon became demented and eventually died mysteriously, lying before the open door of the ranch house safe, leaving the money and other important papers of temptation exposed."

"Yes," Jacqueline Oddmeyer broke in, "According to his journal, Apollyon was the first to discover the body. He didn't consider it foul play since nothing was taken. I read that Apollyon Zane didn't take the money because, if he had, he'd be suspect."

Eb looked up abruptly, "Journal?"

"Yes. I read it, but it seems to have been lost or stolen maybe by the student who wrote the biography. However, as he perused the documents," she continued, "he discovered the deed and title to the ranch wherein the only blank spaces were the lines for the name of the owner. Apparently, the old guy had left it blank intending to insert the name of his son or sons if one or both survived the war. Zane concluded that, since Exelon considered him a son, he'd inherit the ranch, but, in his senility had forgotten to fill in his name. That being the case, Apollyon took them, left the corpse, the money, and the rest of the papers for the cook to discover, and did his best to mimic the old man's writing. Practicing it several times, he wrote, with the spirit of Exelon's guiding hand on blank sheets of paper until he was satisfied that he had channeled Zane's signature to a close resemblance, burned the practice sheets, and filled the blanks with his own name.'"

"Yeah! It says here that the cook was found with the money and accused of murder," Eb read on, "but in the end, was only charged with theft when there was no indication of foul play... Oh! But he was hanged anyway!" The room acquired a deep silence for five seconds until he resumed reading. "Apparently, Zane later produced the title and deed stating that the old man had given it to him with the promise that Apollyon would not claim the ranch until after Exelon died. Zane quickly sold the ranch for a huge profit."

"Yeah," said Ms. Oddmeyer, "I figure that before anyone could suspect him of any wrong-doing, or another relative showed up to grab what he felt was rightly his, he fled North. It wasn't long before he staked his land claim in the 1889 land rush and established a ranch near here. His journal revealed that he cheated and paid someone else to ride ahead and stake out the claim of this very large area soon after the stampede for the land began."

"So he founded the town and named it Zanesville?" Molly asked."

"Yes. He built the saloon, the general store, established several other shops and services, and brought a doctor in from

Chicago. The townsfolk established a school in 1910, and the library was built in 1920."

"What happened to the guy he sent ahead to grab the land?"

"In his journal, he stated that he shot him to be certain his secret was safe."

"What did he do with the body?"

"According to his journal, he burned it and scattered the ashes over the entire claim."

Ebenezer Thornbird said, "According to his Will and Trust, Zane established the western portion of his land as a permanent wilderness in his Will. One day, or so he said, he had realized in one very long fitful, Nostradamus-like, prophetic nightmare, of mechanical monsters, he interpreted as the railroad and eventually automobiles, bringing strangers to the area and ruining the natural landscape. His Will and Trust stated that the forest was never to be used for any commercial purpose and should be maintained as a park."

There was a full minute of silence before Ms. Oddmeyer spoke. "It was rumored that Zane recruited a local tribe's Medicine Man, the town Priest, and a traveling Buddhist Kung Fu trained Monk from the Shaolin Temple, who was in search of the American father that left his pregnant Chinese mother to die in China. He persuaded them to bestow their blessings on the small forest. In fact, some years later, he asked the Medicine Man, Jay Thornbird, to place a protective curse on the park to seal the bargain. The remainder of the Trust left the rest of his estate to his wife, son, and daughter.

"But," Said Ebenezer Thornbird, "I read in the genealogy that his wife and daughter perished in the Spanish flu pandemic of 1918, and his son died in a freak accident when he was sodomized from behind on the horns of an infatuated bull."

"Yes," Ms. Oddmeyer continued, "the odd thing was that no one ever understood why, just prior to the curse, Zane had the body of a mysterious relative brought from his original Texas home to be buried in the woods. I saw the Railroad receipt, but it didn't list the contents of the box. No one was ever allowed to see the corpse and, wrapped in a Native American blanket presumably to keep the body erect, it was interred in a hole in a standing position. I've always wondered if it was the poor creature who was captive in that out building I visited at the Zane home in Texas. The only people present were the ranch hand who dug the grave and the native Medicine Man, Jay Thornbird, who placed an amulet he had imbued with mystical powers, in the blanket before it was interred in the tubular grave. Both men are long dead now. The grave was rather shallow since they struck a little water at the bottom. They filled it in, and a ring of stones was placed around the grave to mark it. The rumor was that the reason for keeping the forested area preserved was, at least in part, because Apollyon Zane had buried something there, possibly a treasure, instead of a body, and he had the place cursed because he didn't want it found. He certainly did not set the property aside, they reckoned, out of the goodness of his heart, since he was no Theodore Roosevelt progressive conservationist."

"If he demanded that the area remained wild, how did it end up developed into tract houses?" Ebenezer Thornbird puzzled.

"Apollyon Zane's Will and Trust was conveniently forgotten, or so they said, for the next half-century until it was rediscovered too late, after the town of Zanesville expanded into the only place the town had jurisdiction. The forested area that was officially within the purview of the town and under its protection."

"What happened to the ranch?" Molly asked.

"When he died, Apollyon Zane's distant relatives sold the ranch to a granary, and the shops were sold to some St. Louis entrepreneurs. The forest was left untouched at first, but eventually sold to land speculators and converted to subdivisions of tract houses."

"Let's see if there's any of that family left." Eb was eager to investigate further, if possible.

Molly was silently turning red in the background.

"The Zane family had practically died out with the demise of the ancient patriarch Edward Zane." Eb turned the page looking further into the genealogy, stopped, stared at the book, and abruptly looked up. "The only remaining branch, according to the genealogy, is that of the Everharts. Molly, that's your family!"

"Yeah. My mother's maiden name was Joan Marie Zane before she married my father, Dennis Everhart." She looked embarrassed.

Ebenezer Thornbird looked back at the genealogy. "Molly, didn't you say your nanny's name was Artemis?"

"Yes." She was wide-eyed now.

"It looks like, from what I'm reading here, that she was a descendant of the native Medicine Man Jay Thornbird!"

"Well, I'll be....." Molly's voice trailed off into the fog of time and disappeared at the end of her tongue and, after a few moments of thought, she said, "She never told me her last name. What a coincidence!"

CHAPTER TWELVE
HELL WORLD

In his walkabout through town, fully aware of the sheriff's vehicle standing poorly hidden behind a nearby building, Eb encountered an elderly gentleman who introduced himself as Reese Brown. He was sitting on a bench in front of a small drygoods store, the hair he had left was snow white, and he no longer cared what people thought about his disheveled grooming habits. Clearly, a man who had fallen on hard times. His teeth, those that remained, were so yellow that they looked brown matching his surname. He was receptive to Eb's questions though and supplied additional history. Eb asked him, "Have you lived here in Perfection very long?"

"Yes, Sir! Most my life son, but it was Zanesville when I was born. I used to be a history teacher in the high school here, but that was a very long time ago. I taught part-time at the college in Orson too, for a few years, but now I get along dependent on God, a minuscule pension, and the good graces of the townsfolk, most of whom were my students at one time. Mr. Brown did not mention that he was now a recovering alcoholic who poured booze on his life savings, squandering it after his wife died while living in Orson Wells. Sober now, he moved back to Perfection.

"Can you tell me what you remember about the town's history? I'm especially interested in that tract of land west of here."

His eyes narrowed a bit as he peered into the distant past trying to focus on his remote memories; "Well Sir, just at the Western outskirts of Zanesville," he said, "a subdivided tract of land two miles wide and three deep, the size of some small towns by itself, was destroyed."

"Yes. I heard that it had been destroyed. It was completely devastated?"

"Yeah. That's right." The old man took a moment, tipped his head back as if searching the sky for permission to continue, and offered a slight Mona Lisa smile. "First, land speculators cut down all the trees, tore out the vegetation and built tract houses," he said, chuckling under his breath. "They were not just cheap in the sense of monetary worth, but also in the sense that they were poorly constructed. After the homes were built, they planted trees and vegetation."

Ebenezer Thornbird laughed. "You mean they cut down all the trees and then planted trees?"

"Yep! The owner, his name was Jack Ketch, ordered a giant rock to be placed at the entrance to the tract. It was supposed to be a landmark and a symbol of solidity and permanence, or so he said in an interview for the local paper. What a laugh and a half! Actually, there was a rumor that the boulder had been used by a Native American Medicine Man in various ancient rituals." He looked down the road to his left, then to the right before he said, "They don't use it anymore."

"Why not. If it was sacred, what would have changed that?"

"Because they believe it was cursed!"

Reese Brown went on about how just three years later, there was a biblical infestation. A certain virulent type of termites, sometimes called green ants, were somehow brought here from Australia, that presumably hitched a ride as stowaways on some wooden furniture. The Termites struck the tract so viciously, that, along with native carpenter ants, no one could exterminate them no matter what was tried, and the homes had to be abandoned. "The speculators had named it Westland," he said, "because it was actually the western half of the town, but it soon earned the title 'Wasteland.'"

"Wasteland?" Ebenezer Thornbird perked up and leaned toward the only guy who could tell him what he had been seeking.

"Yeah, some homeless people had squatted there who, trying to keep warm, accidentally burned down some of the empty houses, and some of the adjacent homes caught fire, as well." He continued to speculate that several of the houses were burned on purpose by vandals, and arsonists burned some of them for those who had insurance. "At least that was the rumor."

He painted a picture of a time when it was as if fate had cast a grudge. "Tornados came through and ripped up most of the remaining structures while the rest fell down from disrepair and succumbed to the pestilence of ants, termites, and misfortune."

According to the old man, it only took twenty years of the cursed attacks for that half of the city to convert to desert dust and wind. "The few trees and foliage that were left," he said, "were dead or dying from the lack of water that had been promised. A diversion of water had been slated for delivery from a lake one hundred miles to the North, "But that never materialized," he continued, "due to political wrangling in the state legislature and then it got hopelessly lost in entanglements amidst the quicksand of confused bureaucratic senescence." The few wells connected to natural springs," he went on to explain, "couldn't serve the overpopulated subdivisions alone and dried up in protest from the unfair demand for over work. The founding company threw up its hands, gave up the ghost, filed for bankruptcy and, as though the curse was incomplete, the owner soon died an untimely death. It was officially called a suicide, but no one knew for certain."

"You mean," Eb asked, "it wasn't a suicide?"

"Mr. Ketch was not at all poor, and he had other successful companies in trust and other vast financial holdings, so the reason for his apparent suicide was a mystery. Following his death, his wife and children disappeared, and people gossiped and debated their fantasies about what had happened. One man said he saw them hurrying out of town looking terrified as if they were being chased by a demon. This was not the only loss he had survived in his life either. He had weathered worse financial storms and disasters without scuttling the good ship entrepreneur. He was mysteriously found hanging in his garage amid much debris strewn about."

"Why were they certain that it was a suicide if there were so many things strewn all over?"

"The authorities concluded that he had been overcome by a fit of rage and despair, threw objects around in the garage, left the car running, the key in the ignition, the driver's door open, and summarily hanged himself. These facts made it appear as though he had been dragged out of the car by brute force, but were never adequately explained."

"That's weird! They just ignored these facts?" Ebenezer Thornbird frowned and shook his head.

"Besides his lynching, the authorities decided that he was trying to asphyxiate himself to ensure that even his ghost could not survive. There was a never proved rumor, however, that a vigilante group of angry homeowners had perpetrated the deed. There was some speculation that the authorities covered it up because some of them had homes in Westland."

"What do *you* think happened?"

"I don't know. I suspect the homeowners had something to do with it, but there is no way of knowing for sure," but then," he smiled, "there is that pesky demon!"

"You mean the legend that there is a malevolent force lurking out there?"

Yeah. It's probably just a silly rumor."

Ebenezer snickered, "What happened to the ownership of the land?"

"The property was thrust back into the unsuspecting city's public domain when taxes were left unpaid, and there was no way to collect them, but no one knew what to do with it. Obviously, it was not conducive to building another subdivision, and there was not enough water to sustain industry or farming, even a co-op urban farm was out of the question for the same reason, even desert animals refused to live in that sterile environment, and people began to avoid it."

Ebenezer Thornbird had already discovered that no one could remember who named it *Hell*, but the moniker gradually caught on. "Someone," Mr. Brown speculated, "it must have been adolescent wags, painted *Hell World* on the giant rock at the entrance to the barely recognizable road still leading into to wasteland as though it was an amusement park."

"The culprit graffiti sign painter was never revealed even though the Sheriff at the time, in his draconian approach to the problem, interrogated everyone over the age of eight and searched over fifty percent of the homes. After a generation or two, the moniker of *Hell World* stuck and, of course, the land was perpetually for sale, but no one bought even a grain of sand."

"Wow! What a weird story."

After a moment of reflection, Reece Brown said, "Many years later, on his deathbed, Elmer Edgerton, one of the workers who had operated a large earth mover during the construction of the tract houses, confessed that they had inadvertently unearthed some buried bones wrapped in a blanket. He said they were secretly reinterred somewhere else in the tract away from the housing, but he didn't know where. There was a rumor," he said, "that they had difficulty burying the rug and the bones because they seemed to push up out of the ground whenever it rained." Reese Brown thought for a minute, traveling through time into the past against the known laws of physics and said, "The only other remarkable thing Elmer remembered was that the *Hell World* rock had been moved out of the middle of the tract and left at the entrance where it would be out of the way of the construction."

"Thank you, Mr. Brown. You've been very helpful."

"Glad to meet you Eb. I'm glad to help. I hope your writing goes well. Good luck."

"Thanks again." Ebenezer Thornbird slowly walked away trying to fill in the gaps of information he had already accumulated.

CHAPTER THIRTEEN
PREPARATION

Molly Everhart had returned to work at the *Wake-Up! Coffee Shop* the next day while Ebenezer Thornbird continued to peruse the important pages of documents he had copied in the library, the notes he took there, and the information he gleaned from Reese Brown. At exactly three o'clock, Molly's quitting time, Eb stumbled into the coffee shop preceded by his blazing red eyes that were still difficult to focus after hours of reading. While he and Molly drove to her parents' home so she could change clothes, Eb told her that there were certain items he would need her help to purchase, and he summarized his encounter with Reese Brown; how it meshed with what he had learned at the library, what she and other townsfolk had related, and reiterated his plan to check out *Hell World* before he went in there. "Can you help me to purchase the items I need?"

"Of course, but how can you explore *Hell World* before you go in there?"

He just said, "You'll see" and left her floating in the soup of anticipation and wonderment, deepening her taste for a great adventure with this enigmatic man.

She introduced him to her parents who were cordial, but obviously not pleased that Molly was spending so much time with this itinerant stranger. "This is my dad, Dennis Everhart. Dad, this is my friend Ebenezer Thornbird. Eb, this is my mother, Joan Everhart."

"Good to meet you, Mrs. Everhart," and, reaching his hand toward Denis Everhart, he said, "Mr. Everhart." But he was met with hesitation before Molly's father offered his own hand as though he wasn't used to this ritual. When he finally shook hands with her father, Eb felt that same odd feeling of emptiness, of something missing, flowing into his hand that he had noted from everyone else in town. Mr. Everhart didn't look him in the eye, Joan Everhart simply nodded and looked away as if she had forgotten something important and desperately had to go find it. They appeared distracted as if called to a distant undefined task.

Finder whispered, *she seems afraid you'll try to shake her hand, or worse, hug her. She's terrified of us, and he is simply befuddled.*

Molly's father suddenly looked up at Ebenezer Thornbird for what seemed like a very long time without the blink of even one eye, as if he wasn't actually seeing him but looking at something in his own mind instead. Finally, as if he could think of nothing else to say, he offered, "Have a seat." Assuming Mr. Everhart meant for him to sit on the couch, he headed for the sofa.

Mr. Everhart was a clean-shaven, five feet ten inches tall, sporting wire-rimmed spectacles. He was a thin man wearing a beige dress shirt barely visible under his V-neck argyle sweater that revealed his brown bow tie peeking out timidly at the outside world. He wore ordinary tan chino slacks, matching argyle socks, and brown wingtip shoes. His receding brown hairline was closely cropped, so his ears stood at attention at a thirty-degree angle from his head which made him appear elf-like.

Molly's mother was a thin rather stiff-postured woman wearing an apron over her way-out-of-style dress with a tiny flowered print that looked as if there were hundreds of tiny insects randomly crawling all over it when she moved. Her hair was pulled into a neat brownish bun that sat atop her head like someone who peeked through from a previous century. Her face was full of frown lines of bitterness partially camouflaged by her thick horn-rimmed glasses. She quietly entered the room and sat stiffly with hands in her lap, on a straight-backed chair off in the corner of Ebenezer Thornbird's eye as if she was a ghost who desperately wished to be invisible.

Mr. Everhart sat in his easy chair across from Eb, facing him in an awkwardly silent stare down until Dennis Everhart looked away and Eb broke the impasse. "Have you lived here long?"

He looked at Eb over the badly smudged glasses that had surreptitiously slipped down to the end of his nose. "Just all my life. That's all," he said as he pushed his spectacles up only to have them drop to exactly the same spot where they began. Despite the words, his response didn't seem angry or sarcastic, just emotionless and matter-of-fact. *Something is missing in his zombie-like responses.* Finder whispered, *it's as if he's missing a soul for lack of a better term.* Eb nodded subtly. *Not in the religious sense, but more like lacking a depth of connection between himself and others around him. There's no flexibility there at all.*

Eb said, "You're fortunate to have such an intelligent and compassionate daughter."

He stared at Eb as if he was trying to comprehend this and how to formulate the right thing to say. He definitely wasn't spontaneous. "Yes. I suppose so," and, as if he remembered something he learned in a book or at a seminar, he added, "thank you," which seemed to be a novel idea, displaying a subtle underlying reluctance, and his demeanor seemed to belie an emotionless, but almost disgusted tone. It was as if he didn't recognize those traits in his own daughter.

Mrs. Everhart wrinkled her face in a slight wince as if she was trying to cover up the fact that she had just swallowed something nasty, but was too polite to vomit it up in front of the host who served it to her. She simply gulped it down and endured the taste of discomfort. She nodded a polite, but insincere acknowledgment, and said, "I suppose so." She started to arise nervously from her perch, obviously restraining the urge to run.

Turning to Joan Everhart before she could get two steps toward her kitchen sanctuary, Ebenezer Thornbird said, "You have a lovely home here, Mrs. Everhart." She stopped in her tracks as if she had been caught with her hand in the cookie jar, turned her head toward him over her shoulder, offered the obligatory smile, a slight nod, and finally turned to face him for an anxious fraction trying to project an air of politeness. Her nervous fiddling with her hands, smoothing her dress and apron and touching her hair increased until, without excusing herself, she slowly made a stiff-legged retreat and disappeared into her safe-haven. Her hasty withdrawal was preceded by an almost whispered "Thank you" that seemed to fight its way past the constriction in her throat. Ebenezer Thornbird was beginning to realize that he was on enemy turf and his mere presence was a painful disturbance in the Force. In fact, when Molly's parents did occasionally look at him, he felt the sting of daggers flying in his direction.

"Is she alright?" Ebenezer Thornbird inquired with some concern.

"She's okay. Just not feeling well. She has to attend to dinner." The sound of pots and pans were soon heard clanging too loudly in the kitchen.

Finder said, *that anger is covering the anxiety of not knowing what to do when her routines are disrupted.*

"Dinner sounds like it is taking an intense effort," Ebenezer Thornbird probed.

"I guess," said Dennis Everhart.

The noises were accompanied by loud running water, and high decibel pounding and frustrated chopping noises reminiscent of the Queen of Hearts yelling, "Off with his head!" as if his metaphoric neck was under her chopping blade trying to rid herself of the intrusion.

Ebenezer Thornbird and Dennis Everhart sat in the living room mostly starring at each other while Molly changed her clothes, freshened up, and discarded the debris of the incalculably boring day at the *Wake-Up! Coffee Shop.*

"Nice neat little town you have here," Eb tried.

"Yep."

"I've been trying to do research for my articles and journal about this wonderful town, but I'm having difficulty finding out why its name was changed to Perfection. Do you have any insight into it? Do you have any idea why it changed from Zanesville to Perfection?

"Nope."

There was a complete absence of curiosity; not even a spark of interest was hiding in his responses. He was totally uninterested in small talk; maybe of talking at all. "What line of work are you in?"

"Accounting."

At least he has a vocabulary that includes polysyllabic words! "What drew you to that profession?"

"I was good at math," he reverted to monosyllabic speech.

"So, you find math interesting or exciting?"

Dennis Everhart sat, wallowed in the silence for a full minute, so still that his unwelcome guest wondered if he had fallen asleep with his eyes open or, God forbid, if he was dead. At long last, he emerged from wherever he had retreated and said, "No. I don't think so. I'm just good at it." It seemed to both Eb and Finder that this had been so difficult to answer because he failed in his search for some internal visceral reference to the words "interesting" and "exciting." Both words had more than a single syllable, and it was as if he had to refer to an internal dictionary for the definition of words without even a hint of emotional reference.

To be fair, there were some initial ritual questions from Molly's dad like, "How do you do?"

Eb said. "I'm good. Pleased to meet y…."

When Eb tried to answer, he was interrupted with, "What do you do for a living?"

Ebenezer Thornbird could only get out, "I'm a travel write…" before Mr. Everhart asked the next question as though the goal was to dance as fast as possible to get the waltz over with before the music ended. He clearly was uninterested in the answers.

"Where are you from?"

"I'm from Massachus…."

"What are your plans?"

"I'm going to publish a book about my travel...."

It appeared to him that Denis Everhart was simply trying to get through his tiny repertoire, a memorized script of rehearsed responses kept in reserve in case something distasteful like this should ever intrude on his life.

Dennis Everhart's responses were mostly confined to, "Yes," "no," "I don't know," "good" or "oh?" After a fifteen-minute attempt, Ebenezer Thornbird surrendered and tried not to return Mr. Everhart's very odd stares. He wondered if Molly's parents even remembered her name or that of each other, for that matter. *Too many syllables!* Finder joked, and Eb tried not to smile.

Joan Everhart tiptoed back into the room, a shadowy shade from Hades, a ghostly presence, a shell of a self, barely noticed, reemerging from the kitchen and reclaimed her stiff, nervous perch in the corner. They sat there in a statuesque, distant and unemotional tableau for an eternity.

Eb said, "Mrs. Everhart, I see a picture there on the mantle. Is that your family?"

She said, "It's my mother and father and me."

"Lovely looking family," he said, noticing his extreme discomfort causing him to wipe away the perspiration forming on his face.

She looked stricken as if she was forced to have an unsavory conversation that she desperately wished to avoid. "Thank... you," was all she said as if it left a bad taste in her mouth.

He looked away, mostly trying to distance himself, trying to avoid being sucked into their black hole-like emptiness, but he did occasionally stare at them to reassure himself that they were still breathing. Feeling the tendrils of their eyes coming at him full force, a relentless and emotionless Medusa trying to paralyze him, dragging him toward their world, strangling every interaction as if something was gripping his throat, and causing his discomfort to reach an unbearable pitch. There was nowhere to run and nowhere to hide from the scrutiny that was gripping his soul and draining his heart. He was older than Molly, but they were more worried that he was a stranger, a drifter who was likely to distort their already misguided offspring, not to mention their ritualized, orderly life. He and Finder sensed that his mere presence disturbed their tightly constructed and managed matrix. Eventually, Joan Everhart, having nothing to say, arose and floated silently toward the kitchen once more where she could be heard banging and clanging pots, pans, and dishes again, apparently the only way she could express her irritation toward an invader such as Ebenezer Thornbird. Dennis Everhart remained in the living room, eventually elevating the newspaper in front of his face, thereby blocking himself from view in the ensuing cold war, the snub providing a temporary relief from their staring contest.

Several strong competing odors began to emanate from the kitchen which Ebenezer Thornbird could not identify. Finder wondered, *is it eye of newt and wart of toad!?*

There was an occasional emotionless utterance emanating from behind the journalistic iron curtain such as, "I see the High School won another bowling competition over the Orson team." He seemed to be informing Mrs. Everhart because he raised his voice loud enough for her to hear in the kitchen, or, "The price of grain has dropped by two points," but she was making such a racket that it was doubtful she heard anything he said. Eb had flashes of the days of the concrete, if not symbolic, Berlin Wall separating East from West.

In the ensuing silence that hung like a ton of bricks in the room, Ebenezer Thornbird looked around at the very traditional pictures hanging on the walls, apparently placed there merely because of some rule that there "should" be pictures on the walls rather than the desire to beautify the place with thoughtful interior design. They didn't seem to match the rest of the color scheme. There was little rhyme or reason to the décor, and the couch had a large flowery print that clashed with the color and design of the Oriental rug on the floor. Mr. Everhart's chair was old and threadbare with a totally different busy design that matched nothing else in the room. Mrs. Everhart's chair was a straight-backed thing that was a refugee from some other unidentifiable century unlike anything else in the room, possibly a fugitive from some medieval torture chamber. The walls were painted a neutral beige, and the curtains were an odd shade of gray pulled tight against the onslaught of the outside world.

To Eb's great relief, Molly came to the rescue an interminable twenty-five minutes later, a striking vision with her perfect makeup, Denham jacket, and pants with a light blue T-shirt, matching blue tennis shoes and socks. Her hair was let down, beautifully coiffed, and there were sensible silver earrings that dangled next to her long slender neck accented by the elegant thin silver chain with a dangling heart pendant.

Eb smiled in reaction to her radiance and for the thankful relief of being rescued.

She said, "Did you guys have a good talk?"

"Why yes dear. Very enlightening." Her mother lied.

Her father offered an unconvincing, barely audible, inanimate, and monotone, "Of course."

"I'm so glad you all got along." Molly forced a smile, offered a subtle shrug aimed at Eb, and a brief "hum," belying the fact that she was not fooled. She flopped down next to Eb on the unforgiving couch causing it to bounce him a little. "What did you talk about?"

"Oh. You know dear. Just the usual stuff. The ordinary... you know," her mother managed.

"You know, work and what we do...You know," said Dennis Everhart, snapping his iron curtain newspaper without lowering it to look at them.

The temperature of Eb's anxiety reached two hundred when he thought they might be stuck with her parents for a while longer. His very red face looked at her with wide-eyed non-verbal pleading.

Molly got the hint and said, "Mom, Dad, we'd better get going. We have things to do while the stores are still open."

They said goodbye to her parents, "Goodbye Mr. and Mrs. Everhart. It was nice meeting you."

"Yep," said Mr. Dennis Everhart.

"Of course," Mrs. Joan Everhart followed her husband's lead with a deadpan smile that didn't rise to the level of her eyes.

They shook hands as briefly as possible, acceptable to all parties, and Eb tried not to run out the door. Finder was screaming, *don't run. Just walk to the nearest escape hatch, hold your nose and jump!* Eb thought ... *or die trying!*

Molly didn't hug or kiss them even though it seemed as if she wanted to, but somehow displays of affection were *verboten*! She drove Eb in her worried noisy van to the local stores and one in the nearby town. They were more than happy to take his money in a whirlwind of purchasing the necessary items for a quest Molly had not yet fully grasped. Eb was as focused on the tasks as Ahab on the trail of his white whale. Molly was afloat in a surreal world that she had never encountered, treading water in an ocean of excitement mixed with confusion, trying to keep her head just above the surface.

Ebenezer Thornbird had a cell phone, but there was no reception. There were no towers near enough to Perfection, besides phones are too difficult to conceal and cell phones drop calls. So, he bought a small audio and video transceiver that could record anything picked up by the tiny tethered microphone and an infrared camera he could wear in secret.

"These," the salesman said in his enthusiastic anticipation of the sale, "are guaranteed to transmit over a five-mile radius!"

Molly feigned understanding but had no clue what he was talking about when he began spewing tech-talk minutia about specs and the like. In fact, her interest in these gadgets was waning, and she began to wander around the store mindlessly examining other items she had no real interest in.

Eb obtained a small drone with an infrared camera aboard. It was controllable from up to four miles at an altitude of a half mile and could be monitored like a ghost for a three-mile radius at that altitude. The salesman said, "It's practically silent."

Molly was wide-eyed, "What is that for?"

"I'll show you later," he reassured her. She stood by, more puzzled than ever, reckoning that it had to do with *Hell World*, but she wasn't sure what. He bought a small flashlight and binoculars and, at the drug store, a pack of paper face protectors that people wear over their nose and mouth to filter out germs and particles in the air, a gallon bottle of pure natural spring water, and a small spray bottle of cheap cologne. At the checkout counter, he bought two candy bars.

Upon leaving the store, Molly said, "I don't understand everything you're doing, but I really don't understand what the candy is for."

"One's for you, and the other is for me."

"Very thoughtful, Sir," she beamed an eye-wrinkling smile, dipped her head slightly to her right looking up into his eyes with a slight skip in her step. She wasn't used to people being thoughtful in such a genuine way and her heart responded as if it were trying to break out of her chest to reach him. She was like a giddy little girl again free for the first time without the blockage of parental and societal inhibitions she had endured all her life. *I can't let this one get away!*

It was an unseasonably balmy day for that time of year. They drove out of town with their purchases for their clandestine meeting in a remote field East of town where they could test all the equipment in secret. Molly said, "I haven't been out here since I was a kid when I used to come here and read my books lying in the grass and watching the clouds."

****

Molly traveled back to the times when she imagined that she could reach up with her finger and paint faces and patterns in the clouds, pretending they wouldn't have developed like that by themselves without her assistance. *Or would they?* She saw the shapes of faces, animals, and demons. Sometimes she imagined herself ascending to the sky in an attempt to escape from the tether, the heavy weight of rules and demands that, like a straightjacket restricted her soul. As a girl, she imagined herself in one of those myths her nanny, Artemis, told her about in which people were rescued by one of the gods, ascending to their realm, and sometimes transformed into gods themselves.

****

Eb plugged the chargers into the multi-receptacle adaptor he had purchased, inserted it into the van's power outlet, all those wires making it resemble an octopus. Waiting for the full charge to develop, they unpacked the purchased items, assembled the apparatus, rewarded their work with the candy bars and, while sitting on the blanket Molly kept in the van, Eb explained their roles in this endeavor. He said, "If it's okay with you, I'd like you to be the covert ops engineer, monitoring what I do and everything that happens, while I follow my fated quest of search and rescue."

"Search and rescue?" she asked.

"Yes. There's something out there longing to be returned to its rightful place, but my Finder sense detects a powerful force preventing its escape and return. I'm going to find it and liberate it. I need you to monitor and record the entire quest."

"Okay. I'm game. What can I do?"

A small bird landed atop the van unnoticed, hopped back and forth, bobbing its head in a curious examination of the scene, its feathers ruffled in the light breeze blowing in from the West. There was the fragrance of flowers even though it was too early for any blooms. Eb thought, *could there be some flowers beginning to bloom in this unseasonable weather*?

Molly was such an eager and quick learner that she seemed to encompass everything that he thrust at her, absorbed it deep into her being, open and happy to receive whatever he gave her as if her body was learning it before her mind could process it. Besides, she was with Eb, and there was the fact that nothing interesting or exciting ever happened in Perfection in all of her twenty-five years. She had the pent-up energy of an adventurer ready to burst forth into the exciting unknown, taking in all that was presented to her and was excited to give everything she had to Eb and his quest. The warm breeze of anticipation filled her sails, and she drifted off into her ecstatic reverie filled with the possibilities that her relationship with Ebenezer Thornbird offered.

"I'm trying to be prepared for anything out there," he explained. "I've got face masks in case I encounter smoke or fumes, cologne for covering the smoke and any foul odor I might encounter, a flashlight to illuminate the night, and the water if I need it to drink out there in that arid land. Of course, the recording equipment goes without saying."

"Okay, but what about the drone?"

"That's how I'll make a surveillance of *Hell World* before I go in there. I'd like to know as much of that place as I can before I put my life on the line."

"Put your life on the line? "She felt her anxiety reach geometric proportions as her body shuddered, her head swirled a little, and her knees became rubberized.

"Yes. Like I said, I detect something very powerful and dangerous out there. Probably the same thing you feared that kept you away."

Eb showed her how to use the receivers and recording equipment and explained her role in the plan. It was as if her brain was an absorbent sponge soaking up his instructions exactly in one swoop. It was single trial learning at its height, as well as a fairytale fantasy land that captured her full attention more than her novels ever had. Like her novels, however, it inflamed her passions and desires that burned deep in her soul.

When all the equipment was fully charged, Eb tested the drone and practiced using it to be sure he could reliably control its flight and taught Molly how to assist in the reception and recording of images from the drone's camera. He showed her how to use the transceiver to monitor the audio and video feed he planned to wear on his clothes and how to record it. She practiced monitoring and recording while he practiced flying the drone until he knew he had the hang of it, and Molly continued to catch on as though she had experienced it all before. She was an empty vessel being filled with the ecstasy of her new relationship and the promise of liberation it engendered. Molly was delighted to help, and Eb was a good teacher. "I have to find what's lost out there, whatever it is." He explained, "It's what the town's folk lost on the cusp of adolescence, and I have to be ready in case someone or something out there tries to thwart my effort with fumes, smoke, or something worse." If there was a bond fire out in *Hell World*, he wanted to be prepared. No one would have been concerned about a fire because there was no longer anything left to burn down and no one cared if a homeless person or some kids had a fire going anyway. Besides, there was no water to extinguish it. He didn't really believe what some of the adolescents, intent on scaring the younger kids, used to say about there being a demon and witches out there tending the fires of Hell, but he'd be ready for anything.

Molly was uncertain about Eb's plans, but she was ready to do anything she thought would help and keep him safe.

After Eb carefully emptied the contents of his pack, he methodically placed the newly purchased items of need into it for their readiness, put everything back in the van, and drove to the motel. After Molly dropped him off, she floated home on her rusting metal mounted on a clattering cloud of nuts and bolts, unaware of the bumpy ride. Passing the Sheriff's flashing squad car as it flew by in the opposite direction, going nowhere pretending to investigate no crime at all, looking important like he was actually enforcing the law against imaginary crimes, and speeding by so fast that her wave was left hanging in midair unnoticed.

Finder In Hell World

CHAPTER FOURTEEN
PEERING INTO HELL WORLD

Standing on the boundary between *Hell World* and the rest of the town, the next afternoon on another surprisingly balmy day for that time of the year, Ebenezer Thornbird peered into that wretched empty space. Molly Everhart was dozing in her van after working until two, and after an ecstatic, insomniac night thinking about the insoluble bond she felt with him. Neither of them had slept much. Molly for worrying and fantasizing, and Eb planning his quest.

There was nothing to see, but Finder felt the cry for rescue more strongly than ever, but Eb didn't cross the boundary into *Hell World* yet. Instead, he stood for an hour at the intersection of the bypass and the overgrown barely recognizable road to *Hell World* leaning on the rock, trying to decipher the message. But no matter how long or how hard he tried, it was too jumbled and chaotic with too many voices calling out at once. The sun was at a forty-five-degree angle, and he had already reckoned that the best time to enter would be after dark since that's when the kids went there for their supposed ritual rites of maturity. He stood by the side of the road for a long time while the shadow of Bunuel's "Exterminating Angel" flew by as silently as a thought in the shadows, carrying with it the feared trap of death, settled behind the rock, peered out and licked its chops in anticipation. There was a strong breeze blowing that smelled sweet like flowers when he thought he heard something in the bushes behind him, turned, and for an instant he thought he saw the shadow of that vaguely distorted figure he had seen in the West Virginia coal mine disappearing in the shadows. But, he decided his mind was playing tricks on him in cahoots with the wind rustling in the weeds.

Ebenezer Thornbird tossed a stone into *Hell World*, and it seemed to vanish in a kind of very light, almost unrecognizable shimmer; so, he picked up another one, careful to choose a round one, and rolled it, noted where it seemed to disappear and marked the spot with a line of pebbles. He went into a trance-like concentration in search of the stones with fierce, focused intensity until he saw them as well as a lonely old wheel cover. *Is this a psychological phenomenon, an illusion, a mirage, or is there some kind of barrier here?*

He started the drone, gently nudged his co-conspirator and said, "Molly, wake up. I need you to monitor the video feed."

"Aye, Aye, Sir!" She crooned sleepily as first mate on the voyage of a lifetime. *This is fun! So far.*

He turned on the equipment and flew off over the barren wasteland of *Hell World* passing back and forth in a grid pattern covering every inch of it. Molly yelled, "There's no one and nothing there, with the exception of two rings of rocks, one that looks like an extinguished fire, the other a well, and there's a log close by, a fallen dead and rotting tree trunk." From the aerial perspective, she saw the ruined outlines of the foundations, phantoms, left over from ancient leveled houses. The only indication that there had ever been any structures there was the rectangular patterns of discolored soil in the shapes of houses and other structures as though the Earth had swallowed everything in sight. "There are a few dead trees scattered throughout, but nothing else," she hollered to Eb who nodded. "There certainly are no people or animals out in the open." The drone returned to its base as it was programmed to do when the battery had only enough charge left to do so.

Looking at the recording, he said, "I don't see anything out there, do you?"

"No," Molly responded, "All I saw on the monitor was what I told you. The only other thing was what looked like a cover on the well with a rock on top of it and, see there," She pointed to a spot on the screen, "that might be a rope or something, too."

Eb's brow was furrowed when he said, "You told me that the kids go there at night around Halloween, but there have been other times too, like during a full moon and maybe a blue moon?"

Yes, but after all, a blue moon is just the second full moon in a calendar month."

"Maybe there's some stronger power or pull during a blue moon than a regular full moon" Eb tried. "It is an anomaly in a natural cycle. Maybe Halloween has a strong pull too."

Anyway, the kids go there as a rite of passage, she reiterated." She shuttered at the thought and visions of horrors that preadolescents might encounter out there.

"And there's a bonfire too?" he yelled over his shoulder.

"Yes, sometimes. At least that's what people say, and, as you can see, there is an extinguished fire in a pit out there."

"So, we should come back at night when there will be activity out there," he decided as he turned to face the van. "I think there's a full moon tonight."

"Yeah," she said, "I heard the radio announcer say it's a blue moon, so I guess that would be when things are most likely to happen if they're going to happen at all." After hesitating for a tenth of a second, she said, "Are you sure you want to do this?"

Eb's forehead looked like a freshly plowed field. "Of course!" and after a long, thoughtful pause, he said, "Okay. It looks like we need to come back in the evening. Let's get something to eat, but we should get some sleep too so we can be alert tonight. You can drop me off at the motel and pick me up at six, so we can eat dinner before we head out."

Molly couldn't hide the flash of disappointment etched like a neon sign of drastic signals on her face. She said, "Why don't we stay in the motel together rather than running around like that?" She was surprised at her own sudden burst of bold assertiveness.

See. There it is, Finder whispered, *her strength is peeking out, like Oz, from behind her curtain of inhibitions. This woman has the deep untapped strength and magic in her bones.*

"I suppose we can do that if it's okay with you," Eb smiled, showing no resistance at all.

"Oh, it's definitely all right with me," she fluttered. "I'd have you stay at my place, but my parents wouldn't approve of it or any of this whole operation, for that matter. Besides, they think I'm working late."

They drove into the motel lot, stumbled into his room exhausted from too little sleep, fell into the bed atop the covers fully clothed, kicked off their shoes and boots and dozed for an hour. Eb woke up first. Molly felt him stir and sat up. He said, "Do you mind if I touch your back?"

She was delighted and surprised at the same time. *This is getting more interesting by the minute!*

"No. I don't mind. Be my guest!" she said with a little too much enthusiasm. Maybe gusto is a better word as she presented her back for contact.

Why do I feel so comfortable with him?

Sliding his right hand under her top, causing her to feel the deep stirrings of anticipation, he gently palmed the small of her back and moved his hand slowly lower in small decreasing circles until he heard Finder say *there!* He stopped.

Molly felt the rising excitement of a longing that burst forth in her core. "MMMMM, that feels nice," she swooned.

He moved his left hand slowly around under the front of her shirt, placed it on her abdomen and moved it slowly lower to just below her navel.

Molly swooned a little more, *Oh, oh!* She went all rag doll limp to his touch.

He whispered in her beautiful left ear, "Inhale, relax and Just exhale slowly."

A flash flood of excitement headed south, enveloping her mind and body, a warmth emanating from his hands causing her to let go of her tension, and she did as he requested. Just at the end of her very long exhale, his left hand still firm on her abdomen, just below her navel, he made a sudden sharp push with his right like driving a stapler into a ten-page pile of paper. An electrifying arc, a thunderbolt passing between his hands, passed through her accompanied by a low crackling sound emanating from deep in her Soul. Molly let out a yelp.

What the...? she gasped. There was a full body quake, a ripple shot through her that she recognized as an orgasm, but there was an additional very warm wave that went way beyond orgasm, and, rolling onto her back, she looked up at Eb with a puzzled surprise on her face through heavy fluttering eyes. A warmth, replacing her surprise, radiated out from her Hara, the site of the procedure, through her body filling the room, and the known universe. She felt her muscle tone leaking out, and she melted into a pool of flaccid tissue, spilled into a heap on the bed, and drifted off into oblivion. He lay next to her and exactly two minutes later the atomic clock found them both in a mutual, deep, dormative state.

Molly dreamt that she and Eb were standing naked, but there seemed to be two of him facing her, looking into her eyes, Eb and Finder smiling knowingly, beaming proud support. She knew, she didn't know how she knew, but she felt his excitement for her. Still in her dream, they stepped toward each other, their bodies fused together into one, and she felt an instant coupling at the level of her navel.

Ebenezer Thornbird awoke at five o'clock, shook off the remnants of sleep and felt Molly Everhart softly nestled in his left arm, looked down at her, smiled and lightly kissed the top of her head. She stirred with a slight smile in her dream sleep. *She is lovely,* he said to his brain, and the rest of his anatomy agreed. Slipping his numb and deadened arm out from under her neck to regain his circulation, he relieved himself in the bathroom and splashed cold water on his face and neck. He sat in the chair next to the bed and observed her sleeping innocence knowing that she was no longer so innocent. She was even more beautiful in that relaxed, tranquil state of sleep with one ear exposed, her hair drifting down over her forehead and across her cheek. He felt the glow surrounding her body as it spread out and engulfed him as if they were encased like twins conjoined in a womb of energy. He smiled and basked in the warmth of their mutual aura. *I'm grateful for her. I've never encountered anyone like her.* She rolled over in her sleep, and he felt a protective closeness just as he dozed off again.

Drifting into dream sleep, he saw the back of an old, wrinkled, naked, Native American man sitting cross-legged on the dirt floor of a sweat lodge in front of a kind of altar that had a bird, an unidentifiable flower with thorns and the picture of a young woman. He couldn't make out the woman's face, but he had the definite impression that it was Molly Everhart. The man turned his head slightly and said over his shoulder, "You have all you need now to complete your mission with only one last detail. You must give away something precious; something you treasure. After that, your success or failure will depend upon your skills." Eb felt the sensation of falling and falling a long way. It seemed as though the sensation went on forever.

Molly awoke at five-thirty-five in a haze of sleep-heavy lids, looked at the empty space in the bed next to her, felt the nauseating sensation of tiny animals roiling around in her stomach, gripped by the fear that he had left her, reminiscent of the cowboy student several years ago. She turned over and saw with relief that Eb was asleep in the bedside chair. *What was that strange feeling when Eb pushed on my back?* Then she remembered her dream and felt a more profound sense of herself than she had ever known. Somehow, this feeling of connection with Eb and a simultaneous sense of liberation sent grateful tears to her eyes, and she became slowly aware of a mild tingling like a slight electric current in her navel. When she got up and went to the bathroom to freshen up, Eb, shaken from the arms of Morpheus, heard her stirring and felt as if he had finally landed on solid ground. He checked the time and pulled on his boots just as Molly emerged from the bathroom. He noticed a feeling in his navel and smiled when Finder said *contact!*

They silently grabbed their jackets, and as if of a single mind, headed out to the restaurant, their quiet reciprocity remaining all the way through their late afternoon breakfast of over easy eggs and pancakes. Molly couldn't remember the last time she ate so much, let alone breakfast at supper time. She felt as if she was going to burst with her stomach full of food, her expanding freedom, and her deepening intertwined relationship with Ebenezer Thornbird and his Finder. She was amazed that they had invited themselves to sleep in the same bed of longing and Eb made no advances. She didn't even remember that she had nuzzled up to his arm, or in the total amnesia of sleep, that he had kissed her on the head. Ready for whatever happened, but disappointed that it didn't, she wasn't sure what to make of it all. On the other hand, she was aware that there was a deepening bond between them that went beyond the physical. Sleeping in the same bed though, without the sexual intimacy that she had so strongly desired, in fact practically offered him, only to have him do whatever he did to her…. *This is very confusing. Maybe I'm not interesting enough sexually, maybe he's gay, maybe he's not attracted to me, maybe I'm not pretty enough, maybe my pheromones are incompatible with his or maybe he is from some other planet where they have sex that way. I did have an orgasm. Did he say he thought I was beautiful just to appease me?* Frustration got the best of her, *ARRR!* She only knew that, beyond her very strong desires, she was emotionally connected to him and wanted to help him more than ever. The intensity of their connection seemed stronger than the most intense sexual experience she could imagine. Oddly though, she also felt a new sense of herself as a strong woman suddenly freed from her bondage.

Eb sensed her puzzlement and spoke first. "Molly. You know I feel very close to you, and we both know that we are very strongly attracted to each other. Under other circumstances, I'd pursue more, but I must wait until the danger is over. I can't let you get so involved that you might be in danger too."

She was stunned that he knew the stirrings in her heart, her longing, and even more impressed that he was being so gentle about letting her know the possibility the future could bring. *At least he's not from outer space!* She would never again, she realized, sink into self-doubts and self-loathing, but she had been left on the frustrated precipice of unsatisfied desire. She said, "Thank you Eb. You're a kind and perceptive man." *Maybe a little too perceptive for comfort, though,* she thought, but *I've let others dictate what I think and feel and especially what I do for too long. It is time for me to make my own decisions.* She was feeling her new sense of self so clearly now that it surprised her. *I know there are risks, but I've never felt so free before, at the same time so connected to anyone, and I want to experience this for as long as I can, even if it has to end sometime. So...* "Ebenezer Thornbird, don't you try to make decisions for me," she said, hearing more gusto in her voice than she intended. "I'll make my own mistakes thank you very much!" She was shocked to hear her sudden attack of assertiveness and the comfort she felt with it. "I'll be involved as much as I like, Sir!"

Ebenezer? Sir? She means business! "Okaaay," he said in surprised wide-eyed agreement holding his hands up and leaning back slightly in a posture of surrender to the metaphorical swing she took at him. They sat in a vacuum of stunned silence staring at each other until they simultaneously burst into raucous laughter, a laughter that set them free of misfortune and trepidation. Finder whispered, *bingo! Now she's free.* After they calmed down, Eb said, "Did you ever hear of Aristophanes's fable in Plato's *Symposium* where humans used to be attached to each other with two heads, four arms and four legs into single cartwheeling beings?"

"No," she said. She was looking at him with interest accompanied by a surprised but skeptical expression. "Do tell."

"These beings decided to storm Mt. Olympus, the dwelling of the gods, and Zeus got pissed off to the point that he sent thunderbolts to split them in half. They were condemned to spend their lives searching for their other half." He waited for exactly the count of one thousand and five for her to catch up while he left the money on the table for the tip. They were standing now. He paid the bill at the register, and they left the restaurant. "Molly, I felt you calling."

She stopped and stood there stricken and silent for a century that lasted at least thirty seconds while two tears of the relief, recognition and overwhelming love leaked out in the form of a single drop from her left eye. Once Molly had recovered from her blissful paralysis, she hugged Eb too tightly restricting his breathing. She felt the full measure of her nascent strength along with the excitement of finally surpassing her life-long wish for such a relationship. Suddenly, she stopped and turned toward Eb, "What the hell did you do to me back at the motel?" she demanded. Her voice sounded pleased and filled with curiosity, but Eb detected nothing off-putting in her tone.

"It was the Finder in me that did it. There was something in you that needed to be found and liberated. It simply needed to be done."

"What are you talking about? What had to be done?"

"My finder sense, so to speak, felt the need of something inside you crying out to be found and set free. I felt around on your back until Finder found its location. I pushed to crack it open, and I felt you open up, in a manner of speaking. It really wasn't against your' will, though."

"That's true. I did tell you it was okay, but the push you gave me!"

"Yeah. I didn't think it would hurt you, Finder detected the part of you that needed to be returned to you, and it needed to happen that way so you could be freed up to feel your completeness; to achieve your true potential. I didn't add anything. The maneuver simply retrieved what you had lost."

"Well, I sure do feel different; more full... sort of." *Or is it those pancakes?*

"That's great!" he said with a sincere sense of total support.

There was a five-minute silence while Molly mentally searched herself and allowed the new "her" to integrate further before she asked, "What now?" *I do feel a new sense of fullness. A kind of freedom to be completely me that I've never known before and, at the same time, I have a profound connection to him. It's like we're glowing, two complete entities, but voluntarily attached together somehow. This is very strange!* They were on the same wavelength, so to speak, and there was no one else dwelling at that frequency. There seemed to be a seamless flow of understanding passing between them. Molly knew what Eb was experiencing, and he seemed to know her more completely than anyone ever had.

After a silent but mutual shift of gears, Eb asked Molly more about the history of *Hell World*. "I know you told me about *Hell World*, but can you tell me any more about it?"

"As I said," Molly reiterated, still with a loving but slightly shaky voice of leftover shock, "The kids seemed to be in a daze when they returned from their *Hell World* rite of passage, but I thought it was because they were exhausted. Now I'm more certain than ever that they were transformed afterward in some way. Not one of them could tell me or anyone else what happened except that they just fell asleep, woke up before they came back, felt funny, and they were sort of blank for a few days afterward. That really scared me. Later, they talked about nightmares of demons, etc., but I thought that it was just to scare the younger kids who hadn't gone yet. Now I don't know." She paused in suspended animation while four seconds slipped by looking like a deer in the proverbial headlights before she said, "Actually, if I remember it correctly, they were talking to each other in front of me, and I think they assumed I had gone through the rite of *Hell World*. Maybe they really did have shared nightmares because they all sounded very similar." She recognized now that she had acquired an enhanced and deeper intuitive understanding of things around her and in her past as though someone opened a window and a fresh spring breeze had cleansed the air. It wasn't that Eb had added anything. He simply breached the dam that held her back. A resurrection of sorts.

"Why did virtually everyone go there?" Eb asked.

"The seventh graders and a few of the older sixth graders went there, as I already told you, for a kind of primitive ritual," she seemed mildly irritated to repeat the story. "The idea was that, if they survived there all night in that dead primeval hell of a place with the alleged demons, they would enter adulthood. You know, "pass Go and collect adulthood." I guess they did, sort of. I mean they soon became cyborg clones of their parents anyway."

In college psychology classes, Molly began to see it as a kind of mass hysteria that they all bought due to the belief in demons and the expectation that they would enter adulthood after they passed the test. "The older kids," she said, "who had already gone, made up all kinds of stories about demons, apparently gleaned from their own nightmares, that supposedly lived out there to scare the younger ones trying to get them to chicken out, but none of them did except me, as far as I know." She imagined that the mass hypnosis, or whatever it was, along with every generation going through it, made it more believable as a rite of passage. "My professor said, 'If you repeat something often enough, people tend to believe it and start living their lives as if it were true. Just look at politics for example. Lies become accepted truths!" After a moment of reflection, Molly said, "I wonder if there was an intoxicating natural gas out there like that which some archaeologists, according to another professor, think was extant at the Oracle of Delphi, causing hallucinations, or at least, bad dreams?"

"You may be right about that, but, why did virtually everyone go? Eb asked. You'd think that maybe the majority would, but everyone? You know, like Lincoln said, 'You can fool all the people some of the time and some of the people all of the time, but you can't fool all the people all the time.'"

Eb thought, *many cultures around the world have ritual transitions into adulthood, but this seems like an anti-rite. A passage into some strange condition unlike, say…. a Native American ritual where the kid faces hardships and comes through it more focused, but not so inflexible and distant. They're just not childish and… It seems to me that males and females have their separate paths in all other traditions.*

"I know it's irrational," Molly said, "and it's probably just a mass hysteria after all, but I'm still terrified to go near there." She thought for an entire minute, "I don't want to get caught up in anything like that whether it's real or not" *I'm not willing to lose my independence even if it's imagined.* She returned to the current space-time coordinates and said, "I don't really know any reason beyond the peer pressure angle," and stopped for ten beats before she continued, "I think I overheard someone say they felt something trying to pull them there or something like that. Maybe there's something in *Hell World* attracting them. Mass Mesmerism… maybe."

"Did you ever feel compelled to go there beyond the peer pressure?" Eb was puzzled.

"No, but like I said, I always stayed far away."

Eb asked, "How did you resist? I'm sure other kids were scared too."

A faraway look invaded her eyes. "Well, my nanny, Artemis, always taught me to think independently and question the pressures of the world. She was very protective, but not overly so. She helped me think for myself and not to follow the rest of the goats in the herd." After a momentary vacuum of blankness, she continued, "After Artemis left, I now realize, I suppressed her teaching in my failed adolescent attempt to fit in."

They began swimming upstream in a torrent of the pent-up volcanic lava of sexual energy, but the eruption had to wait... for now.

Stopping at the rock of *Hell World* and floating through the equipment setup trying not to be distracted by the seismic waves of carnal desire, they felt as though they were operating from a single mind separated only by their bodies longing for total unity. *Maybe Plato was right*, Molly speculated, *and we have found our soulmates,* so to speak. At least it was exciting to think of it that way, so she decided to believe it was their destiny. *But, nothing lasts so don't count on it*! She heard a recorded voice playing back in her head, the voice of her mother's warning, trying to discourage her. She stood straight up, took a symbolic step away from that interloper, that spoiler of the moment her mother had always been, and, "No!" slipped out at a volume that made the ground beneath her rumble, or so it seemed. A vision of her mother that had loomed over her forever began to shrink until it occupied only a tiny spot in her mind, more like a memory now than an ongoing experience. She looked around to see if Eb heard her, but he did not falter from his tasks. Her posture remained tall and straight, but relaxed, unlike her previous self-consciousness.

He tested the hidden mic and video clipped to his clothes as well as the video feed from the drone. She monitored it all, signaled that everything was ready, gave the thumbs up and said, "Everything's 'A-Okay Eb!'" For a moment, she was Neil Armstrong on the Moon.

That odor of flowers appeared again briefly on the breeze from the East, but eventually as darkness blanketed the area, the wind shifted coming from Hell World, and it changed to a competing pungent noxious odor; a mixture of ammonia, sulfur, and burning tires that repelled him. It all seemed to foretell a pending battle between sweet and sour, good versus evil, light versus shadow. The sun descended turning to blue and crimson, then past yellows and pinks before the strange cloudless, but totally starless darkness had settled in. Ebenezer Thornbird saw off in the distance, perhaps a mile or maybe two, what looked like a bonfire, a flickering dancing blaze silhouetted against the tarpaper blackness of night. It was blurry, like looking through a foggy shield *or, maybe it's more like peering through hot air rising over a fire or looking through the steam of a boiling pot.* He thought about this image for another twelve seconds. *There seems to be a rift in time and space. No wonder the stone I threw in there was almost invisible during the day. There's an aberration. Apparently light goes in, but not much of it escapes its captor, perhaps only that which is allowed to; maybe a barrier reflects much of it back from shining through from Hell World.* He sniffed the air. "Whew!" *Maybe what I smell is burning trash, but it's getting worse; definitely foul and malodorous.*

"Hey!" He suddenly wondered aloud, "Why aren't there any kids out here ready to enter their rite of passage?"

Molly stood in a pool of puzzlement. "I don't know. It is strange though."

Despite the wonderment gripping him, he waited a while longer, observing the fire's lapping tongues that were clearly, he realized after some time, the images of beckoning arms and hands of undulating exotic dancers trying to lure him in. However, he knew that they were not responsible for the urgent voices calling him. Those were still there, but they seemed to be blocked, muffled, or maybe partially burned off by the fire, like the natural gas wells of perpetual flame he had seen in oil country while working the rigs several years ago. The voices were less clear now as though the flames had ignited them in an attempt to prevent his notice. He feared that the voices would all be incinerated into a mass of mute sadness and despair in time if he did not stop the conflagration. However, Finder knew somehow that he should wait so Eb continued to look through his binoculars at the fire. "It looks like there's a person out there tending the fire," he said. "He seems to be throwing things into it. I can't make out what it is through the haze, and even though the colors of the flames seem to be shifting, there is a thick, very black smoke that, against the starless night, blends into the colorless sky."

Handing the binoculars to Molly, he said, "What do you make of it?" Peering at the fire, she not only saw but felt the flaming arms beckoning her and, despite her resistance, she was pulled, entranced, compelled to follow the beseeching incendiary arms, taking three gradual unconscious steps toward *Hell World*, feeling the tug of a firm and steady cord. Eb noticed a feeling in his own gut emanating from behind him, and turning, he saw Molly being slowly dragged toward the flames, grabbed her arm, and wrenched the binoculars from her grasp.

She was startled back to corporeality not realizing where she was for twenty-three very rapid beats of her heart. "What...? What happened?" she asked. Her voice was vibrating, her heart was racing ahead of her thoughts, and her breath was the rapid and shallow hyperventilation of panic.

He stared at her for a very long thirty seconds. "Have you ever been out here at night before?"

"No," Molly said. Anxiety was intermixed like a DNA helix with her fascination. "I never even came this close to it!" she exclaimed, "The closest I ever get is driving by as fast as I can. I never even drive by at night," she was visibly shivering. "I especially avoid it on Halloween and full moon nights."

He said, "You seemed drawn to the fire out there."

"Oh, my God!" she said. "That's terrifying! I didn't know… I… I…"

"I can imagine!" he said with such compassion that her heart magically slowed down along with her breathing, and taking her in his arms, swaddling her so tightly she felt herself melting into his embrace, cleansed of her fascination with the fire. She was more aware of the solid, growing connection with him now. She hugged him in her grateful arms with her ear on his chest, felt his strong, steady heartbeat causing her breath to deepen and decrease its velocity even more.

After they pacified their tensions enough to step back, they looked at each other, temporarily put aside their passion and silently went to work, Eb booting up the drone, Molly grabbing the controls and the receiver from the van. With renewed urgency, she watched for his signal to start monitoring the drone and his hidden transceiver. He signaled, and she started recording.

She felt like the radar operators and signalmen she had seen in movies or, she imagined, a Mission Control operator at Cape Canaveral.

She said, "Ready Eb!" Offering a thumbs-up.

"Okay," he responded and tested the drone to be certain the whole thing was working. "Looking good!" he yelled over his shoulder and sent the craft up and out over *Hell World*. "Here goes!"

She looked at his silhouette backlight by the fire of *Hell World* and felt the excitement of achieving something far outside of any previous experience. Somewhere deep inside, coupled with her new-found freedom, before she knew it, her unbridled elation emerged in a high pitched, "Weeeeee!"

They both laughed so hard that Eb nearly lost control of the aircraft.

CHAPTER FIFTEEN
ON THE EDGE OF HELL WORLD

Despite the lack of stars, the blue moon hung heavily like the weight of a shining treeless Christmas ornament in the still balmy night sky. Ebenezer Thornbird knew that the moniker "Blue Moon" was a mere metaphor; blue originally meant "rare." It wasn't really supposed to be blue, but there it was, a strange bluish almost purple tinted halo around this one. Finder said, *Odd that the Moon is so bright, there are no clouds, and yet the stars over Hell World are blacked out. It's as though the gods extinguished the stars, leaving the moon as a spotlight waiting for the Gladiators to enter the arena.*

Looking through the binoculars, Ebenezer Thornbird had confirmed that there was a figure, probably a man, sitting on the log by the fire and a short way from him, a wide hole ringed by rocks, probably the well they had seen in the daylight. Now, the man seemed to be waving to Molly through the drone's camera eye. It was not so much a wave as a come on, an enticement. Then the smoke seemed to shift in response to the man's next gesture and obscured the view. Bringing the drone back to its docking platform, Eb stepped into the van, set it down inside, grabbed the tiny camera and super sensitive microphone and hid them in his shirt. He placed his backpack over his shoulder, feeling like it weighed fifty pounds with the gallon bottle of water and the rest of his equipment in it. Molly pled with him once again, "I don't want you to go. I'm afraid for you." *Us!* she thought. She realized it was a predictably futile effort, but she wanted to convey her loving concern and fears of potentially losing him again. *Again?*

Turning to her with eyes of deep sympathy, he engulfed her in a hug and said, in a low guttural Schwarzenegger-like imitation accent, "I'll be back."

Molly was not amused. She said, "I know you will, but I'm worried about what condition you'll be in. I'm afraid for you. You might return as a shadow of yourself like everyone else around here. Now that I'm thinking about it, I wonder if no one ever leaves Perfection because they can't bear to part with a piece of themselves they left in there."

"I know Molly, but I need you here to monitor what happens. You don't realize what a tremendously important part of this quest you are." He hugged her again, more tightly this time, and said, "I think this is what I was supposed to do. I don't know why, but it just feels right." He gave her a last squeeze and pulled back with his hands gripping her shoulders and looked her in the eye. "Promise me you won't go in there, no matter what. Your destiny lies here. Mine is out there no matter what happens. Whatever is out there is trying to draw you in. That may be why there are no kids waiting to enter *Hell World* tonight. You're the only holdout, the only one who resists the pull to enter that hellish place. Finder thinks that you are the key to something, we don't know what it is, but we're going to find out. You can't give into it regardless of how you feel. Promise?"

"All right," she agreed with the conflict between reluctance, her fear of *Hell World,* and her desire to help and protect this man; her man, her soulmate.

He lightly cradled her left cheek with his right hand "You are my anchor to this reality, Molly. I need you just the way you are. Do not enter *Hell World* under any circumstances while I'm out there. There's more at stake than our relationship. If you give in, Finder feels you'll be lost forever, and I don't know what other disasters that would cause!"

"Okay." *No one has ever felt that way about me. No one wanted me just the way I am!*

Remembering the words of the Medicine Man in his dream, *was it my Great-grandfather? "You have all you need now to complete your mission with only one last detail. You must give up something precious."* Ebenezer Thornbird pulled up a small leather cord from around his neck and over his head. There was a small ring threaded through it, worn as a talisman since Pati had given it to him when he was twelve. It had been handed down through generations and given to his birth mother by his grandmother. Handing it to Molly, he said, "I want you to take this. It is precious to me. I don't know whether it has any monetary value, but it's the only thing I have that belonged to my birth mother. It's a talisman handed down to me through the fortune of time and legend. It'll keep you safe."

She was shocked and simultaneously flattered. She stood there, mouth agape for twenty seconds. "I can't take this!" she protested.

"No. This is important. I need to give it to you, and you must accept it. Please take it. You're the most important person in my life right now, probably ever, and I can't think of anyone better to have it. I really need, and I mean need you to take it. It *will* keep you safe."

She just stared at it for twenty-six more seconds. Her words remained stuck in her throat as she searched for them, but they were almost too far away to reach. "It's beautiful," her hoarse voice finally forced passed her partially paralyzed vocal cords. It was a silver band sporting an inscribed arrowhead inside that his grandmother had given his mother the year before she died. Molly slid it off the cord and slipped it onto the ring finger of her right hand. It fit perfectly. She remembered Artemis' words, *say thank you when you are given a gift even if you don't believe you deserve it*. So much had changed, and continued changing so rapidly in her life that she was so overwhelmed with the flood of emotions welling up from her gut to her leaking eyes that, despite opening her mouth to speak, nothing but a raspy squeak came out. "Thank you."

Changing the subject, he said, "Everything will turn out all right, but I still need you to do your part."

Suddenly, she looked up, "Wait! If this ring will keep me safe, it'll keep you safe too! You should keep it. You're the one who is going out there to face danger in *Hell World*."

"I understand your logic, but I've had a dream, a premonition if you will, telling me that I would need to part with it. Please accept it. I know it's counter-intuitive, but it'll help me complete this quest. Besides, it is you he wants, not me."

"Okay," she said in a brave whisper looking down at the ring, but with a voice stunned by his beautiful and touching generosity.

The drone had been returned to the van, so they tested the transmission of the recording devices attached to Eb as he suited up, checked that he had everything as a final measure of safety, and gave the thumbs up to Molly. She returned her thumbs up signal. *If I'm going to help him make it through this intact, I need to concentrate so, FOCUS!*

CHAPTER SIXTEEN
DEMONS OF HELL WORLD

Ebenezer Thornbird peered out across the *Hell World* wilderness while he rocked forward on his left foot and then back on his right. He repeated the movement three times in the anxious but energized motion of a long distance runner surveying the track ahead while waiting for the call to the starting line. He was ready to go, but something was pulling him back. He had stopped at the threshold of *Hell World* feeling pulled between his destiny ahead and Molly's need tugging at him from behind. He turned to her and said, "Molly. Let me go. I will return to you intact." Making a promise with good intentions, but one he wasn't sure he could keep. He no longer had his talisman to keep him safe, but he knew it would keep her safe. It was a sacrifice he was willing to make; one he knew he had to make.

He returned to the rocking motion of a marathon runner anticipating the snap of the phantom starter's pistol in his head, stepped forward, cut through the air that constituted the borderline between two worlds and immediately felt the change from the cool night breeze to an arid, hot stifling desert. A boundary in time and space was crossed, and Eb felt disoriented, confused, and consciousness seemed to fade before he regained his bearings. He staggered a bit, shook his head violently to regain his focus, and thereby shook off the disorientation.

After testing the receiving equipment, she stood next to the van and watched him step beyond the invisible boundary into the gloom as he disappeared into *Hell World* and she wiped away the three tears in her worried eyes. Until that moment, it seemed like a dream to her, and she feared it could soon become a nightmare. She felt the numbness of disbelief, took three steps in his direction, but she had to pull back and let him go with trust in her heart that he would keep his promise. *He'll return to me,* she tried to convince herself. Step by step, Ebenezer Thornbird felt the past, present, and future suddenly collapse into his increasingly labored breath that Molly Everhart heard on the monitor.

A sudden unexpected downpour the likes of which could only be described in biblical verse separated Molly from *Hell World* and her man. The deluge was so heavy that it knocked Molly Everhart to the ground as if she were standing directly under Niagara Falls. She looked down and saw the electronic gear drowning in an immense puddle after it had been wrenched from her grip in the torrent. The rain was so intense that it was digging a small lake in the earth beneath her feet. Managing to retrieve the soaked equipment, dragging it through the deluge, the likes of which had not been experienced since Noah, she found refuge inside the van. *Talk about raining buckets!* She fiddled with the power switch on the device. Nothing happened. "C'mon! C'mon!" she yelled as if it would heed her demand. "C'mon!" The equipment was dead. Starting the van's engine, she turned on the heater to dry it out, but it never worked again. Feeling despair, all she could do was wait and fulfill her promise to Eb not to enter *Hell World* under any circumstances. She turned her attention to the apparatus again in a futile attempt to reestablish contact with Eb. She wiped it off thoroughly, but no matter what she did or how many times she tried, it was no use there was no return transmission. She had already activated the recorder several times after it had dried out, but there was only electronic snow and static where picture and sound had been. She sank into the quicksand of fear and anticipation that there might be a long radio silence. *Is he all right?* She was beside herself. She looked around the van and saw that the drone and its controls had been left inside before the hellish onslaught of the crushing liquid outside, but she couldn't fly it until the lashing rain and wind that had started kicking the van around, as if a monster was rocking it, had stopped. As she sank deeper into helplessness, to add insult to injury, the van began to slip deeper into the muddy sinkhole.

In the dry heat of *Hell World*, Ebenezer Thornbird saw a huge cloud of billowing smoke speeding toward him, a wavering and shifting face, reminiscent of the drifting clouds of childhood looking up from the grass; but these faces were dark, foreboding, and menacingly sinister, and he had the strange sensation that they were laughing. "Are you seeing this Molly?" he asked the microphone. There was no response. A shiver coursed through his body that traveled up from his stomach until it stuck in his throat causing his voice to quiver. "Molly? Molly?!" Still no answer. "I don't know whether you can hear me. If you can, just keep recording. I think something is trying to scare me away." He started to worry that something had happened to her, but it was too late to turn back. He had to simply believe that she was all right and that she could hear him, even though he couldn't hear her. He experienced a moment of despair as if he were talking to some anonymous person and felt the sadness of losing contact with Molly as though she was separated from him in another world where they could no longer touch. He had no time for the sadness and fear of loss welling up from somewhere deep in the core of his being. Instead, he had to press on and believe that she was safe.

Molly Everhart was frightened and tried to swallow the stone in her throat, shuttered when the lightning flashed nearby, and the thunder that followed sounded like the gods were ripping the fabric of the universe apart in one jagged, dysrhythmic renting motion. *ZzZzZzZzip... Boom!* Shocked by the strength of her emotions, Molly's nerves seemed to snap, crackle, and pop with the thunder and lightning. Her stunned brain experienced an electroshock treatment of the *One Flew Over The Cuckoo's Nest* variety, her follicles cramped up, making her hair stand at attention while her skin, rippling in *St. Elmo's Fire*, was fizzing like a newly opened can of soda pop, and she fell into a kind of stupor.

Eb said, "Please remain calm no matter what happens," as if she could hear him, but of course she could not. When he said, "I need you, Molly," she thought she sensed his phantom dream-like voice whispering in her ear from some far distant land, but the radio silence continued. Her breath had stopped, causing lightheadedness when her diaphragm was paralyzed for a second catching her unawares, and the universe was suspended for an instant.

Deaf, dumb and blind to Eb's situation, there was a fluttering in Molly's chest, her pores succumbed to the piloerection of goose pimples that crawled up and down her arms and legs. Her hair stood on end, while gremlins kicked her in the stomach, and she forced herself to focus more closely on her intuition. She checked the video feed and the audio again like Eb had instructed, but there was no reception. It was turned on and seemed to be in working order now, in fact, it was still tuned in just as it was when they tested it, but there was no incoming signal *Damn! Ruined! Or is there something else blocking the signal?* She sat back in a lump helplessly surrendering to the circumstances and drowning in a tide of fear and trepidation. That is not to say that she had given up. She just had no options at that moment. There was a small hope though that the drone could work once the storm had passed. She just had to wait. She did feel intuitively that he was all right but wondered if that was truly intuition or simply wishful thinking. She chose to believe the former, so she sat back, grabbed a bottle of water out of the cooler she had packed with food the day before and nervously waited. Although food did not appeal to her, she knew she needed to ward off dehydration.

Despite the rain's slightly diminishing rate, the ceaseless wind was still blowing so hard that it rocked the van in dangerous gusts making the whole thing shiver, vibrate, and sing, like a droning of an out-of-tune Greek Chorus, commenting on the hopelessness of her situation. Her helplessness was pulling her into a black hole of irrelevant time and space as she was buffeted about in the hapless vehicle.

Despite the loud rapidly approaching sound of buzzing ahead, Ebenezer Thornbird couldn't determine its origin until a mass of giant insects he thought might be locusts smashed into him as they fled the smoke. He turned his back against the onslaught, pulling his bandana up over his nose, put on his wraparound sunglasses to protect his face and eyes from the swarming pestilence blasting into him, and wished he had brought goggles. The swarm passed, but there was still the fast approaching dark billowing smoke, and despite his burning eyes, he was forced to take off the sunglasses to see in the dark,.

Nearly losing his bearings, save for the pleading sounds ahead, he stepped boldly into the cloud, intending to head straight toward the terrified faint crying voices that Finder could barely detect through the cloud of interference. The smog was increasingly pungent. His throat began to tighten, as he felt the fingers of the foul odor choking him, smelling increasingly like burning tires and sulfur, trying to strangle him from the inside. He knelt and found the face protectors in his pack and soaked one in cologne to cover the odor before he put it on.

Without warning, thousands of birds were strafing him with guano and then, one by one, they fell from the sky causing him to pull his hood up over his cap and lift his pack over his head for a shield while trying to step over their carcasses. He decided that the flock, sent in for the attack, had been inadvertently grounded by the smoke like the unfortunate birds that, trying to warm themselves, are rendered unconscious by the rising carbon monoxide and fall down asphyxiating fireplace chimneys in the winter.

As if slogging through a field of waist-high mud, the thick, dense smoke made it increasingly difficult to walk. He lit the flashlight, but the light was simply reflected back at him from the impenetrable wall of smoke. *Is there something in it that's making me feel this way?* He could barely see the uneven ground, but started to run, stumbling the best he could toward the calling pleading grief he knew was straight ahead. Staggering, he suddenly emerged from the worst of the smoke and saw the fire fifty yards ahead. Across from it, there was a dark, distorted figure of a man sitting on the rotten log, a tree that had long ago surrendered to the malevolent forces of *Hell World*. "Can you hear me, Molly?" he asked the microphone. Silence scuttled his heart, fear increased exponentially, his pulse was quickening, and his eyes were watering. "There's someone near the fire." He kept talking, hoping against despair in the unlikely event that she could hear him. "There's a person there, but I can't make him out clearly yet." His pounding heart was thrumming in his ears now, his nose was running, and he couldn't see anything clearly through his watering eyes. He was flying blind without instruments. "I'm getting closer," he gasped. "I won't be able to talk now and, whether or not you're picking this up, I'm leaving the transmitter on.

He was so overpowered by the smoke that he staggered a bit and fell to one knee, barely hanging on to consciousness as if there was some kind of poisonous gas or perhaps a paralyzing drug that was laced in the breeze, targeting his nostrils like tentacles, filling his disgusted sinus cavities, and creeping into his brain.

His extremely lightheaded vision settled on the strange old man whose visage was wavering in the occasional gap in the smoke. *Is it the smoke or is it the old man that is wavering like that?* The old man was seated on the log atop a rise where the smog was thinning. Ebenezer Thornbird's vision began to clear a bit. He struggled to his feet and staggered toward the log, the Earth unstable beneath his feet.

"Hell... hello," he managed to choke out through the horrific taste of radical fumes in his strangling throat and the spinning in his head. He sat down on the opposite end of the log from the old man who, now that Eb could see him clearly, had a short nose, a jutting jaw and buck teeth. He had a very thin, ashen, wiry-haired six-inch long scraggly goatee and he was mostly bald, save for the tufts of gray, kinky, hairs in the middle of his head and sticking out by his ears, making them look larger than they already did on their own. His mouth circled too far around his face and lifted at the ends forming a slight but permanent smile as though someone had cut them at the distal ends to form an artificial grin, and made him the specter of Heath Ledger's Joker in *The Dark Knight*. It wasn't a happy smile, but a sinister and seemingly diabolical one. His sparse eyebrows were spawned from the same follicles as those kinky pubic-like hairs on his head. His large, dark, empty animal eyes with very long lashes were sunken into his face. He had on black pants and shirt and his legs ended in two misshapen bare club-like feet. He seemed to be wheezing, and Eb thought he heard a burp, a cough, and then a fart. *Quite a welcome from this old Jinn!* "I'm Eb," he said. "They call me Finder." When the old man put a hand up to wipe his slightly drooling mouth, Ebenezer Thornbird saw for the first time that his ancient hands were gnarled and knobby as if he was afflicted with severe rheumatoid arthritis. His skin was extremely dry reminding Eb of the corpse he once saw of a man who had died in the West Virginia coal mine after he apparently lost his way, wandered into an abandoned shaft, and was found after being AWOL for several days.

The old man said nothing. He merely nodded and stared straight ahead at the fire.

＊＊＊＊

Ebenezer Thornbird remembered the petting zoo on an elementary school field trip where, among the farm animals, there were some goats the children were allowed to pet, but he was afraid to approach them. Finder said, *there's something sinister about these animals. I don't think it applies to all goats, but these creatures give off a weird impression.* There was a stout odor in the air that seemed foreboding, and the goats were odd looking creatures with their longish snouts, big ears, and scraggly hair. They were willing to eat anything in sight, including aluminum cans. One of them, an old Billy, tried to eat the pants off a terrified and sobbing little girl until she was barely rescued by the goat keeper before it charged him. After the keeper rescued the girl and narrowly dodged Billy, he turned to see that he was facing a fierce semicircle of goats. He had to jump the fence to escape the pending attack. The Zoo henceforth banned free access to the goats. Eb and Finder both felt the beasts were dangerous when he was seven or eight years old, but the old man resembled the goats.

****

The hellish smoke had diminished considerably. However, the stench of whatever the old man was burning, mixed with the personal bilious odors emanating from every possible pore and orifice of the old man's body, was so strong now that even the heavy dose of cologne in Eb's mask was rendered completely ineffective. He wondered whether the old guy, surrounded by so many gasses, was in danger of exploding if he came too close to the fire. Sitting on the opposite end of the log about five nauseating feet away from the old fart, he said, "I was curious about the fire and who was out here," he coughed. "What are you doing way out here in this barren place?" his voice was raspy. Still no reply. The old man just gazed at the fire. "I'm a finder, and I believe there are things out here to be found." He didn't want to say that what he was looking for was calling him or that he felt it close by.

The old man finally looked at Ebenezer Thornbird with compassionless empty eyes and bleated, "I'm Maara, the Collector." *His tremulous voice sounds a little goat-like!* His eyes seemed empty, and his gaze was bottomless. "I sense your revulsion from my appearance. This wretched form is all I could manage since fate has stuck me with it, thanks to my mother," and after a pregnant pause, "When a part of a person disappears from this world, it enters another form. Somewhat diminished, but with certain other talents. It's damned difficult to get back!"

Eb sat staring uncomprehendingly for six seconds. *What is he talking about?*" I'm afraid I don't follow you. What do you mean?"

"You were not supposed to come here." The old man's goatee waggled on his chin as he spoke, "I was expecting someone else to come and complete my collection; my entry back into the world," he snorted, "but you turned out to be a fine specimen. You were strong enough to make it through the barriers." He turned his face back to the fire.

"Who were you expecting?" Eb asked, "And what did you expect to collect from them? If you don't mind my asking."

"Well," the old man hesitated. "I've been waiting for that person for twelve years, but so far she has resisted my enticements. It has taken me fifty years to get this close" He was frustrated, and he seemed to be sad. "There is only one last item left to complete my collection; my doorway back."

"I think I know her."

"Yes, you do!" His voice revealed a barely controlled rage coming through clenched teeth. "And I thought you'd bring her to me!" What little fists he had were clenched.

Finder said, *this guy isn't trying to retrieve something he lost, it is he who is lost; afraid he'll die if he is returned to wherever he belongs. He's trying to take on things that belong to others; things they lost because he took them, and I think they're down in that well. He needs more of it, only it's not his to retrieve.* "What do you collect from people?"

"It depends on how you look at it... Mainly, in a manner of speaking, I guess you could say they are..." He hesitated while he looked back at the fire with dilated vacant eyes trying to find the words for six beats of Ebenezer Thornbird's rapidly galloping heart, "wet things, I guess you'd say," he said with a tone of irony.

"Wet things?" Eb displayed his puzzlement with a wrinkled frown. "Out here in this dry place? Where do you keep these wet things?"

"In the well." He pointed to the circle of rocks that formed the curb around the hole with a rope snaking out from under the wooden cover.

Eb swore he saw the rope slither on the ground like a boa constrictor, *but, on second thought, it reminds me of an umbilical cord attached to its placenta.* There was a large rock atop the cover presumably to keep his collection from escaping. "How do you find these collectibles?"

"I don't go looking for them," the old man exclaimed in a slightly disgusted tone. "They come to me like a cat chasing a string. You don't chase a cat, you lure it, entice it to come close to you, just like you were lured here by mistake." Turning abruptly to look at Eb with an angry red face, he screamed, "You are the wrong cat!"

Eb stared at the crippled old guy with still burning eyes complements of what remained of the smoke.

"I guess we're alike in that regard," the old man continued, "You said you seek things that are calling you and I lure them to me."

"No, I'm nothing like you. Lost or stolen things call me to return them to their rightful places. You lure them away from where they belong for your own selfish purpose."

"I suppose you have a point." He seemed to be smiling, but it was difficult to tell.

"So," Eb said, "I sense that *you* are lost, but you don't want to be returned. You are trying to steal things from others, so you don't have to go back to wherever you belong, but what you took does not belong to you."

"Well," the old guy sounded angry, "you can talk all you want, but I have my collectibles, and I only need one more to accomplish my goal!"

"You keep them, your 'collectibles,' down in the wet well away from this arid place?"

"No, the well is dry," he snorted as if to say, "You're so stupid!"

Ebenezer Thornbird stared for a full uncomprehending minute. "How do you keep wet things wet in a dry well?"

"It absorbs the wetness." The old man grinned. "It preserves them; something like the Latin American Mummies."

Eb was puzzled by this old man. *This is bizarre.* "Oh! You mean like freeze dried food that you can reconstitute by adding water? You collect wet things that are lured here, capture them and put them in the well, and it sucks the wetness out by osmosis or capillary action? I suppose you intend to reconstitute them with water later when your collection is complete."

"In a manner of speaking, not exactly, but that's the only way I can describe it to you... Soul food, maybe." He laughed so hard that he began to choke on his own joke, but it was so loud that it hurt Ebenezer Thornbird's ears.

Soul food? Does he snack on whatever is in there? Maybe he'll eat them all when he has the full complement. Maybe he needs to digest them to achieve his purpose. "What's the cover for?"

His goat-like reflectionless eyes turned and stared at Eb as though he was infinitely more stupid than he thought. In a condescending and sarcastic tone, he said, "To keep them from escaping and to keep curiosity seekers out, like you," his bony arthritic finger shot sharply toward Eb causing him to flinch as if it was a knife. "Besides," he said, "the more I collect, the more perfect the town becomes! A fair exchange wouldn't you agree? So you see, there is mutual benefit."

"Benefit? Perfect? You mean the emotionless rule-bound disinterest in others?"

Already lightheaded, Ebenezer Thornbird lost muscle tone and, propelled to the limits of awareness, he nearly fell off the log barely avoiding the emptiness of unconscious oblivion. The old guy suddenly closed the distance between them, as if he disappeared from his position and reappeared next to his victim without actually moving, and caught his arm. *Did he just do something to me with his bony pointed finger or is this the effect of a contact high from the hallucinatory smoke?*

"I need more collectibles," the old bleating voice came out of the ether. "You'll do for now, but I have to have your girlfriend!"

"How do you know whether I have an interest in someone?" Eb slurred, sounding far away from the voice that must have been his own. He knew exactly to whom this ancient devil was referring, but he wanted to minimize his connection to Molly to protect her.

"I have my spies," he said, and after a minute of diabolical reflection, he said, "I'll still collect her now that I have you," the old demon laughed. "If she values your life and her relationship with you, she'll come to me. She's the cat now, and you're the lure!"

"Oh no, you won't!" Ebenezer Thornbird's adrenaline pushed him closer to consciousness through the smog filling his head that had the consistency of cotton batting. "She'll never come to you!"

"Yes, she will. She's a Zane! Besides, if she doesn't, I'll extract what I need from you and add it to my permanent collection!" the old man continued, swollen with determination, "Mark my words, she'll come looking for you to prevent that!" He was yelling now. "Stupid love will conquer all, but it'll be my conquest!"

"Not a chance! I won't give in to you, and I won't let you have her!"

"I seeeee," he said as he lifted his chin high with an aloof and sarcastic tone. "Well, maybe you'll change your mind when you meet my daughters." It was difficult to tell because of the abnormal shape of his mouth, but Eb could have sworn that the disgusting old beast had an ironic smirk on his lips. "You might find them much more practiced in the art of lovemaking." He pointed a very gnarled and crooked arthritic finger toward a spot in front of his victim. Eb followed it in the direction of what at first appeared to be five naked young women, but his eyes soon focused to see that only three had materialized. The old man said, "Meet my daughters Devaputta, Maccu, and Kiles." They tried to tempt him with the fermented fruit of Bacchus, but he declined the bottles of alcoholic beverages this unholy trinity offered from which they had been imbibing. Trying to entice him with their undulating suggestive dancing, they rubbed their nakedness against him, but when he fended them off, one temptress kneeled at his feet, unzipped his pants and grabbed for his private self. He was barely able to push her away in his weakened state.

He resisted his body's fermenting temptation that was growing in his pants. Finder said, *be careful, resist this! If you don't, we're lost!*

Speaking in turn, the trio said, "We can make you very happy, we want you, we will do anything you want us to do." And in unison, "We'll give you anything you want! We will please you beyond your wildest desires! You only have to ask." Their voices seemed to ungulate combining into one voice and then into separate ones again.

They rubbed him with their naked skin in an attempt to flint the fire of passion and lust while the one in front of him sat her naked self on his lap and wrapped her arms around his neck. She felt like a feather, solid but ghostlike simultaneously. She grabbed his hand and tried to force it between her legs. It took all of his strength to wrestle it free. She tried to kiss him on the mouth, but, turning his head, her lips landed on a rejecting cheek. Resisting all temptations, despite their efforts, he kept the vision of Molly Everhart, his virtual shield, in the forefront of his mind, along with Finder and his mission, against uninhibited enticements.

His head was spinning, and he felt as though he was teetering on a mountain plateau. "Go on!" the old man screamed, trying to push him over the cliff of Mount Temptation, "Take her. No one will know! Your pants are screaming for her!"

"I'll know!" Ebenezer Thornbird yelled, closing his eyes and feeling his inseparable connection with Molly. He heard the voice of Finder, *remember your mother's mistakes under the influence of intoxicants and the fact that you are being manipulated, something we've never allowed.*

Barely able to speak, after a herculean effort to clear his head, he beckoned the women to come close. One, Devaputta, stayed on his lap, and the other two bent forward on either side, pressing each ear close to his mouth while he felt their breasts gently pressed against his face. The one on his lap said with husky words of seduction, "We'll do anything your heart desires."

Nearly overcome by the gasses and their stiffening temptations, he was barely able to whisper when he managed to ejaculate a question. "Anything?" he wheezed. He was swooning closer to unconsciousness from the intoxicating fumes.

"Yes baby, absolutely anything." she said, "Your wish is our command; anything you ask." She slipped his nearly unconscious hand between her thighs again and writhed a little.

"You all agree?" he managed to squeeze out.

Their breathy seductive answers were simultaneous and definite. They said, "Oh yes! We'll do anything!"

"No exceptions? You'll submit to me and carry out my orders?" he whispered.

"Absolutely, no exceptions baby!"

"No questions asked?" His head was drooping now.

"Anything you want."

His eyes looked up, "Okay I'll tell you what I want you to do for me," barely able to push it out and, Limp wristed, he gestured them to move their ears even closer to his barely whispering mouth.

"Your wish is our command." They're voices, and seductive gestures were eager to pleasure him as they hugged closer.

He pointed at the old man and barely hissed out, "Kill that old goat." Their widening eyes nearly fell out of their heads and, stunned into paralysis for three extremely long seconds, eyebrows stretching high, they stared at Ebenezer Thornbird through the gap in time. Their terrified heads turned slowly in unison toward the old man whose face was turning into such a loud blaze of crimson that Eb thought it might bleed or explode.

Old Maara gave a loud belch, and a snort as the fumes of evil greenish purple gasses erupted from his body distorting the air around him before he roared, "You son of a bitch!" He stomped his feet. "And you Bitches," he pointed a gnarly finger at the girls, "you are going to pay for your failure!" As suddenly as they had materialized, they evaporated into the terrified flames and smoke, mere shadowy whispers of hallucination, leaving only their fleeting phantom images on his retina.

Slumping on the log, Ebenezer Thornbird fell into a stupor, his arms and legs feeling as if they were stretching while his body burned in an oven of fear, and the entire spectrum of colors danced like a prism in his brain. The old man threw some fuel on the fire, bundles of sticks that, in ancient times were used to burn people at the stake. There was something in the smoke that produced odd colors. The gasses from the bonfire had turned his head into a viscous liquid that felt as if it was slowly solidifying into a gelatinous semi-solid, heading he thought, toward rigor mortis. Consciousness fleeing from his brain, feeling as if he were in a tall tower overlooking an unreachable forest of thoughts, emotions, and impulses, he was certain that he was dying. However, to his surprise, he suddenly awoke to find himself in a circle of angry men in military fatigues insisting he place his John Hancock on a document that he was in no condition to read, let alone sign. *Is this a nightmare or a hallucination?* They had clubs and knives threatening to beat him to death, cut him up into little pieces, and give the meat to their snarling dog. Through the haze, he thought, *that dog from hell looks remarkably like Eddie's Jake.*

He said, "I can't read that without my glasses, and they're back in the motel," he lied, "and besides, I can't see in this smoke or with my dizzy head."

"No need to read it! Just sign it!" they yelled in a menacing tone as they stepped closer.

When he declined, the minion charged him, but he closed his eyes and Finder said, *stay still no matter what happens.* He remained still and, although terrified on the inside, he acted unafraid. True to his credo, he did not question his fate. Finder said, *they feed on fear for their strength.* He was doing what he was meant to do and would do, even if it endangered his life or if it was coming to an end. His body was stretching out infinitely in all directions like Gumby as if he was being drawn and quartered. He suddenly realized his stark insignificance in the universe. He heard the men yelling a chant, threatening and pounding their weapons on the ground and the log next to him, but he didn't feel anything, and their words lost all meaning. He wondered if he had been so anesthetized by the fumes that he couldn't feel whether he was actually being beaten and cut to ribbons. The ground seemed to disappear beneath his feet, and he could no longer feel Finder. *So, this is what it's like to be dead.* He was lost in an empty space for how long, he had no idea. Time and space meant nothing anymore. He had lost all sensation, and there was the most total silence and darkness he had ever encountered. *There's nothing left but a silent hollowness; a spot filled with nothingness. It's the opposite of presence. It can only be inadequately described in words as... as... an absence.* He was all alone with himself when, relieved to feel Finder fading back into his awareness again, he heard him say, *remember what that shade in the mine said and your nanny Parcae told you. You'll be faced with unimaginable danger, and you must remain calm in the face of it.* He seemed to fade away again deeper into a place where there was nothing at all, save pure consciousness. He had no idea how long this timeless state lasted, but all at once, the silence he assumed was death was supplanted by the old man's roars as he awoke from the nightmare of martyrdom.

Ebenezer Thornbird opened his eyes, the soldiers were gone, and the old man was furious, more enraged than ever. Pawing the ground in equine madness, he galloped toward his captive, but Ebenezer Thornbird held his ground, unblinking in a smoke-filled eye-watering stare down. Instantly, the old man was in a nose-to-nose fury, teeth clenched in a grimacing smile. The fog in his head was lifting, and, regaining his wits, he flexed his hands and legs to regain their connection. It was then that he realized the limits of the old man's power. *Finder is right, it is fueled by fear and hatred, but he's impotent in the face of calm, fearless courage, and love.*

The old man ran to the well, grabbed the giant rock from atop the wooden cover, raised it over his head with superhuman strength, and with raging eyes ablaze, he smashed it on the ground causing an earthquake that shook everything nearby, despite there being no fault lines for hundreds of miles. "How dare you! Who gives you the authority to oppose me?"

Eb reached down and touched the Earth, the only reality he felt certain of, with three fingertips that kept him from falling off the log causing the tremors to cease. "*This* is my authority!" he said, feeling more grounded now. Reality came rushing back, clearer than ever, and confidence rose to giant proportions. Life became more solid as he gave his final word, "The world will go just where it wants regardless of your unearthly taunts!"

The old man yelled, "You've conjured up all kinds of wit, but none my friend is worth a shit!"

The old man pointed to the fire. Ebenezer Thornbird saw Molly Everhart burning in the flames like Joan of Arc tied to a post. The old goat said, "Look you into the flames and observe, peering back at you, love's burning desire." There was a deafening lugubrious laugh followed by a howl that rang as echo's ghost in Eb's ears long after it ended. "What did you see in your flames of passion?" The old man screamed in Eb's face. Eb was close enough that the old man's laugh smelled of death.

"I saw her in the fire and heard her scream!"

"I can remove your suffering! Bring her to me!"

Even though the apparition looked like Molly, there were subtle differences. She was almost a caricature. Her features were slightly off. *Maybe it's the old man's image of her as a younger girl.*

"Well, what do you think of that malicious scene?" the old goat screamed, took one frantic hop and slammed his feet so hard that it caused the ground to rumble.

Ebenezer Thornbird struggled to remain conscious. "I say, fight fire with fire. The fire of the fullness of life and love will destroy your incendiary evil deeds!" Eb opened his pack, extracted his gallon of pure spring water and arose from the log. He stared at the old demon with the intensity of a fire hose which served to extinguish his flames. "Get out of my way!" screamed Ebenezer Thornbird as he pushed the old man behind him, staggered to the fire, poured the water of life on it leaving only a smoldering remnant, and strode toward the well.

****

Back at the van, Molly was buffeted in a frantic hurricane of emotions matching the raging tempest outside. She felt trapped in her metal box, or was it a casket? She had lost audio and video contact and, up until then, she had felt a foreboding; but now her intuition told her that, more than just the equipment failure, there was something else very wrong. Her now enhanced intuitive connection with Eb told her he was in trouble. She just knew it without a doubt. They had that kind of empathy right from the first "hello," but it was magnified now since his liberating push on her back. She was too upset to eat the food she packed, save an occasional bottle of water and half of a sandwich that seemed to taste like fear. She had drifted off into sleep several times too but was startled awake by Thor's hammer. As soon as the thunder diminished, the interminable rain turned into a light mist, and the wind ceased, she grabbed the only pieces of equipment that had been protected in the van from the body crushing rain and sent the hopeful drone aloft as soon as the rain stopped. The water, still above her ankles, she couldn't rest the equipment on the ground, so she placed it on the edge of the van's open sliding door and the drone on the cooler that barely kept it above the lake beneath. Eb hadn't taught her how to use the thing, but she had watched him closely and had absorbed the general idea. She had to practice pitch, yaw, and roll, struggling to keep it steady and, once she had the hang of it, sent it out on an unsteady course over *Hell World* in the direction she reckoned the fire had been. Soon she saw Eb on the monitor staggering toward the well, lifting the cover and the old man was behind him.

****

Ebenezer Thornbird, feeling his head clearing, still unsteady on his feet, dragged himself to the well, lifted the wooden cover and heaved it aside. He looked at the large hole in the Earth, the leftover smoke from the fire, the rope, and the cast aside lid, turned briefly to the old man, "It's over! Stand back!" he heard himself yell at the old man and turned back to the well.

The old man screamed, "No! You don't know what you are doing! You can't do this to me! I'm so close! You don't know what you're going to cause. You're ruining everything!"

"You don't belong here!" Eb screamed over his shoulder as he peered down into the darkness, the origin of the cries for help. The fragrance of flowers followed by the musty dry odor of a New York City alleyway on a hot day arose to his nostrils, and closing his eyes as if that would diminish the stench, he pulled up the rope to liberate whatever was down there. Just as the huge bucket emerged and, about to carefully set it down on the curb of the well, he opened his eyes and saw what he thought was a bird dash past his left ear. He flinched, and the bird was followed by the drone that was headed straight for his face. He saw it just in time to duck and turn aside to dodge the drone. The old man, with murderous rage on his face and fire in his eyes, had been running toward him from behind, intending to push him into the well, but was distracted when the bird flew right into his face at the same moment Eb dodged the drone and stepped to his right. The old man shot past him at full bore with the furry of all his might and fell into the dry cistern instead. Eb thought he felt the breeze of something else shoot past him on his right as if something was following the old demon down the well. He stared into the darkness as a cacophony of yelps, screams, and screeching terror emerged for two minutes followed by a dry silence. A stench arose that was more overpowering than even the smoke that by now had died down to a low-lying fog. Ebenezer Thornbird looked up as the bird landed, perched on the curb of the well, bobbed and nodded, chirped, and flew away. "Live long and prosper little guy," Eb said, as he peered into the dark chasm, shook his head in the attempt to clear it, looked toward the fire pit and noticed that the smoke had receded to a thin trail. By the time he looked into the bucket, it was empty. Its captives had escaped, but Finder detected the damp residue of timid Hope lingering at the bottom.

As he stumbled toward where he had left Molly, he looked down to his right and saw what appeared to be dog tracks that led to and ended at the well. He started to say, "I'll be da...." but stopped abruptly and revised it to, "I'll be darned!" He shifted his gaze, offering a thumbs-up to the drone that responded as if to nod in the affirmative up and down action, then wings tipping left and right. Finder said, *the lost have been returned to their rightful places in town. Healing can begin.*

Ebenezer Thornbird's attention was captured by the sound behind him, a gurgling emanation from deep in the Earth that graduated to a rumble, then a roar. He ran nearly falling with still-staggering steps under the remaining difficult influence of the gasses. He was only fifty yards away from the well when the geyser erupted spewing what Eb hoped was merely water from the well. He was stepping over thousands of flowers on the ground that had replaced the dead birds that had fallen from the sky. The deluge chased him all the way to the border of *Hell World*, and his boots were sloshing through the rising tide bubbling up through the soil until it reached his boot tips. He was slogging through a swamp by the time he stepped out onto the road in front of Molly's van. The air was suddenly cool. The flood water from the rain of Molly's captivity was beginning to mingle with that of the streaming remnants of the diminishing deluge behind him. The invisible force field separating the two worlds had disappeared allowing the tide on Molly's side of reality to surge past the flow from behind Eb upstream into *Hell World* forming a tidal bore.

Eb had no idea how long he had been gone as he staggered back toward the van. He detected the faint sweet smell of spring grass just as he stepped through the invisible, but diminishing barrier between the two worlds, when Molly ran and threw her arms around his neck. "Are you all right? I was so scared for you when we lost contact. There was a terrible storm here that

~ 210 ~   Finder In Hell World   Charles R. Stern

drowned the equipment, but I'm glad the drone worked," she gushed.

"A storm?" He looked around at the remnants of the downpour. His boots were soaked and sloshing through the river flowing beneath his feet. There was silence for an awkward three seconds.

"I think I'm okay except for the drum-line in my head from whatever was burning out there," he said looking at her with a mixture of relief and appreciation. "Thanks for helping with the drone."

The weight of his body began to sag, and she tried to hold him up while, with her help, he staggered to the van and, brushing aside the drone controls, sat down inside the open sliding door. "How long was I gone?" he finally asked.

"Almost three days! I didn't know what to do when the equipment failed. Fortunately, I brought enough to eat for a couple days, but I lost my appetite. I was going to come after you, but I agreed not to no matter what happened." She handed her dehydrated man a bottle of water and a sandwich. "The rain and wind were too strong to fly the drone until an hour and a half ago so I couldn't hear, see, or know your fate until then, but I knew somehow that you were in trouble. So, after I practiced, I flew the drone over that damnable place as soon as the rain let up."

"I'm glad you did! You saved my life." Sandwich in one hand, he hugged her with the other, "Thank you, Molly Everhart."

"I couldn't communicate with you so I could only send the drone toward your face, hoping you'd duck when the old man charged you. But, it looked like a bird flew into his face. I think the drone helped to distract him too, after you ducked out of the way."

"Well, you did great. I can't thank you enough."

She thought, *I would have gone in there after him if the drone hadn't worked,* but she didn't say anything.

He hesitated for ten beats, looked around, and said, "There was rain here?"

"Yes, it was horrendous. It was so sudden and heavy that it knocked me down. When she felt his arms and his voice surrounding her, she realized that he was still her Eb. *He hadn't ended up like the good citizens of Perfection after all!*

"I'm so happy you're okay!" She choked back her tears of relief, but the fear she held inside for days was still there, and her heart was pounding like a bird trying to escape its cage. She sat next to him and hugged his arm with both of hers, but he turned and, freeing his arm from her vice grip, put it around her, pulled her close and kissed her deeply. Having let go of her stranglehold on his arm, she encircled his neck, surrendered to his love, and responded to his kisses in kind. They lay in the van for ten minutes of reconnection holding each other, trembling with a mixture of relief, excitement, and the damp cold before they fell asleep, legs dangling out the van door.

When they awoke, they gathered the equipment and themselves and drove to the motel.

"I think we make a good team," Eb said.

"Good?" Don't you mean EXCELLENT?" They laughed a deep stress-relieving laugh until tears began to drip and their bellies hurt.

"I guess you're right!" Their laughter settled down to a chuckle and then to a smile that reached all the way to their twinkling eyes.

By the way, Molly said, "I just remembered, I had the strangest dream. I saw a grotesquely deformed man standing in a shadowy corner. He seemed to be asking for my help."

"I had the same dream a few years ago! Well, it was more of a vision than a dream. It was when I was working in the West Virginia coal mines. I don't know what it means. Maybe it has something to do with what we're doing out here."

Driving through town, the streets were empty even though most people should have been at work or busy performing the tasks of the day. Arriving at their destination, Molly closed the door and embraced Eb and boldly kissed him more deeply than either of them had ever felt in their lives. Kissing with a connection that lasted for a century in that three minutes of intensity surprising her for her boldness, trying to make up for their three days of harrowing separation. Reading each other's minds, they helped one another strip off the soggy, muddy remnants of *Hell World*, entered the shower, washed themselves and each other with copious amounts of soap, scrubbing away what seemed like a decade of evil stench and sweat that clogged their pores. He dried her off and tasted her longing breasts, the milk of human kindness, the nipples of love and desire. Her dilated eyes peered up at him wanting to take all of him inside her. He looked her in the eye as they silently pulled back the bedcovers of reality and fell into a deep, intense and intimate sexual embrace. Moving slowly at first, savoring it like inchworms and gradually accelerating into the synchronous ecstatic undulations of thoroughbred race horses straining for the finish line. The raw desire that had been held back breached the dam that had built up over the decades of the past week and flooded the bed with love. All of Molly's sexual fantasies were dredged up from her novels, concentrated and then surpassed, in that moment of toe-curling, back-arching ecstasy that accelerated beyond the depths of which she had ever imagined possible. None of her novels prepared her for this nor had her practice sessions! Spent, their intertwined bodies were about to fall slowly into a satisfied slumber, "You are so beautiful," Eb whispered to the top of Molly's sleeping head.

She said, "You're just saying that!"

"I thought you were asleep," he smiled.

She looked up at him and said, "I'm glad you're a blind man."

"I'm glad your hearing is so good." He looked her in the eye and said, "Like a Lotus, your beauty rises above the roots of reality, and its blossoms reflect the elegance within."

"Who said that?"

He looked her in the eye and with the total sincerity of a straight man and said," 'I did! Just now. Pretty good huh?"

She laughed, "You're a terrible poet! Don't quit your day job. Oh, wait! You don't have a day job. Rumor has it that you're just an unemployed drifter!" They laughed themselves back into a deep embrace. He fondled her breasts while their kisses deepened along with their mutual trust and desire to give pleasure and ecstasy. His hand migrated to her thighs, and slowly, very slowly, he found her clitoris and felt her body respond with an intense orgasm that dominated her entire body. She reached for his hard self, was excited beyond possibility, and guided him to her vaginal opening wanting to swallow every bit of him. Her heart was about to burst when he entered her. She swooned, and he felt her surrender to her need, the need to be filled, taken and, simultaneously, fulfilled by giving to him. She felt his arousal increase and that caused her excitement to escalate to new peaks beyond her wildest dreams. She couldn't help her crooning utterances, and she didn't try to hold them back. This was bliss built on trust and true intimacy along with a mutual desire for each other's happiness and, of course, carnal pleasure. For a while, they were both weightless in the stratosphere above the plane of existence beyond mere love; beyond words to describe what even surpassed simple experience. There was neither space nor time. There was nothing in the multiverse but the confluence of two imerging into a single body and soul.

When the wondrous storm finally passed, and their bodies washed ashore on the raft of exhaustion, and after a three-minute breath-catching pause, he said, "I think I'm in your dream, and you are in mine." She smiled and nuzzled his neck before they fell into a satisfied, well deserved, and rejuvenating deep slumber.

CHAPTER SEVENTEEN
CONSEQUENCES

The next day, when she awoke, Molly hugged and kissed Eb who responded with a smile that rivaled hers. She took her video recordings from the drone to the town newspaper, *The Perfection,* the headlines of which later proclaimed the *LIBERATION of HELL WORLD!* The front page named Ebenezer Thornbird and Molly Everhart as the heroes who had perpetrated the miracle. The editor, the paper's only reporter, was shown the recording from the drone's camera. A fuzzy picture of what looked like it might be the deformed old man who called himself Maara "The Collector" trying to push Ebenezer Thornbird, the Finder, into the well, only to be swallowed up by it instead. He, therefore, confirmed that the nightmares of the kids who went in there were not dreams, but actual memories. It was now clearly seen on the video screen when the stop-action was used, that there had been someone out there affecting the youth with enticements and noxious gasses. In addition, there appeared to be an animal, possibly a dog, but it was mostly just a blurry streak. Despite the light of the full moon, the image wasn't clear due to the dark conditions and the speed of the thing that flashed by Eb and down into the well. The sub-heading read, FINDER DEFEATS COLLECTOR IN BATTLE TO FREE PERFECTION! The newspaper article was accompanied by a quarter page size picture of Eb and Molly standing next to the *Hell World* rock. It revealed that Ebenezer Thornbird, the ostensible journalist, was really a "Finder" who had sensed something missing in Perfection and, with the assistance of their own Molly Everhart, braved *Hell World* to set it free. Molly probably revealed too much in her well-meaning, but guileless way, however, everything seemed to be going well for a few days, but only for a few.

****

The lost collectibles had been set free from the deep well of incarceration and took joyous flight straight toward their original benefactors in town. The video feed from the drone captured something that looked like a purplish stream of slithering currents escaping from the bucket Eb had pulled up from the well and was racing toward the town. The article declared, "Now Perfection will be more perfect than ever!"

Surprised, the good citizens of Perfection awoke transformed. Experiencing such a devastating hangover, they felt paralyzed; nailed to their beds for three days. The dawn of emotions and the accompanying passions, missing from their souls since adolescence, began to peek through the clouds of memory. They experienced the wet plague of zits, confusion, self-doubt, hormone-driven lust, and angst. They laughed, cried, made love, and experienced themselves, and life in general, deeply for the first time since childhood. They became lost in a simultaneous tsunami of wet emotions and sensations that swung from the ecstasy of love and passion to anger followed by the devastating doldrums and stagnation of sleepy despair. The floodgates were thrown open with a vengeance, and the town was swept away in a deluge of fire and ice in such mythic proportions that they were left without the resources to handle it. They became aware that their nightmares of demons in *Hell World* were terrifying memories, and the shock of this realization created a post-traumatic stress reaction that added to the overwhelming flood from the return of adolescent emotion, anxiety, and confusion.

Couples awoke next to their spouses, who suddenly seemed like strangers, wondered how they ever got together in the first place and found themselves attracted to other people's spouses, boyfriends, and girlfriends. Jacob Renfrew was startled when he awoke, turned over in bed, suddenly face-to-face with his wife of twelve years and blurted out, "Who the hell is that!?" realizing that he had never really looked at her or even thought about who she was all those years. Startled, his wife awoke just as shocked as he was. "What the…" It was as if awakening in bed with a stranger after the blackout following a drunken stupor. Couples began to have horrific arguments, and some escalated into third-degree physical fights that landed several people in the hospital ER and others in jail, neither of which could handle the onslaught of victims and perpetrators. This was followed by devastating torrents of guilt and remorse. Debauchery was rampant, and adults were acting out long-repressed pranks, some of which were dangerous, followed by heart ripping guilt and shame. It seemed as if every emotion was exaggerated and expressed in the form of intense, deep-seated passion.

Ellen Jaden flirted with her neighbor, Flint Embers. Both had spouses, but passion gripped them, and they began secret rendezvous at the motel. They began having explosive arguments with their respective spouses and secretly met in deep sexual embrace every day until they espied their spouses emerging from different rooms in the same motel. Unrequited and hitherto unconscious libido erupted with volcanic force throughout the town. Unbridled alternations between lovemaking and murderous rage were typical, but there were no normal adults to exert external controls on the town that had been converted overnight from the dryness of autism to wet emotional waves of manic adolescent behavior. They oscillated between the experience of drowning in the deep troughs of shame and depression and dizzying heights of elation. Even the sheriff was too lenient or too brutal depending upon the whim of whether he was having a good day or a bad one, and they were all bad now. Minor riots broke out as did drunken brawls in a previously peaceful and tea-totaling town where the only drinking had been a single glass of wine with meals. No one could hold their liquor, and the sidewalk was a veritable vomitorium. Some citizens soon turned to hard drugs. Their attempt to extinguish the newly experienced emotional growing pains of belated adolescence. The nightmare of unfettered behavior fueled by the stench of uninhibited passion tore apart the previously well-ordered social system and infected it with chaos and anarchy. Rationality was at war with emotional passion and strong positive emotions with their negative counterparts, as were chaos versus control. Optimism never dared to step out in the open, fearing destruction, but instead hid from the overwhelming tumult.

The world and time were suddenly spinning backward. Everyone was dizzy and confused. The fallout from the accumulated debris from nearly five decades of circumspection was scattered throughout the town that could no longer pretend to be perfect. The return of the adolescent deluge thoroughly routed rational thought and was more addlepated than the mere onset of puberty. It made the ungoverned and delinquent juvenility of the *Lord of the Flies* look like a carnival, sans the wild boar's head on a stick.

Only Molly Everhart, Ebenezer Thornbird and, surprisingly, Junior Ketchum held enough insight that they could see what had been wrought by the liberation of the captives. Junior Ketchum had entered the *Hell World* rite of passage in early adolescence, but he came out unchanged. Apparently, he had nothing worth collecting. According to Molly, "Junior was an odd child, always more interested in machines and inanimate objects and to some extent with animals, rather than in personal relationships. In elementary school," she recounted, "he could always be found sitting by himself in the corner of the room in his own world, playing with the toys or constructing something out of anything he could use within reach." She giggled a little, "One time," she recounted, "he harnessed a cockroach to a tiny wagon he constructed out of paperclips, string, and odd scraps of construction paper. It was pretty impressive, but the teacher was not amused. It was rather sad because he sat for the longest time staring at the dark, disgusting spot she left on the floor after she squashed the roach and banished the rig to the round file."

Normal adolescence, Molly and Eb realized, was filled with peaks and troughs; waves of emotion. However, normal development was typically overseen by adults who loaned their own values and ego constraints to the kids as if they were at least somewhat effective governors on the raging engines of teenage hormones. At the very least, emotionally stable adults would have provided diversions from the overflowing cauldrons of the "double, double, toil and trouble" that drives budding youth. Teenage rebellion exploded into all-out war, but with the ferocity of nostalgic adults. However, Eb... Finder... realized that there was something else going on. There had been a kind of artificially induced autism that had been reversed. It was as if a blind person had become instantly sighted, literally overnight. The citizens of Perfection had regained the ability to connect with their fellow human beings, but this, it seemed, also exacerbated the intensity of the return of adolescent rebellion, chaos, and insecurity.

Eb and Molly felt responsible to do something to save this wretched town, but they were at a loss for a solution. Eb was haunted by the town crying in agony and begging for relief. Molly tried to elicit the assistance of the Sheriff, but Buck was too caught up in his own problems. He was playing cop rather than being a cop, and his version of the game was the brutal one seen in movies in which the local constabulary take baseball bats to the criminals, but the entire town was criminal since they were, to a person, breaking laws and moral codes right and left.

It was especially difficult for Molly when she realized that her parents, after being cold and distant all her life, were suddenly too warm, too caring, and too expressive to the extent that she felt the need to get away from them before she was asphyxiated under their overzealous and smothering helicopter love. It was as though they were ill-prepared teenaged parents with a small helpless child. They doted on her, and she chafed at the thick and very heavy sickeningly sweet molasses of their controlling oversight. It was even more shocking to her when she was awakened one night by the sounds of intense sexual activity emanating from her parents' bedroom. She tried to put the pillow over her head in an attempt to eject it from her mind to no avail since the ruckus was louder than her bed could endure. She realized the next day, that her mother and father had been close as children and that they were simply picking up their adolescent lust where they had dropped it over thirty years ago. However, as much as she understood it, she was repulsed by the thought of her parents as sexual beings, let alone enjoying it with such gusto.

The Sheriff was, Molly remembered, a little bully as an elementary school child, terrorizing the other kids, especially the younger ones. By middle school, however, he had changed, and in high school won the student council election for the misunderstood position of "sergeant at arms" on his campaign of being "tough on crime," despite the fact that it was really a powerless, symbolic, and purely parliamentary role. His parents had treated him as though he didn't exist and he seemed determined to be noticed by any means he could find, and by everyone whose attention he could attract. But this drive continued to plague him like the inertia of movement after his stint in *Hell World,* compelling him forward long after there was no emotional force behind it. He was a pretend cop. A caricature copying the actors in the movies. Like everyone else in Perfection, he became motivated by the allure of the power to control things and other people, so the position of constable served him well, but now he was the bully he was in grade school but with the adult authority of the law behind him.

J.C. was still demented, but there was an anxious tremor to his demeanor now and Elise, his adoptive granddaughter, started yelling at him for doing things he couldn't help due to his dementia. He became distraught and withdrawn, and his confusion and disorientation escalated.

Old Bill, who quietly sat in the back of the coffee shop every morning drinking his 'usual,' was suddenly given to fits of complaining. The coffee was too hot, the coffee was too cold, and he disagreed with just about everything anyone said no matter their point of view. After so many years of silently observing everyone's flaws, he began to point them out and was so intrusively demanding, that the townsfolk became irritated to the extent that some of them threatened to attack him physically until he became frightened and ran away.

Gert and Kurt Johnson still owned most of the town in their perpetual game of Monopoly. Now, however, they oscillated between Scylla, the rock of giving large sums of money to charity and Charybdis, the whirlpool of angry outbursts toward anyone who was below their social and economic status.

The shopkeepers started raising and lowering prices seemingly at random, and they became dissatisfied with their own merchandise. They had huge sales that nearly no one bothered with because many of customers rudely stated their preferences for up-to-date styles and started to order their items online and from catalogs. However, when they raised the prices unreasonably, their sales increased. Apparently, if it costs more, it must be the best, and therefore, worth more. It seemed as if the previous obsession with comparison shopping had become too time-consuming.

Eddie Renfield awoke drooling, sitting in the middle of the street in a marsh of his own waste, cars dodging around him, when

Sheriff Buck pulled up with the red gumball machine flashing atop the cruiser and blocked the traffic from running him over. The Sheriff stepped out of his sacred chariot and walked over to the young man. Eddie looked like he had been stunned by a Taser or something just as powerful and lost control of every physical and mental function. When the constable stepped out of the patrol car, he left the driver's door open as he walked with a bowlegged swagger toward the unfortunate young man. Apparently, his rash hadn't improved. "What's the matter, Eddie?" He inquired with an uncharacteristic expression of empathy.

"I don't know." Eddie was looking down at his body, lifting his hands in front of his eyes and said, "What the...?"

Sheriff Buck asked, "What's wrong Eddie? Are you hurt?"

Eddie's glazed and dilated eyes squinted up at the Sheriff with a look of deep bewilderment and said, "Is that you, Buck?" Eddie was shocked, "You're all grown up!"

The officer stood trying to clear the cobwebs of confusion that were filling his head. "Of course I'm grown up Eddie, and you are too!" Eddie looked himself over again and, after the two-way silence that settled like a low-lying fog in the timeless dead space between them, the Sheriff asked, "Where's Jake Eddie?" while he thought, *if he's running loose. I hope that mutt hasn't hurt anyone or eaten them, for that matter.*

Eddie was stunned for a full thirty seconds, a look of misperception creeping over his face, glancing around apparently seeking an answer from the surroundings. "Who the hell is Jake?" Eddie slugged out with a puzzled look of incomprehension.

"Your dog. Jake."

A look of amazement shot through his face. "What dog?" He looked down at himself, raised his hands in front of his face again and said, "But I'm only twelve...I don't have a dog."

The Sheriff stepped back, slipped on some vomit, stumbled over some debris in the road, and nearly fell into the slime. "Twelve? What the hell?" He took three slippery steps forward, gripped Eddie's arm, lifted him up and, after placing a newspaper to protect the seat from the mess, stuffed him into the squad car. "Riot victim found in the street. Taking him to the hospital in Orson," he reported into his microphone to no one but the dead air and drove off.

Almost as soon as Sheriff Buck returned from Orson, the fiftyish Countess, Queen Lilith, whom Eb met earlier, was overwhelmed with a frenzied attack of mania that nearly killed her. She threw off her clothes and ran *flop, flop, flopping* down the street brandishing her umbrella as if it were a sword, yelling something unintelligible. She was stopped only when the Sheriff and five strong men corralled and subdued her. They swaddled her in a king-sized bed sheet as if it were a strait jacket that had been happily provided by the disgusted owner of the Textile Emporium. Of course, it was the least expensive item in the store for which, naturally, she would receive the bill. Once they sequestered her in the back of the squad car, the Sheriff said, "Captured runaway psychotic female. Taking her to the hospital" into his microphone to the phantom dispatcher. As he drove away, a fierce fight broke out between two men who had no clue why they were engaged in combat, but they were seriously intent on it.

Alice Dinglemunger, a prominent citizen, heretofore considered to have the perfect marriage, let loose the floodgates of pent-up complaints and invectives that rushed headlong and nonstop for three days toward her husband. Her harangue streamed out the windows and doors, down the street, past three houses, and across the intersection. Even at that distance, it was still loud enough for Mr. Eggsworth, the proprietor, ensconced in his convenience store and gas station, to make out every word of the diatribe. She cried, moaned, gnashed and ground her teeth like a captive tigress in the cage at the zoo, gnawing on the bones of the sloth that she accused her husband of being. She expounded on how he had grown old and useless before his time and, she might add, had become a poor example to their children! "How," she asked, with loud rhetorical gusto, "could you justify sitting around the house in your underpants and slippers whilst I tore my nails that, by the way, are ruined, working my fingers to the bone? I have worn myself out, bruised, burned and scraped all over my entire body doing the laundry, cooking your dinners and fixing every little thing that went bust around the house. Besides, I have transported, like a bus driver, the children to their ballet and soccer practices and games as well as kid's birthday parties all alone! I have taken care of you and *your* brats all their lives, never pursuing a post-high school education, never having a job outside of my home, performing my wifely duties whenever required, and all without a complaint." She was lost in a world of imposed ignorance, fear, and loneliness. She had trundled down the tracks on a predetermined route through the stations of life until the train derailed and the tracks were taken up before she had any idea how to steer this racing locomotive! "Oh! And, don't forget, I have taken all the insulting invectives and pontifical edicts targeting me from your parents who 'tried and tried to teach me' (she made the most violent air quotes in the history of mankind) how to raise the children, cook, care, for the house and, most importantly, how to pamper their selfish, wimpy, lazy, and worthless son. Not to mention your insensitivity. And by the way, you have never, never mind you, defended me!" She ran out of breath and took a moment to perform the longest and deepest inhale humanly possible.

There was a collective sigh of relief when the neighborhood thought the quiet moment that erupted meant the storm had passed, but it soon became clear that it was merely the eye of the hurricane and she was merely catching her breath. She unexpectedly started up all over again about all the stupid boring business award dinners she had to sit through where, she pointed out like a razor aimed at his genitals and cutting his self-esteem to the quick, he had "never, never you understand, received even honorable mention for perfect attendance!" She even threw in the weight of religion. She said, "When you die, and I hope it will be sooner rather than later, I will shit on your grave. Someday in the distant future, I will, with a smiling gaze look down upon you from my perch atop a cloud of God's grace while you suffer the humiliations of Hell. I shall laugh at the sight of you in a headstand with your melon buried in the crap you have expelled on the world during your meager existence on this Earth! "And," she couldn't help adding, "Watch you rot in it for eternity!"

As previously mentioned, this vicious attack went on nonstop for two more days and, although one would expect the epithets to diminish over time, she was just getting started, and in fact, escalated to the heights of vulgarity that would have embarrassed a sociopath, for another day. But, there is not enough space here, dear reader, or maybe not enough paper, or even enough trees to manufacture the sheets, in order to chronicle it all. For the entire time, there were no birds, dogs or any animal seen or heard anywhere in the town. Suffice it to say that by the end of a three-day spectacle her husband was so demoralized and disoriented that he forgot to put on his pants when he left for work on Monday. The Koto drummers were banging away inside his skull serving as the backbeat for his wife's incessant and explosive missiles hurled at him from every corner of the house. For there was no escape from her scorn. He was allowed no respite even in the privy where she would stand just outside shouting laser-like bombs of derision at him through the door where the only benefit he received was the fact that it cured his constipation and scared him shitless. When he left for work, pant-less that Monday, he discovered, thanks to the sudden impact of the vinyl car seat, that there was a humiliating lack of closure below his waist and reluctantly returned to his inflamed bride of twelve years to retrieve his slacks. He found her crying and wrung-out flaccid and limp because the spring of her fury had finally run down. But both of their nervous systems, like alarm clocks that wouldn't stop buzzing, were still vibrating so strongly that he grabbed her up in his arms, against no resistance and took her to bed for the energized makeup sex of jack rabbits for two more hours until they exceeded their surprising physical and emotional capacity. They lay limp and totally spent in a pool of flaccidity. It took two days to recover until the cycle of war, punctuated with truces and sexual reconciliation began again. They were caught in a kind of weird cycle of solidarity in the ups and downs of their combativeness alternating with the relief of sexual passion. They oscillated between the intense connection offered by love and the negative attachment of their mutual hate.

There was an outbreak of similar, but somewhat less intense episodes in town. Sometimes it was the husband or boyfriend who claimed to be the wounded party, and some couples alternated roles between offender and offended, but with the same basic pattern of the verbally abusive mental tennis match of lobbing balls of explosive accusatory energy back and forth with some cheating and foul play mixed in. This was often followed by the tension relieving compromise of lovemaking. There were plenty of others, however, who did not play this exhausting mind wrenching game, but instead, simply packed up and moved in with their new lover, their extended family, or to the home of a friend.

The tumult escalated to the point that there were unconscious men in the streets bloodied by fistfights, and one was the victim of a gunshot that, thankfully, was not fatal. Eb saw a woman, mad with grief, kneeling next to her seriously injured husband, hands grasping her hair, straining so much that the veins and sinews were distended on her neck. Her mouth was impossibly open wider than any human was capable and her eyes were red saucers of fear, rage, and grief. Her head jutted forward in silent open-mouthed screams that remained knotted in her throat, trying unsuccessfully to disgorge her sorrow. Her blood-flushed face was strained and paralyzed while chaos rained down around her and throughout the unsuspecting town.

An emergency session of the town council of five members met for the unprecedented second time that month. This time, one hundred sixty-three citizens attended, eighty-one of whom were exercised over Ebenezer Thornbird's interference who, they believed, brought chaos to the illusion that their beloved Perfection had been perfect. But eighty-two of those good Citizens present were pleased with their new-found freedom and wanted to give him a medal and rename the town Zanesville in a sudden fit of nostalgia. The issue was tabled, and the council adjourned, not for the lack of a majority, but to escape the violence that had erupted in the streets and was leaking into the town hall. Several uncontrolled individuals stormed the place with absolutely no purpose in mind, or so it appeared, except to create mayhem for their own amusement. Windows were smashed, and chairs and tables were overturned before the building was secured when one of the councilmen emptied the place by yelling, "Free drinks at the bar!" There was no bar in the previously tee-totaling town. The general store was the only place to purchase alcoholic beverages, and they had difficulty keeping up with the current demand. The relieved doors were closed and locked the instant the last of the rioters exited the facility and the council members along with the attendees slinked out the rear exit unaware that in a back room there was a couple engaging in unsanctioned sexual activity for which no vote had been taken.

Vigilante groups sprang up, some of which wanted to run Ebenezer Thornbird out of town tarred and feathered on a rail, while others were so enraged that they wanted to execute him. "Hanging is too good for that S.O.B!" one man was overheard to say. A third group wanted to protect their hero. However, all of these groups, essentially overgrown teenage gangs, having no effective leadership, turned on each other, and a minor civil war broke out. There were fistfights, screaming matches, and in the tragic case of one elected council member, an aggravated heart attack that stymied the citizen council meetings because it now had a fifty-fifty split in voting attendance adding to the total lack of order. They focused so much attention on their emotions and energy fighting against each other that they no longer paid much attention to Finder.

One night, Sheriff Buck's wife, Caroline, awoke to a loud racket. Buck's side of the bed was empty. Fear rose in her heart and, leaping out of bed, she ran to the living room and found him in a state of naked somnambulism tearing drawers apart, raving, and running around the house. He was throwing things around in a frantic search making such a racket that Caroline had to duck twice to dodge the missiles flying past her head. She yelled, "Buck! What in hell are you doing?" but it wasn't long before she realized he was asleep.

He yelled, "Where's my gun? Where's my gun?" stumbling around waving his arms in his somnambulistic frenzy.

She said, "What do you need with your gun right now Buck?" She spied his gun on the kitchen table, but he didn't notice it before she hid it in the cabinet under the sink.

"I want to shoot somebody!" he growled.

He was ranting and raving until his wife took him gently but firmly by the arm, ducked a random swing in her general direction and led him back to bed saying, "You already shot everybody. Now it's time for bed."

He ceased struggling, stopped in his tracks, his face doubling nearly in half, looking like an old worn out catcher's mitt, let out a disappointed sounding, "Oh," and shrugged his shoulders in reluctant resignation.

The scales of the world had tipped toward chaos on a teeter-totter that oscillated between war and compassion, stoic rationality and unbridled sensuality.

Ebenezer Thornbird hid for a while after a near miss with a crowd in search of revenge and, thinking the sheriff was going to be looking for him as well, he took a different room at the motel in the hope that no one would find him there. Maybe they would think he left town. It was good fortune that the owner was one of those people who were happy with their new lot in life since his room renting business had increased exponentially due to clandestine debauchery, not to mention his own, so he was willing to help. Eb feared for his life and that of Molly's by association and wanted the rancor to die down to at least a low rumble before he tried to step out in the open. He had walked out of the coffee shop one day, and a rock flew past his left ear. The missile was large enough to have caused serious damage if the hurler of the rock was sober, and had better aim. Shortly after that close call, he saw a mini-mob of five men approaching with various manual weapons such as wrenches and clubs torn from unfortunate trees. There was no doubt that they were looking for him. They reminded him of the *Frankenstein* movie where the townsfolk were looking for the monster with torches and pitchforks. He ducked down a side street and into an unlocked door of the millinery shop where he hid until the coast was clear. Thereafter, he laid low. It wasn't easy to search for a solution to the problem when the only time it was relatively safe to be out on the town was well after dark.

The Librarian, Ms. Jacquelyn Oddmeyer, let down her hair from its traditional bun, unbuttoned her blouse to show her cleavage, hiked up her skirt, put on excessive makeup, screamed, "I quit!" threw her pen and keys across the room, and headed out of town so fast that the Sheriff stopped her for speeding. Tearing up the ticket, he broke the sacrosanct littering law, and after a three-minute discussion, blasting her new found sexuality at him, they checked into the motel room previously occupied by Ebenezer Thornbird (a joke of the owner) for some extracurricular activity, leaving the town to fend for itself for six hours during four overly excited couplings of the two sexually deprived individuals. They tried every kinky thing they could think of for the first time in either of their lives. Once satiated, the sheriff happily returned to his duties, and Ms. Oddmeyer sped out of town, disheveled and sporting a grin that was too wide for her face. Her windows were open to dissipate the steam, and *Footloose* blasted on the radio so loud it covered up her off-key singing. *Footloose! Footloose! Kick off your Sunday shoes...*

CHAPTER EIGHTEEN
THE PHILOSOPHER'S STONE

Finder began to hear something else in Perfection begging to be found. It was difficult to hear through the din of the unfettered emotions scattered about in the chaos of the mob, but when he listened more closely, at three o'clock in the morning when most of the uproar and exhausted, emotional mayhem was asleep, the quiet pleading cries and whispers came through more clearly. There were only the lingering silent phantoms of the past that Finder sensed, and no one else could see, but they weren't looking for him. Feeling compelled to find the source of the faint, but indistinct longing, Ebenezer Thornbird searched the town in the early morning light of dawn while Finder listened to the signals until they congealed into a direction. He had to stop every few steps to make sure his footfalls didn't mask the barely detectable whispering voice of the lost. He had to follow the beckoning step-by-step as if he were a bloodhound until he found its source. After days of tracking the distant quiet, but desperate signal, and many blind alleys, he found himself standing before the rock of *Hell World*. He climbed up on it, and sitting there for two days, looking like a giant bird on a huge sacred egg, deciphering its message, trying to hatch a plan. The message was simmering but faint, a psychic steam that constantly arose, filling the air with a sweet but unidentifiable perfume. He examined the rock with his hands trying to locate something stirring inside and, frustrated, he climbed down, his back facing away from the rock as he slid down and sat on the ground listening for hours. He reckoned that the signal was so faint because it was muffled in some way. *It seems to be buried inside this monolith.* It seemed ancient as if a very old one was desperately trying to penetrate the present time and space.

****

Molly Everhart wondered what happened to Eb and came up empty handed when she searched the town. He wasn't in his motel room. In fact, she arrived there just in time to see Sheriff Buck tucking in his shirt around his utility belt followed by a somewhat disheveled Jacqueline Oddmeyer straightening her clothes and smoothing her hair, exiting Eb's old room. *What the...?* In order to protect her, Eb hadn't told her where he was in case someone tried to get her to inform on him. He trusted her completely, but the way things were going, he couldn't be certain that some vigilante group wouldn't stoop to kidnapping and torture. She found herself back on the streetcar named despair heading for the event horizon of a black hole that had nearly swallowed her up since seventh grade. Discouraging and disappointing thoughts assailed her, *has Eb fled after feeling responsible for causing the reigning chaos?* She felt partly responsible for it too, and there was the rejection she felt from many of the townsfolk who thought she had been duped by this stranger and, although she was held responsible, neighbors did not blame her to the degree they did Ebenezer Thornbird. At least, no one was trying to murder her. Not yet anyway. She made herself scarce while she did her best to secretly search for Eb whenever the opportunity arose, but felt discouraged by her lack of success and panic arose like a rocket blasting off from the Cape. She knew that there were vigilante groups roaming about looking for him, as was the Sheriff. But the Sheriff had his hands full with the chaos and had little time to look for Finder. Certain that she had lost Eb, she tried to keep working at the *Wake-Up! Coffee Shop*, but she couldn't concentrate on her jealous and disappointed Java machines.

Following two days of confusion, worry, and despair, Junior Ketchum sauntered into the shop and asked, "What's Mr. Thornbird doing out at the *Hell World* rock? I passed him this morning when I drove by in Lizzie." Molly's eyes became saucers of excitement, and her jaw dropped so low that Junior had to look away when he could see her uvula at the back of her throat. She hugged and kissed him, he flinched. Running out the door, she forgot to throw off her apron, jumped into her tin can on wheels, and drove to the rock.

Eb, prompted by Finder, thought back and saw some fateful connections.

****

Does my name, Thornbird, connect me to this place? My attraction to Molly certainly did. Apollyon Zane was connected to Jay Thornbird, the Medicine Man who he hired to place the protective curse on Hell World for him. Adam Thornbird, a descendant of Jay Thornbird, disappeared out East, and probably was my grandfather. J.C.'s name is Jesus, probably John Crow's illegitimate great-grandson and possibly my father, but I'll never know that for certain due to J.C.'s advanced dementia; another possible connection. Molly's family was connected to the Zane's through her mother, and her nanny was Artemis, a descendant of Jay Thornbird through Billy Thornbird. And what about my ring/amulet that allegedly was blessed by my ancestor Medicine Man? Was that Jay Thornbird? Am I the descendant of two powerful Medicine Men? Am I caught in the circle of fate, Parcae, my nanny, has foretold? Is it our fate that Molly and I were to meet and am I the nexus of the Thornbird and Crow lines? Molly's nanny was a Thornbird!

****

Rushing out of town, shuttering to a screeching halt at the rock of *Hell World* in her rattletrap, Molly was alarmed to see Eb on the ground leaning against the monolith. Hoping he was merely asleep, she offered a gentle shake to awaken him while calling his name, "Eb, Eb? What are you doing? What's going on? Wake up!" She was frantic.

He opened his dazed eyes. "I'm not asleep, I'm listening."

"Listening? Listening to what?"

"I'm listening to the rock."

"The rock? What are you hearing?"

"I'm not certain yet, but I had a dream earlier that may be an omen for the direction we need to take."

"What's that?" She said, while wondering, *has he finally gone mad? First a talking town and now a talking rock!*

"Well... I dreamt that that phantom I saw in the coal mine, possibly the one in your dream," said to me, 'You are the liberator, but there's more to do.' I think there was something left behind that still needs to be found for the social fabric and sanity of this town, and it is here, somewhere nearby. It was too faint to detect before underneath the cacophony of what was out in *Hell World*."

"But what does this rock have to do with it?"

"I'm not exactly certain yet, but I'm quite sure this rock is involved. I'm picking something up from it, but it's still too faint and vague. It has remained here unchanged throughout time with the exception of the painted sign. Even though it's the same rock as before, in the same position, there seems to be a change in it, subtle, but a change. Something seems to be emerging from it, making me think that's what is still begging to be freed, and I think it's the solution. I think it might be trapped inside the rock...."

"Okay, but what do we need to do?" Molly asked. He welcomed the help of her intuition and was pleased that she included herself in his quest for the solution.

"I'm still working that out."

Walking thoughtfully around the rock examining it, she suddenly stopped, knelt down, and brushed away some thick, foreboding weeds that served as camouflage. "Look." She said, "Eb, come here!"

He slowly arose, stiff from his crouch, rounded the monolith, and Molly pointed to a petroglyph carved into the back of the rock near the bottom where she had cleared some weeds away. It was in the form of an etched Native American arrowhead that pointed to the ground resembling the one on the talisman he gave her. Eb thought for a minute before he said, "What do you make of that?"

She was hunkered down on her haunches examining the sign with her newly improved sixth sense. "It looks like there's probably something buried under here."

There was a three minute and nine-second pause while the Earth seemed to wobble, and the awakening energy of Finder, the sleeping giant deep in his gut, told Eb he felt the rock smile. Eb said, "That's what Finder thinks too!" Molly grinned with delight and surprise as Eb and Finder pulled her to him and embraced her in a near death gripping hug. He thought for the length of time it took a squirrel, holding a nut in its mouth that it had recently disinterred, to cross the road unseen behind them, "I think I saw some heavy construction vehicles in the yard behind the government buildings."

"Yes, they're used for repairing the streets and snow removal in the winter," Molly replied.

"Can we gain access to them?"

Maybe," she thought for a moment, "Junior Ketchum drives those things for a living. Maybe he'd help."

Eb asked, "Do you know how we can find him? We need to move this boulder."

"Yeah, he drives around town in Lizzie, his VW, most days."

They snuck into town and hid in the coffee shop watching the expectant road in that early cloudless and unseasonably warm morning. Eb ran across the street into the hardware for ten minutes and returned. He hid in the stall in the men's room whenever a customer came in, but it was early enough that most of those seeking coffee paid for their beverage as takeout. Old Bill had already gone home. They waited an hour and fifty-one minutes before they heard the chugging of Junior Ketchum's Lizzie laboring along. "Here he comes!" Molly said as she got up and ran out the door to flag down the bug. Startled, Junior swerved, hit the brakes, and ended up stalled across the wrong side of the street. He had to open the driver's door since Lizzie's window was stuck and still needed fixing. Eb watched as she leaned in, said something to him and backed off while Lizzie pulled to the curb in front of the shop, the driver emerged, and he accompanied Molly to the *Wake-Up! Coffee Shop*. "Junior Ketchum, this is Ebenezer Thornbird, Eb, Junior."

Eb reached out to shake hands but felt reluctance in Junior's hesitant handshake. "Mr. Thornbird," he said with a tone of uncertainty. It wasn't as if he had any animosity toward Eb, but rather, Finder surmised, he did not like to be touched. Eb motioned his potential co-conspirator to the seat opposite him in the booth and Molly slid in next to Eb. Everyone leaned in with their elbows on the conspiratorial table in a clandestine Mission Impossible moment, and Eb said, "Junior, can I call you Junior?"

Junior Ketchum hesitated, nodded and said, "Sure."

Eb said, "Great, thanks. Please call me Eb." There was a moment of mutual sizing up to see if the measurements made a good fit before Eb began the secret, barely audible negotiations, "We don't like what's going on and I can see that you don't either."

Junior cut in, "I heard that it's your fault. I saw the two articles in the paper. The first one said you were a hero and the second one blamed you for all this trouble. I guess now you're the goat." Ebenezer Thornbird grimaced, but Junior's countenance wasn't angry or even irritated, just a simple, matter-of-fact monotone.

Sitting back for three quick breaths, Eb tried to decide his next move with this very concrete thinker who only speaks when he has something to say. Finder said, *Junior doesn't like change or disruption and wants it fixed as quickly as possible, and the chaos around him is driving him mad, but he blames us for it. We need to persuade him to come over to our side. We have to allay his anxiety. He needs a solution.* Then Eb's mouth began before his conscious self could catch up, "Junior, I think we can agree that no one likes what's going on here. It's certainly upsetting. I'll admit that we righted a long-time wrong, but it was only a partial victory. Now we know the consequences, and I think I know how we can *fix* it!" Eb emphasized the word "fix" to engage Junior's apparent mechanical mission in life.

Junior's attention was piqued, and he thought for one second before he spoke, "What makes you think that you can fix it when you caused it in the first place?"

Eb spoke carefully and slowly with as much sincerity as he could muster, "Well, Junior," he said, "*you* can fix it with our help. Besides, it can't hurt to try, and we can't do it without you. I believe we corrected only a part of the problem, and the rest is up to you."

Junior sat back, his wheels turning, trying the wrap his gearhead brain around the idea. "Well," he finally said, "I see your point, but how can *I* fix it?"

Molly said, "We'd like to take advantage of your expert skills. You're the only one who can do this part to repair the damage and prevent it from getting worse." Her firm expression didn't leave any room for resistance, the way some women have of getting their way with men while making it appear it is the only possible choice, and the man involved ends up being the hero of the story. Besides, she was one of the few people in town who spoke to him like a human being. During the silence that followed, extending for the eighty-eight-day year it takes the planet Mercury to orbit the Sun in that twenty seconds, Molly Everhart and Ebenezer Thornbird felt the tension fueling the machinery of Junior Ketchum's brain, shifting into drive, speeding forward, and considering the only option Molly had left open. He was caught in the presumptive bind; accept the unsavory task of helping or let things get still more chaotic.

Finally, he said, "Okay... I guess", with a slightly confused wonderment of *How in the world did I end up in this pickle?*

The dust settled in the corner just as the light suddenly brightened, the coffee shop awakened to a new course and a cockroach died an instant death in the roach hotel behind the counter of which no one was aware, not even the roach. The coffee machines were on the edge of anticipation now as a dramatic silence descended over the group of partners in crime for ten ticks of the atomic clock on the wall until Eb said, "We need you to do some..." He stalled for time to search for the right words to fit Junior's frame of reference...

"Road work," Molly interrupted, "in a manner of speaking."

Junior Ketchum shook his head in puzzlement, "Road work?" There was a deepening of the furrows lining the now more fertile but puzzled brow, sprouting the newly planted seeds of conspiracy accompanying his hunched shoulders of confusion.

"Yes," Eb continued, "That rock with *Hell World* painted on it needs to be moved."

Junior Ketchum blinked five times in rapid succession and said, "Why?" Being the man he was, Junior Ketchum always needed to know the reasons why things worked and how to carry them out. His problem was that he couldn't grasp the complexity of human variation. It drove him crazy, and it drove him toward machines and animals.

Eb leaned in closer, "Because we have every reason to believe that the solution to this problem is buried under it." Junior was hooked because he wanted things to settle down and he loved working those machines, couldn't tolerate chaos, longed for things to return to the routine and structured life he craved. Besides, Molly, his only real friend, had offered him no alternative. It was unlikely that he would back out now because he was such a concrete thinker that, once he was committed to a particular track, he had difficulty shifting to a new path of mental constructs. It would be like a locomotive jumping the rails. His train of thought needed the tracks to keep it going in the predetermined direction. Any deviation in forward movement would be too anxiety provoking unless he was diverted to a new one by an external force, and Molly and Eb had thrown the switch at the Fix-it junction.

Eb said, "There's something buried under that rock, and we need to dig it up; so, your mission, if you choose to accept it, Junior, is to move the rock so we can dig up whatever is interred there. Once we do that, we can determine what our next step will be. We need you, Junior."

Not being used to any human needing him for anything, Junior Ketchum simply said, "Okay... I guess." He arose from his confusion and, without so much as a goodbye, exited the coffee shop, fired Lizzie up and drove off to 'borrow' the giant multi-purpose construction vehicle with the huge scoop in front.

"Does that mean he agreed; he'll meet us there?" Eb asked, unsure.

"Oh yes. Once he makes up his mind, which isn't usually this fast, he takes direct action. He'll be there.

Leaving his jealous angrily backfiring Lizzie behind with her engine running on, shuddering, before she stopped in despair, he drove the giant machine right through town without anyone questioning it, and headed to *Hell World* where Eb and Molly were waiting.

Eb showed Junior Ketchum the petroglyph arrow pointing the way and said, "This means there's something buried under here. We need you to use your scoop to move this rock out of the way so we can dig beneath it.

Junior said, "Okay, I understand," meaning he understood the task, but not its complete purpose; but being committed now, he leaped on his machine looking like a mountain lion climbing over the rocks, smooth and surefooted, licked his right thumb and touched the console like he had seen in a movie, not knowing why, but it seemed to be the correct thing to do somehow. He energized the ignition, dropped the scoop aimed it at the boulder, drove forward, slid the scoop under *Hell World* rock, and lifted it. Sitting the rock-filled scoop down fifty feet away from its original position, he shut the machine down, patted the console and hopped off. He grabbed the two shovels he brought, and he and Eb started digging while Molly served as lookout.

There was a shallow vertical grave about seven feet deep with something in it that turned out, on further inspection, to be a rug. They untied the bands that held it together, unrolled it, and there in plain sight of the universe, were the bones of what looked like the remains of an extremely distorted human or human-like body with an amulet mixed in. Eb said, "That looks like a Native American symbol, but if you look at it in a different way, it looks like a 'Z' in the middle of a dreamcatcher." Eb stared at the skull for what seemed to Molly like an hour, but it was probably only two or three seconds. "It resembles the old goat I encountered out in *Hell World*." He said, "But that old demon is down the well out there." He pointed out into *Hell World*.

Finder In Hell World   Charles R. Stern

CHAPTER NINETEEN
BURYING THE EVIDENCE

Prompted by the signals Finder detected coming from the skeleton, Ebenezer Thornbird felt that it needed to be returned to its rightful place and to whom it belonged... *but where?* After a three minute cogitation, thinking over all that he had learned from, Mr. Brown, the townsfolk and his library research, he said, "Junior, we need to take this rug and its remains along with the rock out to the well about a mile and a half into *Hell World*. Can you do that?" Raring to go, Junior nodded, smiled and mounted his excited steed, awaiting his firm, but caring touch.

Junior, like his giant machine, didn't really understand the purpose of it, but he agreed. It was a task, and he was good at tasks, especially those of the manual labor variety. He and Eb loaded the rug and its contents on to the vehicle, drove to the well, Molly and Eb trailing behind on foot until Junior stopped the multipurpose behemoth, patted it again, shut it off, leaped down like a gazelle and helped Eb drop the rug and its contents down the well. A whooshing sound followed its descent, landing with a slight splash at the bottom causing a cloud of some kind to shoot up out of the hole carrying with it the fragrance of flowers. Molly later said, "I could have sworn that I saw something, a kind of mist, emerge from the well, gather itself, and drift toward town!"

Eb looked at her with a surprised expression. *Huh!*

The well, now a barely damp circular grave, had apparently expelled most of its fluid contents that by now had soaked into the surrounding soil.

He said, "Junior, we need to fill in this well and cover it with the *Hell World* rock." They shoveled dirt into the well until it was filled with five feet to spare. Eb said, "Can you knock this curb into the well with that thing?"

"Sure!" Junior said, and, with a mildly insulted look on his face, "Her name is Annie" he insisted and, with the swagger of a proud cowboy mounting his steed, he jockeyed it forward with a "giddy up!"

Eb thought, i*t looks more like a Rex than an Annie.*

He directed Junior, "A little to the right." He pointed to Junior's right realizing Junior couldn't hear him. Then pointed left. Then a two-handed gesture that indicated "Straight on." The curb surrounding the well crumbled, topping off the hole. Junior backed up the prehistoric beast, his metal monster, and awaited further instructions.

"We have to drop the boulder over the hole!" Eb yelled while making hand gestures to mime the procedure until Junior Ketchum understood.

"Aye, aye sir!" Junior yelled with a pseudo-military solute, drove the giant painted *Hell World* rock forward and dropped it in its rightful place covering the well. The hole made an "oof!" in response.

The grave disguised as a well was sealed for posterity, and the rock was its foreboding marker.

Eb reached into his pack and took out two cans of quick-drying enamel paint he had purchased at the hardware, one black and the other white, along with two brushes and painted the entire rock black obliterating the red *Hell World* logo. After it dried, he wrote R.I.P. in white paint and drew an arrowhead aimed earthward and wrote, "HERE LIES THE SALVATION OF A WONDERFUL TOWN. DO NOT REMOVE UNDER ANY CIRCUMSTANCES," Just above the arrow and, in much larger letters, "EVER!"

Eb stepped back to survey his work. "Not bad if I do say so!" he said. Molly applauded, and Junior Ketchum followed suit even though he had no idea why.

"I hope no one ever removes that rock from the well," Molly said. "Who knows what it would uncork!" There was a rumble deep beneath them causing the ground to swell and undulate in ripples, and the Earth seemed to flow as if it were liquid making the three Musketeers fall to the ground. The waves of the Earth were radiating out in all seven directions North, South, East, West, up, down and forward in time. As if a curse had been lifted, something seemed to be trying to replace *Hell World*, whatever had been freeze-dried was being reconstituted, and it was expanding exponentially. Watching the quake roll away, the crew picked themselves up, and Ebenezer Thornbird and Molly Everhart rode, sitting in Junior Ketchum's giant scoop, back to the van. Molly pointed out some sprouting grass, a few saplings beginning to sprout, and a small stream seemed to be bubbling up from the Earth again. There was even a rabbit.

Molly and Eb rode Annie's scoop back to where Molly had parked her van, and they followed behind Junior Ketchum into town. The litter of the previous chaotic week was scattered everywhere. The shopkeepers were cleaning up in front of their establishments, replacing broken windows, returning doors to their hinges, and the local trash collector, Jimmy Englehardt, was emptying the trash cans, sweeping up the miscellaneous debris in the streets, hosing the spilt liquor, beer, vomit, blood, and other bodily fluids down the drains along with some unidentifiable slime. Everyone seemed to be cooperating, and there was no sign of discord. People on the streets smiled and waved at the threesome in their unintended and frankly exhausted parade floats. Junior Ketchum used the scoop to assist in the cleanup, and Molly dropped Eb at the welcoming motel and continued home.

The town's warring couples and divided factions either perpetrated a truce, parted agreeably, or simply went back to their previous lives. Some of the couples who had parted were reasonable, agreeing that they had joined for convenience and profit, had never felt love for each other, and separated amicably. Twelve couples decided to reconcile with the agreement that they were free to have outside relationships if they so choose, but stayed together in principle for their kids and, by lucky coincidence; they were the very ones who were involved with someone in one of the other couples with the same arrangement. A few, like the Everharts, realized that they loved each other after all and reconciled with a difficult, but fruitful rearrangement of their roles and treatment of each other.

Kurt and Gert Johnson were still working on their money-making schemes, but they were earmarking ten percent for charity. Lilith was discharged from the mental hospital on medications. Eddie was in therapy to understand what had happened to him. J.C. and Elise were back in a relationship of mutual caring. J.C. was still strange, but a little more lucid, and he was no longer swimming around in those oversized clothes that he had exchanged for better fitting ones. Bill continued to frequent the coffee shop, was more outgoing and interested in others, and instigated a group of retired men who began meeting at the *Wake-Up! Coffee Shop* every Thursday to talk and argue about sports and politics.

Molly's parents had been in love before their experiences in *Hell World,* and now their relationship simply grew stronger with uncharacteristic love and passion. It disgusted Molly despite her rationalization that they were happy for the first time, and that part of her visceral reaction was because they were her parents. She had never thought of them as passionate lovers, sexual beings, or even as real people and had never experienced them as compassionate and empathic. To her, they were aliens who had been dropped here from some other planet. *Who are these people?* She wondered, *the parents I knew all my life have disappeared in a fading dream. These people don't even look the same! They look ten years younger somehow. Is that because I'm really seeing them for the first time or is it because they're smiling with the looks of relaxed empathy and compassion I've never seen? Maybe it is the more up-to-date, modern clothes.* It was odd to finally have the parents she wanted as a child, but no longer needed them nor felt like they were her parents. *I guess it's too late.* Sadly, she felt a loss, but simultaneously, a sense of liberation and validation. She always knew in her heart that there was something wrong, but always kept it to herself. *Now I feel free for the first time in my life, and it's fantastic!*

The next morning, Molly packed her things and told her parents. "I'm leaving town with Eb. I need to seek my own life now. I'll miss you, but I have to go. It's way beyond time for me to find my own path."

Her mother said, "Oh dear! Do you have to go? We love you so much!" Molly thought she detected genuine sadness in her voice and maybe a small tear drifting down her cheek, outlining her nose.

Her father said, "It'll kill your mother you know." Then, after a ten-second pause, in a melancholy tone "It'll feel empty around here without you." An experience that seemed foreign to Molly. She had never seen him express sadness, love or, for that matter, any strong emotion.

They were upset because they felt at long last they could be close to her, but they realized she needed her independence and, once they understood there was no dissuading her, her mother said. "Please be safe and call frequently to let us know that you're all right."

Now I'm certain they're replicants, exact duplicates, snatched and replaced by space aliens.

"I promise I will," she agreed, gave them awkward hugs and kisses, and drove off to Eb's motel with her much-enhanced intuition, confidence, and sense of freedom.

Eb felt a sense of fulfillment for having faced and survived the most difficult quest of his life, especially since it had benefitted so many people. He and Molly were grateful for finding each other as if fate had brought them together. *Satisfying!* Finder and Eb thought simultaneously. Something felt different now, maybe because he had faced danger, maybe it was because he had succeeded in overcoming his most difficult challenge ever, maybe it was because he found a kindred spirit in Molly, another first for him, but they both felt liberated somehow.

Finder felt a deepening sense of contentment and increased confidence. In fact, there was barely a separation between Finder and Eb now. They seemed to be merging into one tower of rock-solid self-confidence and strength.

When Molly entered Eb's room with a heads up confident stature she never had before, they looked at each other for a poignant moment and, without a word, they stripped off their clothes, entered the shower together as if it were a kind of baptismal, leaving their previous life behind. Reborn into a whole new world, they washed each other off and, despite the anticipating bed, consummated their connection right there, soap and all. After that brief tension relieving diversion, they dried each other off and, with passions rekindled, headed for the bed, making love three more times that day and into the night with a few naps in between.

Eb was thoughtfully silent for five minutes before he spoke, "I've never felt so close to anyone. It isn't just the sex. For the first time, I feel a truly mutual give and take. Love, I realize, is the joy of getting pleasure, giving it is exciting, but giving to a truly joyous reception increases the getting tenfold."

She kissed him and said, "I love you Mr. Amateur Philosopher," and they smiled themselves asleep for another hour.

When they awoke later that day, the Sun was directly overhead and, after another hour of lovemaking, they washed up, dressed, Eb packed up his things, and they left the Motel for good. Molly brought several changes of clothes, and her journals were still in the van from her three-day wait for Eb at the threshold of *Hell World*. They said little at first except for a few "I love you" and other brief affectionate expressions and drove out of town. They both knew, without a word, they were going to stay together. They didn't even notice the growling hunger in their bellies.

While Molly drove up the road, they passed Junior and Lizzie. Junior Ketchum waved, and Lizzie offered a happy backfire. Molly and Eb laughed and waved back. They watched the silent landscape pass by, it watched them back, and Eb said, "I guess Plato was right." Gently placing his hand on her knee, they looked at each other, he smiled, she returned a matching grin, and the van seemed instantly one thousand watts brighter than the Sun.

Eb said to Finder, *I guess the talisman ring only kept me safe because I believed it would.* Finder replied, *yes, it was really the belief in ourselves.*

But Molly felt a glowing warmth circling the ring finger of her right hand and smiled.

Finder no longer sounded separate now. He was Eb's own thoughts; he was Finder and Finder was Ebenezer Thornbird. There was little difference. He remembered his nanny's words when he was twelve, "Make no mistake, you will find yourself facing the very danger you will have been preparing for all your life. When you are ready, you'll be faced with temptation, threatened, and lost with little more than the skills you'll acquire in the meantime to protect you. It may be symbolic or mythic. You'll be distracted by love and anger and wrenched by guilt. It is your destiny to be torn between your good and pure intentions and the unintended consequences of carrying them out. The treatment for this cancer, and all cancer cures, is so toxic that it nearly kills the patient while trying to kill the disease. Destiny is like the Sun. It's always there. No matter where you run, you can't deceive it, you'll never escape it even when you cannot see it through the clouds of unknowing. There's no sense trying to change it because it can't be defeated. So, acceptance is the only choice if you don't want to go mad denying the unstoppable."

The most important thing she said resonated now more than ever, "Mark my words, you will be in danger for your life and your psyche and, if you survive it, there will be a difference in you. What that difference turns out to be will only be partly up to you."

Molly interrupted his reverie, "Do you think that people conjure things into reality through their fears and desires?"

Eb, startled back from planet reminiscence to the stream of current reality, thought for five seconds, "I think everything we perceive are metaphors; representations of reality. Metaphors stand in for reality."

"Metaphors?" Molly was puzzled.

"Yes, what I learned from one of my professors was that one person's perception of an object or situation isn't exactly the same as the next person's. We don't say, "That scarf looks *as if it's* red. We say *it is red*. We may agree that the scarf is red, but do we see the same 'red'?" He made air quotes. "Or do we simply agree that it's red even though your perception is different than mine? 'Language itself is metaphor,' the prof told us. We come to believe that our perceptions are actual reality, make metaphors of them, and start acting as if they're true. I think that we imagine, expect, and believe things based upon tiny pieces in small niches of time and act as if they are real whether or not they are. We believe our own stories!"

"Maybe so," she said and, after a six-minute dive deeper into pools of wonderment, "What do you think the meaning was of those bones, the rug, and the amulet that were buried under that magical rock of ages and their effect on everything? Is there a metaphorical explanation for that?"

After thirty seconds of silent thought, Eb finally said, "Yes I do."

"Really? What?"

"Balance."

They were lost in silent thought as the van disappeared through what seemed like an invisible barrier, maybe a weather front, suddenly warmer, with whiter clouds backed by a deeper blue sky. Molly noticed that there seemed to be hundreds of toads lining the roadside as though they were bystanders for what seemed like a triumphant parade. "You know," Molly said, "This might make a good book!"

Eb looked at her and considered it for three seconds. "Nah, who'd believe it?"

"I suppose you're right."

The sun got suddenly brighter, the air was clear and warmer by ten degrees Fahrenheit. The Earth, and maybe the Universe, seemed to be more stable... for now. Eb looked back through the rearview mirror noticed the toads had closed ranks from each side of the road as the van passed in a kind of roadblock where the Sheriff's patrol car had stopped. Eb noticed a truck with a green cab, the white logo announcing *Donkey Express,* passing in the opposite direction. The toads scattered as the truck catapulted through a deep rut narrowly missing the creatures.

It all seemed like a mirage vanishing into the distance, and it appeared to Eb that the town had disappeared too. *The shadow of a dream? A hallucination? Naw! The road must have dipped below the sightline.* He smiled at Molly and, as if they communicated their exact meaning without words, she nodded and returned the smile. They drove over the horizon and into the sunset following their fate that stretched out before them looking for new adventures.

But that's another story.

Charles R. Stern

Charles is a psychologist practicing in the Detroit area since 1980. He has also taught at every level of education during his career.

Charles is also the author of a children's book, *A Rooster's Tale* and another magic realism novel, *Juxtaposition Paradox*.

For Book Festival appearances, and news about future releases, please visit: **www.CharlesRStern.com**

Charles can also be found on Facebook.com and on Goodreads.com

Finder In Hell World

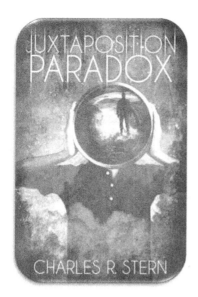

John Doe has amnesia and is seeking help to regain the memories of his past and his identity.

Karl Otto, a man stressed by life, discovers that his wife, Grace, with whom he has just spent the night, has been dead for months.

How are these paradoxes juxtaposed? How is this mystery to be solved?

Available at Amazon.com in paperback and e-book.

The e-book is also available at www.CharlesRStern.com

Finder In Hell World

What happens when two Rooster meet on the battlefield of a sneeze?

Will Blue Triumph?

Or will Red falter in the sand's breeze?

This delightful story, written in rhyme, and illustrated in beautiful watercolor, is perfect for the pre-school and early reader to share with friends, parents, and grandparents.

Available at Amazon.com in paperback and e-book.

The e-book is also available at **www.CharlesRStern.com**

Finder In Hell World Charles R. Stern

Made in the USA
Columbia, SC
20 July 2018